I0598240

BORN FOR ADVERSITY

The CASA Chronicles – Vol 2

Keith Julius

Keith Julius

Published by Keith Julius

Temperance, MI 48182

Copyright © Keith Julius 2016

All Rights Reserved

First edition – September 2016

www.KeithJulius.com

ISBN: 978-0-9969607-5-5

Printed by KDP Select

Cover Design - @pixon_design on fiverr

This book is dedicated to all the wonderful CASA volunteers everywhere. Without your dedication and commitment to the children you serve the world would truly be a sadder place.

Also available from Keith Julius:

Remorse By Degree

The CASA Chronicles:

    Volume 1 – Catch A Falling Star

    Volume 2 – Born For Adversity

    Volume 3 – The Robber Of Youth

    Volume 4 – A Decade Aborning

www.KeithJulius.com
KeithEJulius@gmail.com

Chapter One:

AARON AND Evan Reed never made it to the zoo the bright sunny morning they left the house with their mother.

Walking beside her along Broadway Avenue, the steady stream of traffic on their right a noisy counterpoint to the gently flowing waters of the Maumee River on their left, they meandered along the sidewalk with the pace typical of a couple of nine-year-old boys. They stopped often, pausing to examine the most inconsequential of objects along the way; a shiny stone that caught their fancy, a seagull feather, even a discarded plastic pop bottle. And though the zoo was their destination, and the twins were anxious to pet the rays and maybe even hold a crab at the newly-renovated aquarium, they never reached their objective.

Circumstances conspired against them, interrupting what should have been a pleasant family outing and transforming it into an ordeal that would have deep ramifications for the entire family.

They wound up instead at the Emergency Room at Toledo Hospital.

Laura Reed was feeling the need to get outside. She felt as though she had been stuck indoors all winter, shivering under her layers of clothing as she attempted to stay warm. The only time she got outdoors anymore was to go to work, trudging through the snow and the cold to get to Kroger, where she'd be on her feet for hours at a time running the cash register. Sometimes Ted would pick her up at the end of her shift, depending on his schedule and whether it coincided with hers, but it seemed some days she never even saw her boyfriend other than a few minutes in the morning or at night before they crawled into bed together.

He was sleeping now, upstairs in their room. Mondays we're always tough on Ted, having to readjust to a second shift schedule after spending the weekend with Laura and the boys. She tried to let him sleep in, in anticipation of the beginning of his evening work shift. It was easier for him that way.

It had been a long winter for all of them, Laura reflected, and she was glad it was finally over. She wanted to be warm again, and open the windows and enjoy the smell of fresh air in the house. She wanted to wear her light capris, and her sandals, and the loose fitting sleeveless tops with the airy feel to them that she enjoyed so much.

Spring had failed to alleviate the condition. If anything it prolonged her misery, teasing her with signs of good weather but never quite fulfilling the promise. Below average temperatures and above average amounts of precipitation hadn't rectified the situation, forcing her to prolong her time indoors.

It wasn't so bad when the kids were at school. At least she didn't have to put up with a couple of complaining fourth graders. But here it was, barely into summer vacation, and they were growing increasingly restless already.

Evan, the most vocal of the twins, summed it up that morning. "I'm so bored." He dragged the word out, to emphasize his feelings on the matter. "There's never anything to do around here."

Sitting in the corner, his attention captivated with the hand-held video game he manipulated, Aaron looked up but failed to comment. Less talkative than his brother, and more moody at times, he was content to ignore what was going on around him. Solitude seemed to suit him.

Laura shook her head in disbelief. "How can you be bored already?" she asked. "You've only been out of school for two weeks. Is this what the summer's going to be like?"

"Can't we do something?" Evan persisted. "Or go somewhere?"

"How are we supposed to go somewhere when we don't have a car?"

"We could take the bus."

"That cost money. You know I don't get my check 'til the end of the week. And I work too hard for my money to waste it on public transportation to take us places we don't need to get to."

Aaron – eyes still focused on the electronic game he played – spoke up, his voice barely above a whisper. "We could walk to the zoo." He displayed no emotion with the remark, stating it as a simple declaration of fact and nothing more. He then returned to his game, ignoring the conversation around him, fearful lest he miss out on some of the video action in his hands.

Laura considered. It was Monday, which meant the zoo was free to Lucas County residents, so it wouldn't cost them anything to get in. It was a seven block walk, and though it was a bit of a hike she had done it in the past with the twins so she knew they were up to the task. And at least it would get them out of the house for a while.

Maybe it wasn't such a bad idea after all.

"Okay, we'll go to the zoo," she informed them.

"Yeah!" Evan ran for the door, his exuberance obvious.

"But...!" Laura raised her voice to accent the word, the tone bringing her son to an abrupt halt. "I don't want to hear any whining about how tired you are. Or it's too long of a walk. Understand?"

The twins answered a simultaneous "Yes, Mom," as though they were programmed to say the same thing.

"And we can't spend any money when we get there."

7

"Not even for popcorn?" Aaron suggested, the prospect of food breaking him free from his involvement with the video game.

"They charge too much at those places," Laura continued. "I could make you a whole barrel of popcorn for what it costs for one little bag at that place."

Evan, feeling the need to reinforce his brother's suggestion, drew closer to his mother. "But, Mom –"

His whine halted abruptly following the stern look he received in reply.

"Yes, Mom."

"I think there's some cookies in the cupboard. If you want to bring some along, and maybe a couple juice boxes, you can have them on the way."

The kids scampered through the house to the kitchen, Laura following at a more sedate pace.

She passed Grandpa Mike on the way, asleep in his recliner as usual. The noise coming from the television fell on deaf ears, the old man missing the latest round of trading taking place on the game show in front of him as he slumbered his morning away.

Laura considered turning the television off as she walked past then decided against it. The silence would probably wake him up. No reason to disturb his rest. He'd been fighting a cold the last couple of days, on top of everything else he had to deal with; he could use some extra sleep.

Continuing through the clutter that comprised the living area of the house, and from there into the tiny kitchen at the back, she approached Grandma Ruth, who sat at the chipped Formica table, back ramrod straight in one of the wooden chairs as though it was the most comfortable seat in the house. As usual her attention was riveted on the Bible in front of her, though she occasionally pulled her eyes from the printed page to glance at the boiling pot of potatoes on the stove. She acknowledged Laura's presence with a slight arching of her eyebrows, as though wondering what her granddaughter was up to.

Laura walked idly up to the large pan, picking up a wooden spoon from the counter as she moved forward. She stirred the contents, the steam from the boiling water forcing her to step back slightly. "What are you making?"

"German potato salad."

Laura smiled at the old woman. "I should have known."

"It is my favorite," Grandma Ruth replied.

Finished with the stirring, Laura replaced the spoon on the counter and approached her grandmother. "The boys and I are heading to the zoo for a while."

A smile, a gently lop-sided expression that took its shape from the missing teeth on the left side of the old woman's mouth, answered. "That's nice." She glanced at the two boys, who were busily stuffing cookies from the cupboard into a brown paper bag that seemed on the verge of exploding. "Aaron and Evan will like that. Young boys like them, they should be spending more time outside. Instead of playing those outrageous video games all the time."

"It's more for me than for them," Laura admitted. "If I'm gonna keep my sanity I got to find something for them to do. Anyways, we shouldn't be too late."

"Take your time." The Bible laid half-closed on the tabletop, her right hand marking the page, while her left lovingly caressed the cover. "I got my book to keep me company."

"You gonna be okay?" Laura looked toward the living room. She couldn't see Grandpa Mike, though the soft sound of gentle snoring made it's way into the kitchen. "If Grandpa wakes up –"

"Don't concern yourself with that. After fifty-two years of marriage I think I know how to handle your Grandpap."

"I'm sure you do." Laura smiled, bent over to plant a kiss on the other woman's cheek, then straightened up. "Okay. See you in a few hours."

It was a glorious afternoon, the type of day when the sun shone in the sky and the birds chirped in the trees and even the noise of the passing cars and trucks on the busy avenue they walked along failed to dampen the spirits. Laura walked at a leisurely pace, enjoying the mild temperature, watching her two sons as they scampered ahead. They had already consumed their cookies and the juice boxes were empty, which left them time to enjoy the walk in their own fashion.

Occasionally they would stop, and wait for her to catch up, then resume their play. Though markedly different in temperament from one another they were the best of friends, reacting to situations as only twins could, anticipating each others' moods and responding as one to the things around them. It was as though they shared a sixth sense with one another, having developed a capacity for closeness that Laura still marveled at.

As they drew closer to the zoo they approached Broadway Park, an urban playground of green nestled along the river. By peering through the trees along the bank you could just catch sight of the assorted craft plying the waters; tall-masted sailboats, majestically capturing the wind as they sliced through the waves; sleek motorboats, the roar from their engines echoing from the rows of trees lining the banks; the occasional kayak or canoe, their lone occupants enjoying the serenity of the day. In its way the Maumee River was as busy of a thoroughfare as the street they walked along.

The twins paused, eyeing the playground equipment that beckoned from the city park. Laura caught up to them where they stood together on the sidewalk.

They peered up at her, Evan voicing the question on both their minds. "Can we play on the jungle gym for a while, Mom?"

"I thought you wanted to do the zoo?"

"We can still do the zoo," Aaron suggested, in the quiet, logical way he used to approach things. "We'll just do the playground first."

Laura nearly said no, then thought better of it. At least they were outside. And getting some exercise. And she was out of the house for a change as well. Besides, they had plenty of time before they needed to go home.

"Go ahead."

They ran off, screaming in their excitement, and she called out to them.

"But only for a few minutes."

She doubted they even heard her remark.

They both sped off toward the jungle gym, but along the way Evan got distracted. Something at the side of the playground, partially buried in the sand, caught his attention. He couldn't pass the spot without pausing to investigate.

Aaron continued onward, his destination firmly in mind. Within moments he was climbing the metal bars of the playground structure, swinging from rung to rung as though he hadn't a care in the world. He seemed fearless, climbing hand-over-hand with ease.

Laura found a place to sit close by. A young mother occupied the end of a nearby bench, gently rocking the stroller in front of her with her left foot while she leafed through a magazine in her lap. Looking up from her reading, she offered a weak smile as Laura sat down. "Hi."

"Hi." Laura sneaked a quick peek into the stroller, observing the slumbering infant within, snuggled beneath a blanket of pink. "How old is she?"

"Three months."

"She's a cutie."

"Thanks." The recent mother gestured toward the play area, where half a dozen kids were raucously enjoying the equipment at the park. "Which one is yours?"

"That's Aaron, playing on the jungle gym. The one digging in the dirt by the swing set is his brother, Evan."

"They look pretty close in age."

"Eleven minutes."

Understanding showed on the other woman's face. "You mean...?"

Laura nodded. "Twins."

"Wow. I can't imagine." She glanced toward her daughter in the stroller. "And I thought giving birth to one was bad." She shook her head, apparently contemplating having two children to deal with and deciding it wasn't for her. "They must be a handful."

"They can be," Laura admitted. "But it's easier, now that they're older. And more independent."

"I suppose they're pretty similar?"

"Not really. Oh, they have a lot in common and all. But sometimes they're different as night and day. Evan never stops talking, and is always getting into everything. Aaron's more serious. Doesn't say much, but when he does it's like he's been thinking things over and won't say anything until he's sure what he wants to say."

"It still sounds like it must be a lot of work."

"Sometimes it is. But other times –."

Whatever Laura meant to say next was interrupted by a piercing scream from the vicinity of the playground. Laura was on her feet in moments, along with several other mothers in the area, all of them casting concerned glances toward where the children played.

A still form lay on the ground beneath the metal bars of the playground equipment. Even from a distance Laura recognized that it was Aaron.

She also detected the odd way his left leg extended from beneath him.

A moment later his cries of agony resumed as Laura raced to his side.

Chapter Two:

D R. LOIS Tyrone felt weary, worn-out after nearly five hours on her feet. It had been a busy day at Toledo Hospital. No busier than usual, she admitted to herself. But following on the heels of a full weekend of contusions and abrasions and sprains made it only that much more difficult. At least there hadn't been any tragic car wrecks to contend with, or anything as horrendous as the industrial accident she had dealt with back in December when she was working at Riverside Hospital.

Those were the days that tried her skills as a physician.

Though, at the same time, the tough days were in many ways the most rewarding. They were the days where she truly felt she was making a difference in someone's life; when she could apply her knowledge and experience to successfully see a patient through a difficult time. They depended on her to be there. It was a satisfying feeling that she never grew weary of, rising up to the challenges set before her.

Passing a darkened office she caught a reflection of herself, observing a middle-aged woman with drooping hair and sagging shoulders, the signs of weariness obvious. She made a conscious effort to stand straighter while brushing an errant strand of blonde away from her eyes. She wasn't vain; she was content in the knowledge that she would never grace the cover of a fashion magazine. But she was pleased nonetheless with the change in her appearance as she continued her rounds.

Approaching the tiny cubicle at the end of the hallway she forced a smile, hoping it would disguise her exhaustion. The chamber she entered, one of fifteen just like it in the Emergency Room, looked much the same as the last cubicle she had left; the same standard hospital cot draped in white, the same rolling tray of medical implements, the same nondescript curtain encircling the patient and evoking a sense of privacy.

Her previous patient, an eighty-seven-year-old woman who had slipped in her bathroom and apparently broken her hip, was being wheeled down to X-Ray to verify the extent of the damages. She had been difficult to communicate with, owing to hearing loss that substantially hampered her ability to answer questions in a coherent manner. Her son had done his best to interpret for the woman, but as a consequence of his seeming lack of interest in his mother's predicament he hadn't been very helpful. It had been a time-consuming ordeal, ascertaining the extent of the woman's injuries, and had taken her away from other patients. She was anxious to make amends by getting back to work.

Pulling the curtain closed behind her Dr. Tyrone made a quick visual examination of the boy on the cot while at the same time glancing over his chart. He wore shorts, stained with dirt, and a striped shirt with a torn sleeve. The left side of his shirt was torn as well, darkened with what she was pretty certain must have been dried blood. His sneakers were untied; she wondered if that was an accident or just a fad the nine-year-old sported. His face was dirty with brown streaks that ran down his cheeks. She suspected the marks were a combination of dirt and tears, though he was not crying at the moment. For now the boy sat quietly, a look of fear and bewilderment on his face, clearly uncomfortable in his present surroundings.

According to the report the child had fallen from some playground equipment. From the bruising and swelling already apparent on his leg she suspected a broken bone.

The doctor finished reviewing the information on the chart before addressing her patient.

"Hello, Aaron. I'm Dr. Tyrone."

He attempted a smile, but the movement seemed to bother him. He grimaced instead and nodded his head. His face was pale, his breathing shallow.

She approached the cot to examine the injuries. She reached slowly for the swollen leg but, before she even touched the skin, Aaron flinched, attempting to pull away.

"I'm not going to hurt you," she assured him. "I just need to look things over."

"It hurts," the child admitted.

"I'm sure it does. But you're being brave to sit there so quietly."

She flashed him a smile, which he halfheartedly returned.

Something seemed peculiar to the physician. Something that just hadn't seemed right from the moment she entered, and it finally came to her. She turned toward the nurse on the other side of the cot.

"Where's his mother?"

"I asked her to leave."

Dr Tyrone made no reply, waiting for the young girl to continue.

"I made a quick examination, to determine where he was hurt. I was concerned with the blood on his side." As she spoke she moved forward to lift the bottom edge of the boy's shirt. Aaron flinched, pulling back as though afraid, at the same time averting his eyes from the physician.

"Nobody's going to hurt you," Dr. Tyrone repeated, keeping a soothing lilt to her tone.

The nurse pulled gently on the material, exposing Aaron's left side along with a portion of his back. The skin had been scraped raw – just above his waistline – from the fall, though it seemed to be only a surface abrasion. There wasn't much blood, as though it had seeped slightly through the skin rather than bleeding profusely. The blood was nearly dried by now. It was no doubt sore, but nothing some bacterial ointment and time wouldn't take care of.

Dr. Tyrone gave a passing glance to the wound, her eyes attracted instead to some marks several inches higher on the boy's abdomen. A series of jagged lines, perhaps half a dozen or more, crisscrossed the skin, the raised welts glaring against the pale white of the flesh. A patch of discolored skin, light purple from bruising, showed under the armpit. There seemed to be little swelling, as though the healing had progressed beyond that stage and the damage was beginning to mend.

The nurse replaced the shirt material, flashing a weak smile toward Aaron Reed, and faced the physician. "The mother was hysterical when she first came in, which was understandable. But when she saw this she became confused. Almost disoriented. Like she couldn't understand what was going on."

For several seconds no one spoke, until Dr. Tyrone voiced her concern. "Those marks weren't caused from falling off some playground equipment. And they didn't happen today. They're at least a few weeks old."

The nurse merely nodded.

"Take him down to X-Ray," the physician advised. "Let's get a look at what's up with that leg."

She turned, a look of determination on her face.

"I have a phone call to make."

Evan Reed was bored.

An hour earlier he had been scared, following the unexpected events at the park. He hadn't seen his brother fall from the jungle gym. At the time he had been digging in the dirt with a stick, looking for the colored stones he sometimes discovered at the park. Ted – his mother's boyfriend – claimed they were only bits of colored glass. But he chose not to believe that. Instead he imagined them as priceless gems. Pirate booty, perhaps. Like a modern day Tom Sawyer he fantasized all sorts of imaginative reasons to explain why pirate treasure would be at the park, along the banks of the river. In Toledo Ohio, of all places.

Rational thinking seldom entered his daydreams.

It was while he had been excavating in the soil that he heard the startled cry, in a voice he instantly recognized as Aaron's. By the time he had turned around his brother was laying on the ground, screaming in pain, his mother running to assist him while assorted onlookers approached the scene.

The succeeding events were a whirlwind of activities. Evan stood idly by and watched the action progress, forgotten for the moment with all the attention centered on his brother. It seemed to take minutes only for the ambulance to arrive, the shrill blare of the siren announcing its arrival long before reaching the park. The crowd had separated then, stepping back to allow the paramedics to move forward to assess the situation. Rapid motion followed, the ambulance attendants performing their tasks in a manner that seemed unhurried yet, at the same time, wasted not a single instant. Sooner than Evan would have believed possible his brother was in the emergency vehicle, securely strapped in place and ready to be transported to the hospital.

And then they were on their way, Evan and his mother sitting nervously on the low-benched seat that lined the back of the medical vehicle, while Aaron whimpered and moaned on the gurney – a word Evan had never encountered before until hearing the two men in the ambulance use it.

Their motion over the city streets should have been exhilarating, racing down the roads as traffic pulled to the side to clear the way, but the occupants were too involved with other considerations to pay attention to the mad dash. While Aaron fought back the tears, his pain obvious from the paleness of his skin and the tight clenching of his jaw, Evan sat impatiently observing the scene, squirming in nervousness, sympathetically imagining the agony his brother was experiencing. He could almost feel a soreness in his own leg, a throbbing sensation that jolted him each time the ambulance hit a bump in the road.

Eventually the hectic journey was over. The vehicle screeched to a halt and the rear doors flew open, followed by a hustle of activities. Apparently the emergency room staff had anticipated their arrival; Aaron was instantly wheeled away, their mother at his side, while Evan had been instructed to stay in the waiting room. He sat down in a hard-backed chair and watched as Laura Reed disappeared in back with Aaron and the nurses.

That's when things had slowed down. The excitement had passed, replaced by a dull humdrum of leafing through magazines that didn't interest him, glancing occasionally at the television program playing on the set in the corner, and basically just sitting and waiting and wishing he was anywhere else but stuck in a boring hospital.

What had seemed like an adventure had become a dull routine, his fantasies replaced with the reality of the situation.

Eventually his mother had rejoined him.

"How's Aaron?" The words left his lips before his mother even sat down.

She took a minute to compose herself. "I don't know," she finally admitted. "They think he has a broken leg. They're sending him down to X-Ray."

"Cool!" Evan could only sit there and envy his brother's experience. He wondered what it was like inside the hospital. What secret passageways would Aaron be exploring? Would it hurt to get an X-Ray? He didn't think so. He had never heard of X-Rays hurting. But he couldn't be sure.

He and his mother talked for a while – mostly about what had happened at the park – but it was obvious her thoughts were somewhere else. She stared into the distance, biting her lower lip, her replies vague. After a short while Evan tired of trying to talk to her and slumped back into his seat, staring into space, wishing they had never decided to go to the zoo that morning.

Dr. Tyrone entered the waiting room escorted by a nurse from the front desk, who pointed to Laura and her son and then disappeared around the corner. The physician walked slowly over, a look of concern on her face. There was something else there as well, though Aaron couldn't quite place it. It was a sad sort of expression, as though she'd been called upon to do a particularly unpleasant task.

"Laura Reed?"

She had been feeling drowsy, her mind in an almost trance-like state following the excitement of the morning. But the sound of her name brought Laura to instant awareness. She stood immediately. "Yes?"

"I'm Dr. Tyrone."

"My son –?"

"Will be fine, Miss Reed. He has a fractured fibula. That's the smaller of the two lower leg bones. Luckily it was a clean break. He's getting the cast put on right now. I'm afraid he'll be on crutches for the next few weeks."

Evan's face lit in excitement, imagining the fun of walking around in crutches. "Neat!"

The doctor smiled at the boy, a pleasant inflection gracing her voice. "He'll be laid up for most of the summer, I'm afraid. Which means no swimming. Or bicycling. He won't be able to get around much at all. Now that doesn't sound like fun, does it?"

"I guess not," Evan meekly acknowledged.

Laura reached tentatively toward Dr. Tyrone, brushing against the woman's sleeve. "Can I see him now? I'd like to see my son."

"In a few minutes. But there's something we need to discuss with you first. Please come this way."

Without waiting for an answer the doctor turned and started to walk away. Laura and Evan followed; through the double doors behind the nurses' station, down one hall, then another, and again a third, before finally reaching what looked to be a row of offices. Dr. Tyrone opened a door, then stood aside to usher Laura and her son into the room.

Laura hesitated. Something just didn't feel right. "What's going on?"

"We just have a few questions for you."

We?

There were two people already in the office. Sitting behind the desk was an elderly man sporting a finely trimmed white beard. He wore a white lab coat, and sported a stethoscope around his neck like it was some kind of adornment. Laura took him to be a doctor. His face held a stern look, like it was chiseled from stone and it was the only expression he knew. His eyes glared her way, examining her with a look she couldn't quite place. Contempt, perhaps?

The other man was much younger, wearing slacks and a light sport coat and holding a clipboard loaded with sheets of paper. His manner seemed friendlier, almost approachable. But, like the white-coated man behind the desk, there was no humor in his expression.

It felt crowded in the room, especially after Dr. Tyrone closed the door behind them.

"What's going on?" Laura asked at last.

The young man stepped forward. "I'm Patrick Zimmerly, Miss Reed. I'm a caseworker at Lucas County Children's Services."

"I don't understand." Laura glanced from one face to another, her bewilderment growing. "What's this about?"

"We're concerned about your son's injuries."

"I don't believe this." She stammered a moment, at a loss for words. "My son fell off a jungle gym, for heaven's sake. It was an accident. And it wasn't like he wasn't being watched. I was right there. And now you want to make it into some kind of federal offense?"

She shook her head in disbelief. "Don't you people have something better to do with your time?"

She stopped then, at a loss for words, and the man from Children's Services continued.

"Those aren't the injuries we're concerned with, Miss Reed."

"I don't understand."

Patrick Zimmerly indicated the man behind the desk. "This is Dr. Yamal Rahid. He specializes in these sorts of cases, so we called him in to get his opinion."

Laura, speechless, stared and said nothing.

Dr. Rahid stood, presenting an even more imposing figure as he did so. "Has your child had any other injuries in the last few weeks, Miss Reed?"

"No. Of course not. I take good care of my kids. What are you trying to say?"

"There are bruises, and other marks, that we are very concerned with."

"You mean from his fall?" Laura suggested.

"No," Dr Rahid answered. "These are obviously older, judging by the scarring."

Laura, beginning to get an inkling of what they were driving at, searched the faces in the room for a sign of sympathy. None was to be found.

"This is ridiculous. What are you trying to say?"

No one replied to her question.

She continued, her words gushing forth. "I certainly don't abuse my children. I'm a good mother."

"We're certain you are," the caseworker replied, in a tone that seemed much too condescending. "But perhaps somebody else in your household? Or someone the children were visiting...?"

"No." Laura shook her head violently back and forth to indicate her point. "I don't want to hear this. Just let me see my son. We want to go home."

"We cannot allow that at this point," Dr. Rahid said.

"I don't understand." She looked the accusatory trio over one more time, pausing at last to face Dr. Tyrone. She at least seemed more sympathetic than the others. "Can't we just go home?"

Dr. Tyrone slowly shook her head. "I'm sorry, Miss Reed. But I'm mandated to report cases where we suspect abuse. At this point we have to investigate the allegations. The children will have to stay here, Miss Reed, so we can make a thorough physical examination to determine the extent of their injuries. I'm sorry."

"Children?"

Patrick Zimmerly supplied the answer. "We will need to examine both of the children, Miss Reed."

Laura attempted to say more; to point out how ridiculous the entire accusation was. But she wasn't thinking clearly now. Her mind was in too much of blur from all that had transpired. It was obvious the decision had been reached before she even walked into the room. She really had no say in the matter.

Dr. Tyrone drew a step closer. "It's for their own good, Miss Reed. Please understand that."

"I will need to get some more information from you," Patrick continued. "And then you may leave."

"But my kids...?"

"Will be well taken care of. I assure you. And I promise you I will move this through Children's Services as quickly as possible so you won't be separated any longer than necessary."

Laura looked down at Evan, who had remained silent the entire while. Brushing a tear away from his cheek, she bent down to kiss him on the forehead.

"Mommy will see you again real soon. Okay?"

He nodded in reply.

Chapter Three:

THE SLAMMING of the front door instantly alerted her to the new arrival at the house. Inserting a scrap of paper between two pages to mark her place, she carefully closed her book and placed the Bible – ever so gently – onto the end table beside her. Grandma Ruth looked up as her granddaughter stormed into the room.

Laura looked around, barely noticing Grandpa Mike's recumbent form still sleeping in the recliner, as she surveyed the living space.

Grandma Ruth leaned forward in her chair. "What are you so riled up about?"

"Where's Ted?"

"I think he just stepped out back to have a cigarette." It was a routine both Laura and Ted followed, due to Grandpa Mike's poor health. Breathing was enough of a chore for him on good days without being subjected to cigarette smoke and further aggravating things.

Saying nothing, Laura headed toward the back of the house.

Her senses alarmed by now, the old woman forced herself off her chair. She followed her granddaughter into the back of the house. "Laura? What's going on?" She took a quick look around. "And where are the kids?"

"They took them, Grandma."

"What? Who took them?"

There was no answer. By this point Laura was outside, slamming yet another door behind her as she left the house.

Ted Myers sat on a lawn chair, feet propped up on a second chair, watching the glow from the charcoal grill beside him. The heat was hardly noticeable, competing as it was with the warmth of the sun baking down on him. The flames were beginning to die down now, following the initial burst after lighting the fire. The bag of charcoal and can of starter fluid sat off to the side, waiting to be put back in the shed. Ted figured he would get around to it eventually.

He knew he had to be heading into the shop in another hour. It felt good now to relax for a few minutes a bit before then. He held a glass of iced tea in his left hand, shaking the drink in lazy circles and watching the ice swirl around, while the other held a lit cigarette. He took a slow drag, then blew a lopsided smoke ring as Laura approached. As she drew closer he smiled up at his girlfriend.

"Hey, babe," he began. He indicated the grill. "Charcoal's just about ready if you want me to throw some burgers on."

She stood there, glaring at him with an intense look such as he had never seen before.

"What's up?"

She said nothing.

Instead she replied with a two-fisted punch that struck Ted on the left shoulder. The blow did little more than surprise him, causing him to drop his drink due to the suddenness of the attack. The glass shattered as it hit the ground, the brown liquid quickly absorbed into the dirt.

Ted sprang to his feet in astonishment.

"What did you do?" Laura's voice screamed the question, the rage in her eyes locked on his face.

"Slow down a minute! What are you talking about?"

"They took my kids! Because of you they took my kids!"

She attempted to strike him yet again, but this time he was prepared. Ted caught both her fists in his left hand, effectively blocking her motions and deflecting the blow. After flicking the dying cigarette away he reached for her shoulder with his free arm.

"Now just slow down –"

"Don't touch me." Laura jumped back, distancing herself from her boyfriend. She turned away, whirled around to face him again, then began rapidly pacing back and forth in the confined space of the miniature backyard. She wanted to cry. She wanted to scream. She wanted to lash out at something. But all she could do was stare into space and wonder how everything had gone so wrong.

Grandma Ruth, standing in the doorway, could contain her curiosity no longer. She called out to her granddaughter. "Where are the kids?"

Laura turned, preferring not to face Ted again. "We stopped at the park. On the way to the zoo."

She paused, trying to recall the moment. It all seemed such a blur now, the morning's details erased by subsequent events. It seemed as well like it had happened such a long time ago, as though she needed to scour her brain to bring forth the memories.

"Aaron fell off the playground equipment," she informed them at last.

"Oh, no." Ruth stepped closer. "Is he okay?"

"They took him to the hospital. He broke his leg. They had to put him in a cast."

Ruth's face, which moments earlier had registered shock, smiled at the revelation. "Boys will be boys. Laura, them two are gonna turn your hair gray long before it's due. It's all part of growing up. Especially with boys. You can't get so worked up over things. As long as he's okay, that's the main thing."

"That's not what I'm worked up about."

"Then what is is?"

"When they examined Aaron, at the hospital, they discovered something else. There were...." She paused, not certain how to continue, then forced the words out. "There were marks. On his back. And his side."

The old woman's tone turned grim. "What kind of marks?"

Laura turned toward Ted. "Like someone had been hitting Aaron. A lot. And like it's been going on for a while now."

For several long moments nothing was said. Even the nearby birds seemed to be drawn in to the drama of the scene. Choosing to refrain from their vocalizations, the absence of their singing lent an eerie quality to the occasion, as though nature was waiting for whatever revelation was coming next.

Ted broke the silence. "So what are you saying? You think I've been hitting your kids?"

"Have you?"

"Of course not. Why would I? This is the most ridiculous thing I've ever heard."

"I saw the marks on him, Ted. There's no denying someone has been abusing my child."

"What makes you think it was me?"

"You think it was me?" She turned toward her grandmother, who stared in shocked silence from the back doorway. "Or my grandparents? You think they did this?"

"I don't know what to think. But I'm telling you, it wasn't me."

Ted made a motion to approach her and she stepped back, distancing herself from him, as though she couldn't stand to be near him.

"Get out of this house!" Laura screamed. "I don't want to see you anymore."

For a moment they glared at one another, locked momentarily in a battle of wills, each waiting for the other to respond. Ted finally spoke up, shaking his head in bewilderment as he did so.

"Hell. I don't need this."

He walked around her, purposely jolting against her shoulder as he passed, and mounted the three steps leading to the back door, the heavy thud of his footfalls an obvious indication of his frame of mind. Grandma Ruth stepped aside as he passed. The two looked at one another, doubt and confusion on both their faces, and a moment later Ted disappeared from view into the house.

Laura felt her rage controlling her; the anger and frustration consuming her. She took a deep breath and forced herself to calm down. She couldn't believe this was happening. It all felt like a bad dream, a nightmare she couldn't wake up from.

Her gaze lit on the glow of the backyard grill. The red of the charcoal struck her as an angry color, an intense light that mirrored the mood she felt within. She knew she had to cool down, to control herself and examine her emotions, but the rage she felt refused to abate.

Pulling her attention from the surroundings she willed herself to move, retreating to the kitchen. Slumping down onto a chair, her arms folded on the tabletop in front of her, she rested her head and closed her eyes, fighting to hold back the tears that threatened to overwhelm her.

Grandma Ruth entered silently, standing in the doorway, watching the young woman she had raised from a child. "Are you sure about this, Laura?"

"I'm not sure about anything," she answered at last.

"Maybe there's been some mistake."

"I know what I saw. There's no mistaking that."

Above them footsteps sounded, as Ted moved around in the bedroom overhead. They listened in silence, as if contemplating his actions, hearing the occasional slamming of dresser drawers and the shuffling of clothes. Eventually the footsteps retreated and they heard him coming down the stairs. The front door opened.

His voice called out to them. "I'll be back for the rest of my stuff later."

No reply was offered.

"I didn't do this, Laura. You've got to believe me. I would never hurt your kids."

He waited a moment. No reply was given. Without another word he left the house, the door closing behind him and accenting the silence in the kitchen.

Grandma Ruth drew closer, but made no attempt to touch Laura as she spoke. "The good book tells us, *Let all bitterness and anger be put away from you. Be kind to one another, tenderhearted, forgiving one another.* Maybe we shouldn't be so quick to judge what's going on here."

Laura stood, the chair scraping along the floor as she rose, but didn't bother to face her grandmother.

"Not now. I don't need to hear this now."

She left the room and headed upstairs.

Chapter Four:

To: ALL CASA volunteers

From: CASA Office Toledo Ohio

Subject: Can you help these children?

Twin boys – age 9 years.

One of the boys taken to Toledo Hospital with a broken leg following an accident at a playground. Hospital staff detected unexplained bruising and marks suggesting previous physical abuse. Second child examined but reveals no indication of mistreatment.

Mother and boyfriend live with mother's paternal grandparents. Children initially removed from household after incident but returned following Emergency Hearing. Currently residing at home under Protective Supervision.

Father separated from family three years ago. Has had no contact with children in that time.

If you can find it in your heart to be the CASA for these twin boys please let us know. They are in need of someone who cares.

Keith Julius

Thank you.

Rebecca Poole
Lucas County Juvenile Center
CASA – Court Appointed Special Advocates

Chapter Five:

Sounds DRIFTED to the back of the house. Even through the closed panel of the bedroom door – and with the overhead fan spinning above, adding it's rhythmic clatter to the environment – Larry Kendall could still make out what was happening in the rest of the house. His father had left for work hours ago; he was on an early shift at the station and had risen before the sun. His footsteps had sounded through the house followed by the sound of closing doors, announcing Jeremy Kendall's departure. The ratcheting of the garage door seemed to penetrate particularly well to the back bedroom.

Larry had easily fallen back to sleep minutes later.

For a short time after that things had been quiet.

Eventually Larry heard his mother in the kitchen, her preparations accompanied with the smells of morning. She must have poured herself a cup of coffee; the rich aroma seeped into his room, together with the smell of toasting bread. And was that cinnamon he detected? She made no attempt to keep quiet. Her philosophy had always been that daylight wasn't anything to be wasted. There was no sense in slumbering the day away, as far as she was concerned. She was awake, and could see no reason why the entire world shouldn't join her.

A few minutes later she walked down the hallway, her footsteps pausing outside Larry's door.

"I'm heading off to work now," Linda Kendall announced, as though it was information he couldn't make it through the day without.

Larry rolled onto his back, staring up at the ceiling, watching the steady motion of the fan blades as they spun above his head. The breeze they created felt cool against his skin.

"Lawrence?" She was the only one that ever called him Lawrence, determined to keep her father's name alive through her son.

"I heard you." Even though he tried to conceal it, the exasperation in his voice must have been obvious to his mother.

"So what are your plans for the day?" she asked, either ignoring his tone or feeling there was no reason to respond to it.

A heavy sigh preceded his answer. "No plans."

"You've been off school for three weeks now. Don't you feel like doing something?"

"I am doing something. I'm relaxing."

"I meant something productive."

"I know what you meant."

"It just seems like too nice of a day to be sitting inside."

"Yes, Mother."

"Don't yes Mother me, young man." The lilt in her tone betrayed the fact that she was mildly amused with her son's reply, rather than taking offense with it.

By this point Larry realized he wasn't getting back to sleep, so there was no sense fighting it. Swinging his legs over the edge of the bed, planting his feet firmly on the floor, he stood up and stretched, nearly hitting the revolving fan blades with his outstretched arms. Plodding to the door, he opened it slowly.

His mother stood there, waiting for him, sipping from the cup of coffee in her hand. She offered a pleasant smile to greet his awakening.

"That's what I like to see. No sense sleeping the day away."

"I'm not eleven anymore, Mom. You don't need to be getting after me all the time."

"Well, even a twenty-one-year-old should do something with his life."

"And going to college isn't doing something?" He smiled, enjoying the easy banter with his mother. He always felt relaxed around her. It was a comfortable feeling they shared, each able to express themselves honestly to the other.

"Of course going to college is something," she conceded, apparently willing to throw him a bone in the matter. "But after three weeks away from it I'd think you'd be bored by now."

He lifted his finger to the side of his mouth, presenting a pensive appearance, like he was deep in thought and considering the possibilities. "Nope. Not bored yet."

"Well, I'm heading off to work. Have fun doing whatever you find to do today."

"I will. Have a good day, Mom."

As she walked away he retreated to his laptop, retrieving it from the end table. He made himself comfortable, sitting cross-legged on the bed with the portable computer in his lap, and soon was scrolling through his emails, catching up on everything he had missed overnight.

One address caught his eye. It was from the Toledo CASA office. He paused a moment, reflecting, then opened the message.

Three years into his bachelor's of Social Work degree at The University of Toledo, Larry Kendall still found the subject fascinating and personally rewarding. He liked the feeling of doing something important with his life; it made him feel like he could make a difference in the world. It was no doubt an attitude he had inherited from his father, whose work as a police officer had always seemed special to Larry.

Two years ago he had discovered the CASA program. The basic premise had caught Larry's interest when he first heard about it while attending a seminar through the college, and it seemed like a natural extension to the work he would soon be performing as a social worker.

A volunteer program, the CASAs, or Court Appointed Special Advocates, represented children who found themselves dealing with issues at home that required outside assistance to handle. Whenever a case of child neglect or child abuse entered the court system a CASA was assigned to represent the children and look out for their interests. In a legally binding sense they became a guardian of the children they represented, a watchdog over them and the family activities around them. Each month they would visit the children they were dealing with, to determine that suitable arrangements had been provided for their safety and well-being. They had the right, and responsibility, to make recommendations to the court if they weren't satisfied with what they saw.

But the home visits were only part of their duties. They would interview parents, family members, or friends, in an effort to understand the situation the children were going through. They were entitled to talk to medical personnel, and school officials, and anyone they thought pertinent in their investigation into the children's background.

There were hearings to attend, and court reports to write, all tasks designed with the children's best interest in mind. The kids deserved to have a voice in their lives. The CASA volunteer was that voice.

The CASA program was recognized across the country, with local affiliates in each of the fifty states. Larry had taken the training through Lucas County, in a class with a dozen other people coming from various walks of life. There were a myriad of differences between the members of his class, but the tie that bound them all together was the desire to help children in need of a caring adult in their lives.

The training consisted of intensive class time as a group, exploring the issues confronting the predominately low-income families they would be dealing with in their cases. Since the families could be involved in anything from alcohol and drug addiction to child abuse – whether physically, mentally, or sexually – there was a lot of material to cover.

Outside the classroom individual time was devoted reviewing online material, which provided further information by detailing sample scenarios similar to those they could be exposed to. Plus there were required visits to the Juvenile Court, providing a firsthand look at the reality of the justice system and how it dealt with children in need.

Larry had handled two cases since becoming a CASA a year and a half ago. Both cases had ended a few months earlier, which had worked out well with his school schedule. Finals and end-of-semester papers had kept him relatively busy since that time. Now, finding himself on summer break, he grudgingly admitted to himself that his mother was right. It was time to do something with himself.

He re-read the e-mail from the CASA office, which listed three different families with children requiring volunteers. One in particular piqued his interest. Retrieving his cellphone, he punched in the number stored under CASA and, after two rings, a cheery voice answered.

"Toledo CASA office. Susan Grant speaking. How may I direct your call?"

"Good morning, Susan. This is Larry Kendall."

Larry used his real name in his CASA cases, a practice many of the volunteers chose not to do. They had been informed in training that their privacy would be better protected by not giving out their real identity; in the event a case turned sour a disgruntled parent couldn't seek them out. Larry had decided against this practice. His intention to become a social worker made it seem more practical to use his proper identity for everything. It seemed less confusing that way. It was his decision to make, and the CASA office supported him on it.

Susan was speaking again. "Hello, Larry. What can I do for you?"

"I was considering taking on a new case, and was looking at the email recently sent out by the office. I have a question concerning one of the cases."

"Let me put you through to Becky. She can probably answer that better than I can. Can you hold a minute?"

"Sure."

For fifteen seconds background music emanated from the phone, after which another voice came on the line. "Rebecca Poole here."

"Hello Rebecca. This is Larry Kendall. I'm ready to take on one of the cases in your latest email, but I have a question first."

"Certainly, Larry. What's your question?"

"I'm looking at the case with the twin nine-year-old boys. It says the children are in Protective Custody. What does that mean?"

"It could mean a number of things. I'm not familiar with the particulars of the case, but it usually means Children's Services felt the children were in a safe environment, even with the allegations against the parents. So rather than disrupt the family more than necessary, they allow the children to remain where they are, with the understanding that the agency will be monitoring the situation closely."

"That doesn't make sense, "Larry admitted. "If the children are being abused shouldn't they be taken somewhere else? Wouldn't that be safer for them?"

"It depends on the circumstances. Like I said, I don't know all the details. Monica attended the Emergency Hearing for this case. If you can hold on a minute let me see if I can reach her for you. I'm sure she can answer your questions better than I can."

Once more music came on the line.

Even with two cases behind him Larry was still fairly new as a CASA, so while he waited on the line he considered the limited knowledge he had concerning the way cases were handled. Once an allegation of child abuse or neglect was presented to Children's Services an investigation would immediately be undertaken by the agency. Within twenty-four hours – or on the next business day, if the claim came to light over a weekend or on a holiday – an Emergency Shelter Hearing would be held in front of one of the magistrates at the Juvenile Court. Children's Services would present their findings at this time. The parents would be invited to testify as well, with an attorney present, giving them the opportunity to explain the situation.

At this point in the process it was too early to assign a CASA for the children, because no legal case had as yet been established. So instead an attorney from the CASA office would attend the hearing. Monica Perry, one of the CASA lawyers, had apparently represented the office in the case Larry was interested in. The Emergency Hearing would give her the opportunity to voice her opinion of what she felt was best in the children's interest.

Ultimately it was the decision of the magistrate what happened next. Usually a separation occurred, placing the children with a family member outside the residence or, when no suitable relative could be found, finding an appropriate foster family. The children would reside in their new surroundings for the time it took to thoroughly investigate the situation, at which point a final determination would be reached concerning the children's future.

The courts always hoped for reunification with the family, believing firmly that children belonged with their parents.

The CASA office always worked toward whatever was in the best interest of the children, regardless of how it affected the family. The children were their number one concern, and that was where they concentrated their efforts.

A voice on the phone interrupted Larry's thoughts.

"Hello, Larry. This is Monica. I understand you have some questions concerning the case with the twin boys?"

"Yes I do. I've never dealt with Protective Custody before. I'm not that familiar with the term, or how it applies to this case. Is there anything I should know going into this?"

"Fair question. As you're well aware, it's always the goal of the court not to separate families, unless the situation warrants removal of the children because they are in an unsafe, or dangerous, environment."

"But surely in this case, with signs of physical abuse...?"

"I'm going to stop you right there," Monica interrupted. "Yes, there are unexplained marks. On one of the children only. But there are no witnesses to testify what caused the marks."

"What does the boy say?"

"So far he hasn't said anything. That's often the case with abuse. The child doesn't want to betray a family member. Even with the treatment they've suffered the child often has a bond with the abuser, making them reluctant to betray them."

"How can it be betraying someone if the person is hurting you?"

"I know it sounds unreasonable. And it doesn't make sense from a logical point of view. But it's a complicated relationship, sometimes one that has been going on for a long time without anyone else being aware of it. These kinds of situations develop slowly. It's not something that can easily change overnight, no matter how drastic the situation. And often the child feels that he is the one at fault; that something in his or her actions prompted the mistreatment. This makes them even more reluctant to talk about things.

"What makes this case even more frustrating as well is that there are two children in the family – the same sex, the same age – but only one of them shows indications of abuse."

"So what happens next? What's being done for these kids?"

"This is where Protective Custody comes in. The mother lives with her paternal grandparents, who are retired and apparently don't get out much. I understand the grandfather in particular has health problems that limit his mobility. This means there are generally several adults in the house at any given time."

"Yet the abuse was still going on," Larry interjected, still having a difficult time understanding the logic of the situation.

"Don't let your emotions take over, Larry. You need to look at this from a legal point of view. With lack of proof as to the identity of the abuser the court didn't feel justified in removing the children. Even so, they still feel the allegations need to be investigated. They felt Protective Supervision was the best way to accomplish this. Now that the family is aware of the situation there are multiple pairs of eyes monitoring things, as well as Children's Services. The caseworker is entitled – and obligated – to stop in from time to time to see what the home environment is like.

"And you as the CASA – if you decide to take the case – can also stop in from time to time as well."

"To look for what?"

"Oh, you'll know it when you see it. If things feel funny to you, like they're trying to hide something. Or, once you get to know the children better, you may be able to pick up on their mood swings."

He made no reply, considering her words.

"So what do you think?" Monica continued. "Will you take the case?"

"Yes. I think I will."

"Good for you. I'll put Becky back on the line and she'll see that you get all the information you need to get started. Don't hesitate to call me if any questions or concerns come up."

"Thank you, Monica. I appreciate that."

"No. Thank *you*, Larry. These kids need people like you in their lives. We're lucky to have you as part of the team."

Chapter Six:

THE TWINS spent one night away from their mother, returning home the day following the accident at the playground. It was one night too many as far as Laura was concerned. She had gone longer times without them – when the boys had sleep-overs at a friend's house, or the weekend they went camping with their Uncle Paul – but this incident was different from the times in the past. It had been a forced separation, leaving Laura to wonder what Aaron and Evan were going through and unable to check in with them. She couldn't even call on the phone to see how they were doing – to reassure them that everything was going to be alright.

It felt lonely in the house without them. The absence of the ever-recurring sounds of the video games they habitually played brought home to her the fact that they were gone. Their voices were missing from the table at dinner time.

The evening meal with Grandma Ruth was a silent affair, each woman absorbed in their own privates thoughts, each reluctant to disturb the other. Laura picked at her food, finding she had no appetite. She had retired early for the night, hoping sleep would relieve the anxiety, but slumber eluded her. She tossed and turned most of the night away.

She wished Ted was there, laying beside her, comforting her. His presence would make everything more bearable.

Then again, it had been Ted's presence in the household that had been the cause of the current situation. He was the reason her children were gone.

Laura thought back to the Emergency Court Hearing she attended the day following the accident at the playground. It was a confusing situation for her, such as she had never experienced before. And while the people in the court room had been polite enough, and never accused her directly of any wrongdoing, she couldn't help but feel that she was the center of attention. All those in attendance no doubt regarded her as an unfit mother, to allow her son to be subjected to the misuse he had obviously been exposed to. It made her feel guilty, even though she knew she had done nothing wrong.

One thing that had worked in her favor was her initial response to remove Ted from the household. It displayed, in the eyes of the court, her concern for her children and her willingness to do what needed to be done to rectify the situation. Had she not told her boyfriend to leave the children could have very well been taken from her and placed somewhere else. As it was Protective Custody had been agreed on, allowing Aaron and Evan to return after their single night away.

It was a relief for Laura to have the family back together again. She had never stopped to consider how much her life revolved around her children. Having them back made her realize how precious it was to spend time with them. All she wanted to do was be at their side and interact with them; watching them play video games, or enjoying a movie with them on DVD, or just having dinner together, sitting across the table from the twins and knowing they were close.

She didn't mind the fact that they monopolized her time. She enjoyed being part of their world, and the satisfaction of knowing she was a big part of it only made things easier. But there was something missing in her life now, and it was a newly discovered realization to her.

Somewhere along the way she had lost her identity. She was no longer Laura Reed.

Now she was Mom.

She had never stopped to consider the changes in her life since the twins became a part of it. The constant attention they required, the full-time responsibility that came with raising children, these were just things she had grown accustomed to and learned to accept as part of her life. It had never bothered her before the trip to the emergency room, when her world turned topsy-turvy and everything in her life became a shambles. Leaving the hospital brought it all into perspective; spending time away from Aaron and Evan had shown her that she hadn't much else in the world. She had built a life around her children and it was empty without them.

As she mused Laura once more thought of Ted, and the life they had started to build together. They had known each other for about half a year, and in that time she had come to realize what a successful relationship could be. It didn't have to be all one-sided, like it had been with the boys' father. Two people could agree with one another, and get along with one another, and share a life together.

Or so she had thought only a few days ago.

She still couldn't believe she had been so wrong about Ted. There were no warning signs she had detected, no indications that anything was amiss, until the evidence was thrown in her face and she had to accept the truth of the matter. When it came right down to it Ted was no better than Cal had been. He was no good for her, and no good for her kids.

Which meant it was time to begin rebuilding her life. Again.

Laura wandered to the front window, surreptitiously drawing the curtains for a glimpse outside. A smile came to her face as she observed the activity on the other side of the glass. Aaron sat in a lawn chair perched in the center of the driveway, his crutches abandoned on the blacktop beside him. Evan dribbled a basketball, circling around the chair twice before bouncing the ball to his brother, who somehow managed to catch it without toppling from his seat. Leaning over the edge of the armrest, a look of determination on his face, he sent the ball sailing toward the hoop.

It was an awkward shot, particularly while sitting in a chair with one leg held stiffly in front by the cast. The basketball missed the backboard completely, bouncing three times before coming to rest on the neighbor's front lawn. Evan retrieved the errant ball, laughing as he did so, and resumed the game.

As she watched her children it struck Laura again how different from one another they were. She had always known that, but until recently hadn't stopped to consider their unique personalities. Evan was the outgoing one – spontaneous, eager to chat with anyone about anything, enjoying life and making the most of his youth. Aaron was much more serious and introspective. He was cautious about trying new things, taking time to consider his actions before launching into the unknown.

Had he always been like that? Or was this something recent, a personality change brought about by what he had been experiencing? Had his true feelings been submerged beneath layers of hurt?

Laura had spent hours on the computer the day following the accident, researching information online, and was still no closer to understanding child abuse. It seemed unbelievable to her that anyone would intentionally harm a child. They were so innocent, relying on those around them to shelter and provide for them. Grownups should be there to protect children, and take care of them, not to abuse them.

But the statistics she ran across supported the fact that, not only did abuse occur, but it was all too prevalent in our society. One site estimated that on average five children die each day due to child abuse, with the majority of the cases involving children under the age of three.

And, perhaps most alarming of all, in over seventy-five percent of the cases the abuser was the child's parent. The person that should want more than anyone else in the world to care for a child became instead the monster that misused them.

The more she read the more infuriated she became. Her anger against Ted grew, in consideration of the role he had played in the whole sordid affair, but she found herself blaming her own part in the tragedy as well. She should have been more attuned to what was going on around her. She should have been more aware of the changes in Aaron and the reason for his behavior. Things had been happening – in her house – that she had been totally oblivious to. How could she not have noticed?

She knew she had to talk to her son about the situation, in an effort to discover what had been going on, but nothing in her upbringing had prepared her for such a daunting task.

Chapter Seven:

THE PROSPECT of his brother being on crutches had at first appealed to Evan as he pictured in his mind what the experience would be like. His imaginings leaned toward a clown performing on stilts they had once seen at a circus they had attended with their mother. The colorful figure had cavorted around the center ring, displaying an amazing array of tricks and acrobatics to the crowd, all the while perched atop a pair of wooden stilts that gave the impression he hovered over the spectators in the grandstand. Surely Aaron would master the crutches in no time and would soon be preforming similar feats of derring-do.

The reality of the situation, as the twins soon discovered, was anything but exciting. Aaron actually adjusted well to his handicap, and quickly was able to get where he wanted on his own. But he still stumbled from time to time. And had a difficult time navigating through tight spaces or up and down stairs. And, of necessity, he had to slow down with everything he did, hobbling along on his right leg, with the cast constraining his left a weight that threatened to drag him down.

He made no complaints, and insisted on doing as much as he could on his own, but it quickly became obvious to the family that sleeping upstairs wasn't a viable alternative for the injured child. The logistics of traveling the steps proved a burden not easily overcome.

To make things more convenient for him a corner of the living room was cleared away. Somehow Evan and his mother managed to haul the mattress from the bottom bunk bed in the boys' room and maneuver it down the steps, helped in no small measure by the fact they had gravity on their side. The mattress practically slid down the stairs on its own – only knocking over one lamp, which fortunately weathered the experience without breaking – and eventually a makeshift bed was situated in the space they had prepared.

Evan was pretty certain returning the mattress to the upstairs bedroom would be a more difficult chore.

Like any kids their age the twins enjoyed video games, immersing themselves in the colorful and exciting worlds available through the gaming consoles. At least that was one activity that wasn't hampered by having a broken leg. Aaron could sit for hours in front of the television, a practice that normally wouldn't have been tolerated by his mother but, under the circumstances, was deemed an appropriate use of his time. She also felt a certain amount of guilt, as though she had failed her son by not being more aware of his situation, and found allowing him his fill of the games was a way of atoning for her failure. She tended now to accommodate him in the extreme, feeling it was the least she could do considering the circumstances.

Aaron was content with the arrangement, taking advantage of his forced confinement in the living room, making himself at home in the jury-rigged bedroom.

But now that it was summer, and the weather was pleasant, Evan found himself wanting more and more to get out of the house so he could play. He longed to ride his bicycle, racing up and down the sidewalks of the neighborhood. Or climb the big lilac bush in the backyard to his imagined tree fort in the branches, where his fantasies were free to wander. One day the site served as a Medieval castle, and Evan its Lord ruling wisely, but sternly, over the countryside. On another occasion it became in his mind the mast of a pirate ship, a perch to survey the oceans for galleons laden with golden doubloons and treasures of diamonds and emeralds.

Once again Aaron's condition affected things. These were activities the brothers were, for the time being anyway, unable to perform together. And as imaginative as Evan was, the experience was never the same by himself.

With summer temperatures on the increase Evan looked forward to an escape from the heat, but this also was not meant to be. Their mother opted instead not to set up the swimming pool in the backyard, like she normally did. It was a blow-up plastic ring, barely three feet tall. There wasn't even room in it to do much more than sit down. But it was a pleasure to just splash in it and cool off when the days got too hot.

"Please, Mom," Evan pleaded one morning, about two weeks after the accident. "Can't we fill up the pool?"

"It's too much work. Dragging it out of the basement and all."

"I'll help."

She smiled at him. "I'm sure you would. But do you think it would be fair for you to use the pool when your brother isn't able to?"

Aaron, propped up against some pillows in front of the television – playing video games – turned to face them. "That's okay, Mom. I don't mind if Evan gets to use the pool and I don't."

Evan immediately recognized his opportunity. "See, Mom? Aaron's okay with it. So can't we set up the pool?"

"Maybe later. When your brother is able to get around better."

"But Mom –"

His whining ceased following the stern look she administered.

"Besides," Laura pointed out, "we're supposed to have someone stopping by in a few minutes."

Both twins answered simultaneously. "Who?"

"The caseworker from Children's Services. Along with somebody from the CASA office."

"What's CASA?" Evan asked.

"I don't know," his mother admitted, a trace of frustration in her voice. "Somebody appointed by the court or something like that. He's supposed to stop by to check up on things."

Laura had been pacing the room, rearranging things here and there to make the place more presentable, but now she stopped, slumping down on the couch. She let out a sigh.

"I'm just tired of this whole business."

For a moment the room was silent. Grandma Ruth, reading her Bible as she sat on a chair in the corner, looked up for a moment but chose not to say anything. She understood her granddaughter's moods, probably better than Laura did herself, and could see the frustration growing. The young woman was obviously distraught, fearing her children could be taken from her once more if she didn't present the proper appearance of the loving mother.

Evan, feeling suddenly guilty and not knowing why, turned away.

Aaron's voice, meek and barely audible, spoke up. "I'm sorry, Mom. I'm sorry I fell at the playground."

Laura scooted over on the couch to be closer to her son. She reached out, stroking his arm. "It's not your fault, baby. I'm just glad you're okay." She continued in a firmer voice. "But when I think of Ted and what he did –"

Evan faced his mother. Words flew from his mouth, the tone an angry one. "Ted didn't do nothing wrong! Ted was always good to us."

Aaron, saying nothing, nodded in agreement.

"You boys don't have to stand up for him."

"Ted was fun to be with," Evan continued. "I miss talking to him about things."

"What kind of things?" his mother asked, hoping to get Evan's mind off his initial outburst.

"Oh, just stuff, I guess. Like sports. Or superheros. I remember when he took us to see Captain America, and we talked about who was better, Iron Man or Cap. He was just fun to be with."

In spite of herself Laura found herself smiling, recalling the endless debates Evan and Ted would have about a couple of movie superheros. It was like having a third kid in the house sometimes.

Evan noted the pensive look on his mother's face and decided to press his advantage. "You miss him, too. Don't you Mom?"

Laura considered a moment. "Yes I do."

"Then he should come back," Evan said, as though it was the most logical thing in the world.

For a moment Laura said nothing. She did miss her boyfriend. It was nice having someone to share time with. She had felt so alone through much of her life, like it was her against the world.

Her grandparents were great; they meant the world to her. They had taken her in – on two separate occasions – during difficult times of her life, offering comfort and protection and love when life had appeared at its bleakest to her. She could never repay all the things they had done for her over the years, no matter how hard she tried.

But it wasn't like having someone in your life to share the special times with.

For a few months Ted had been that someone, the person she thought she could rely on to be there for her, the person who cared enough about her to be a part of her life.

She glanced at Aaron, sitting in the corner with his broken leg propped up on a pillow, and the events of the last few weeks came racing back to her mind. "No." Her voice was firm with acceptance. "Ted's not coming back."

"But Mom –"

"No buts, Evan. He's not coming back and that's final. If I have to choose between Ted and you guys there's no choice at all. And to think I trusted him –"

"Ted didn't do nothing wrong," Evan repeated, though there was less anger in his voice now, as though he had resigned himself to the truth of the matter.

"I don't want to talk about it, Evan."

A struggle appeared to be waged in the young man's eyes following his mother's declaration, a confrontation between the desire to stand up for what he felt was right and the need to obey what he was told to do. In the end he relinquished the fight, no doubt admitting to himself the folly of doing otherwise. It was a battle he was well aware he stood no chance of winning.

Chapter Eight:

THE CELLPHONE chirped, its tone barely audible above the music blaring from the dashboard radio. Connie Peters turned down the volume then reached over and, with practiced ease, extracted the phone from the purse on the seat beside her. She had a new message, from Larry Kendall. With no traffic ahead of her she chanced a quick look.

Running late. See u in a few.

She dropped the phone casually onto the passenger's seat, then returned to her driving.

Connie had first spoken to Larry three days ago, when he had called her questioning the particulars concerning Aaron Reed and his family. She was the caseworker assigned to the case now, having inherited the matter from Patrick Zimmerly, who had first investigated the children at Toledo Hospital. This was Connie's first visit with the family at their home, though she had spoken with Laura Reed at the Children's Services office.

The mother seemed defensive and apologetic, concerned over what was happening and astonished that there was any kind of problem with her children. She seemed genuinely interested in her children's situation and willing to do whatever it took to set things right.

Or so she said. Connie had heard the same spiel countless times over the years. Often it was sincere. But too many times they were empty words, the parents saying whatever they felt was necessary to get their lives on track again and get the agency off their backs.

Or, in the worst of instances, the entire routine was a cover-up, a way to disguise the awful truth of what was going on behind closed doors. The statistics revealed the truth of the matter. Too many times it was the parent who was abusing the child. Anyone who would do such a think would have little difficulty in lying about the situation, especially as a means of protecting themselves.

Connie had seen it in the past. She had no doubt she would see it again in the future. As such she had a difficult time believing the words she heard, or the stories she was told. There was always another side to everything.

It would be interesting to note the interaction of the family members when on their own turf – in familiar surroundings – where people often forgot to don the masks that shielded them in public. Connie approached the matter armed with the information she had absorbed from Patrick's notes, what little she had obtained from a few short minutes speaking with him on the phone, and years of experience dealing with these types of situations.

She glanced once again at her cellphone. When Larry Kendall had called from the CASA office, saying he too was just beginning his investigation, they had decided to visit the family at the same time, an approach Connie agreed to.

She reflected on the pros and cons of this method.

Connie didn't want the mother to feel like they were ganging up on her. Laura Reed was painfully aware she was under observation from Children's Services. The allegations presented following the Emergency Room visit several weeks ago couldn't be ignored. That was a given. Miss Reed and her family would be under scrutiny for the next several months, particularly during the early phase of the investigation. She no doubt felt tense regarding the situation – regardless of the extent of her participation in the affair – and having a stranger from the department as well as a CASA volunteer show up at the same time could be overwhelming.

On the other hand, she needed this initial home visit with each of them. By Connie and Larry showing up together she could get both meetings out of the way at once. She wouldn't have to go through the stress of awaiting the confrontation twice; cleaning the house, getting the children presentable, worrying about the hundred-and-one things she could do wrong that could reflect poorly on her ability to mother her children. It would be easier for the family this way.

And from Connie's point of view, it was beneficial having another set of eyes and ears for the first visit. She planned to make a point of talking things over with Larry afterward, to get his impression of the case, on the chance she might miss something.

She found the house at last, a two-story bungalow in a neighborhood of small houses and – for the most part – well-maintained yards. She knew from Patrick's report that Laura and her kids lived with the mother's grandparents. No doubt the house belonged to the older couple. And it was also likely, judging by the signs of neglect that were beginning to manifest themselves around the house, that the grandparents were getting up in years and could no longer maintain the place as well as they had in the past. Clinging vines threatened to overwhelm the fenced-in back yard. The wooden gate at the side of the house hung from a single hinge, waiting either the opportunity to fall off or the chance to get repaired. It seemed to beckon trespassers, offering easy access to the family's backyard.

Connie stepped out of the air conditioned car. The humid summer air assaulted her; she felt as though she was sweating instantly. A glance at the heavens revealed not a cloud in sight, so the prospect of rain seemed slim. She would just have to ride out the heatwave like the rest of the city.

She had barely moved away from the car when a battered green Escort pulled to the curb behind her. The young man stepping out of the car – he looked to be barely out of high school – was casually dressed, wearing shorts and a t-shirt that featured a popular video game. She recognized the characters displayed, having observed her fifteen-year-old son playing it on the X-Box, but she had no idea what the game was called. She had no interest in finding out, either. As much as she loved her son – and wanted to be close to him, and share his interests – she just couldn't understand his fascination with video games.

She consoled herself with the knowledge that her son wasn't the only one captivated by the onscreen entertainment. So as long as he kept his grades up, and didn't spend every waking moment with a controller in her hands, she was content to let things slide. There were enough battles to be fought during the teenage years. Video games was something she could live with.

The new arrival approached, a smile on his face. "You must be Connie?"

"That's right. Larry?"

"That's me. Thanks for letting me meet you like this."

"No problem. How long have you been working with CASA, Larry?"

"Just over a year." By now he had reached where she stood on the sidewalk, and together they approached the house. "This is only my third case," he admitted.

"What got you interested in the program?"

"I'm going to UT for a degree in social work. I figured this was a good way to get an idea of what's going on out here. Sort of get my feet wet."

"Good for you. We're always short-handed and can use all the help we can get."

"How about you? How long have been doing this?"

"Seventeen years now." It felt like much longer, she mused, thinking back on some of the cases she had dealt with through the agency.

Meanwhile Larry had continued speaking. "I'm pretty nervous. Meeting new people and all. I feel like I'm intruding on their lives. Does it ever get any easier?"

"Depends on the case."

They stopped at the front door, Connie rang the bell, then leaned closer to whisper to him. "You'll be fine. Just pretend like you've done this a hundred times before. Believe me, the mother will be more nervous than you."

She stared ahead, waiting for the door to open, and muttered under her breath. "She has every reason to be."

Evan Reed answered the door. Connie presented her most charming smile to the young boy. "You must be Evan. We're here to see your mother."

Evan made no reply, his eyes locked for a moment on the colorful video image on Larry's t-shirt. A smile snuck it's way onto his face at recognition of the game portrayed. Then he shrugged his shoulders, turning, and walked down the hallway. "Mom! They're here."

Connie walked in, followed by Larry, who closed the door behind them, and they waited in the front hallway until Laura came out to join them.

"Thank you for seeing us today, Laura," Connie began. "This is Larry Kendall, from the CASA office."

Larry moved forward, offering his hand. Laura accepted it with a weak shake, muttering a quiet greeting, then led them down the front hallway.

"Come on in," she offered, the invitation polite but hardly cordial.

The three entered the living room, Laura continuing in an apologetic tone. "You'll have to excuse the mess." She indicated the mattress and blankets occupying a corner of the room. "Aaron was having a hard time with the stairs so we made a place for him down here."

"Perfectly understandable."

"This is my grandmother, Ruth Franklin," she explained.

Grandma Ruth placed her Bible carefully on the end table, stood from the chair, and stepped closer. Her eyes examined the visitors as though searching for flaws.

"Welcome to our house," the old woman told them, her words sounding incongruous in relation to the stern expression on her face. "I can't say it's a pleasure having you here, considering the circumstances, but you are welcome all the same."

"Grandma!" Laura's embarrassment over Grandma Ruth's words was obvious.

"That's okay," Connie assured them. "I understand your feelings, Mrs. Franklin. Believe me, I would rather we didn't have to go through this as well. But allegations have been made and I have to do my job." She motioned toward Larry. "We both do."

Laura turned toward Larry, a questioning look on her face. "You're not from Children's Services?"

"No. I'm here representing the CASA office."

"What does that mean? The CASA office?"

"The CASAs are Court Appointed Special Advocates. We are assigned through the court, and our focus is on your children. Primarily I'll monitor their living conditions to insure they are safe and well taken care of. I'll be visiting with them at least once a month for however long these issues take to resolve themselves. So I suppose you could consider me the eyes of the court, looking over the safety of your children."

Laura sat in her chair, fidgeting with her hands, as Larry finished his recital. She nodded, as though comprehending what was involved, but her next words demonstrated her confusion. "I just don't understand any of this," she remarked, when he was done. "How can this be happening to us? We're a good family."

"A God-fearing family," Grandma Ruth added, ignoring the embarrassed look her granddaughter sent her way, urging her to be quiet.

Connie smiled – a weak smile of support – and turned toward Aaron, who still sat in front of the television, his attention focused on the video game he played. Except for a quick glance at the new arrivals when they walked in the door he showed no interest in what was going on around him. It was as though he was totally unaware of the attention drawn to the family as a consequence of his accident at the park.

"And this must be Aaron?" Connie asked.

He offered a meek "Hello" without turning away from the game.

Larry shifted position, to get a better look at the youngster, then glanced toward his brother. "They do look a lot alike, don't they?" he commented. "Are they identical?"

Their mother supplied the answer. "Yes. In looks, anyway. But not in personality. Evan's the more vocal of the two. Aaron's pretty quiet. Keeps to himself more. Isn't that right, baby?"

Aaron made no response, other than a quick shrug of the shoulders in acknowledgment. The gesture could have easily been overlooked.

Connie moved toward the couch. "Do you mind if I sit down, Laura?"

"No. Of course. I'm sorry. Please do. Can I get you anything? Something to drink?"

"No," she replied, taking a seat. "I'm fine."

There was one remaining empty chair in the room so Larry claimed it.

"Let's get down to business," Connie began, pulling a notepad from her briefcase as she addressed Laura. "Besides you and the kids – and of course your grandmother – who else resides in the house?"

"Just Grandpa Mike."

"And where is he right now?"

"Laying down" Grandma Ruth supplied, after returning to her chair. "Michael hurt his back at the Jeep plant, fifteen years ago. Got an early retirement out of it, but it hasn't been the same since."

"I'm sorry to hear that."

"It's God's will," she remarked. "Who are we to question it?"

The caseworker jotted something down on her pad. "And no one else lives here?"

"That's it," Laura assured them.

Evan, standing quietly in the doorway and watching the adults, spoke up. "Except Ted."

Larry turned toward the boy. "What's that?"

"Ted doesn't live here anymore," Laura blurted out. "I asked him to leave. Right after...." She paused, searching for the proper words. "Right after everything happened at the hospital."

"And who's Ted?" Larry asked.

"Ted Myers. My boyfriend. Or, at least, he was my boyfriend. But after all this...."

An awkward silence filled the room, the only sound the beeps and whistles from the video game Aaron played.

"I told him to leave," Laura continued. "That he wasn't welcomed around here any more."

"So you think Ted is the one responsible for what happened to Aaron?"

"Who else?'

Lifting his head, a look of defiance in his voice, Evan spoke up. "Ted didn't do nothing wrong."

"Now, Evan –"

"But he didn't, Mom. He wouldn't."

"I told you I don't want to discuss this right now."

"But Mom –"

"I think you better go to your room, young man."

He nearly said something further. But, apparently realizing the futility of the situation, he remained silent instead. Without saying a word he crossed the room and walked up the stairs.

"I'm sorry."

"No need to apologize, Laura," the caseworker offered in a reassuring tone. "Kids often feel the need to speak their mind. Even when it is inappropriate."

"You've got to understand, Evan and Ted always got along good together. Evan has quite the imagination. It's like he's living in a fantasy world sometimes. It's either pirates or superheros or something, where he's pretending he's something he isn't. Ted used to fool around with him about it. Feed into his worlds of make believe."

She stopped, her attention on the stairway her son had just climbed. "But Evan has to face reality sometime." She turned back to her guests. "I guess we all have to."

Tears were beginning to form in her eyes, the moisture glistening from the light in the room. "I still can't believe this is happening. Or that Ted would have done such a thing. I thought I knew him better than that. I thought after our time together...."

She stood, turning away, as though suddenly embarrassed with what she was thinking. "I know six months isn't a long time to know someone. But in that time I just felt so close to him. He made me feel.... Special, I guess."

"You rushed into things," Grandma Ruth pointed out, no trace of sympathy or understanding in the tone. "You always do. You need to slow down and think things through before you jump into stuff like this."

She spun around to face the older woman, defiance on her face. "I don't need to hear this, Grandma. I know it was a mistake. I can see that. Now."

She sat down once more, collapsing on the couch as though exhausted. Her eyes wavered between Connie and Larry, her face imploring them for understanding. "And he was so good with the kids. So patient. It felt good to have someone like that in my life. Someone my kids could look up to. It just seemed so right."

Then she mumbled softly, the words barely reaching across the room. "But it all turned out so wrong, didn't it? The way everything does."

Chapter Nine:

TWENTY MINUTES later, after obtaining more information and reviewing further details concerning the family, Connie and Larry left the house. In silence they walked toward the caseworker's car. As she was retrieving her keys from her purse Larry spoke up.

"So what do you think?"

"Pretty early to tell. Things seem normal enough."

"Aaron's pretty quiet. Do you suppose he's just afraid to say anything?"

She shrugged. "Could be. Abused children often protect themselves with silence, afraid to say anything that might cause further pain to be inflicted on them. Or it could just be his nature. A lot of boys keep things to themselves. And he's obviously hooked on his video games. I've seen kids draw into the games so much that it's their entire world. My son's a lot like that."

Larry thought he noticed a trace of irritation in her voice; as though video games were a sore subject between Connie and her son. "I'm sort of hooked on them myself," Larry confided, his joking tone making light of the situation.

Connie shook her head, a look of amazement on her face. "I just don't understand you guys and your video games. How you can just sit there for hours in front of the television like that is beyond me."

"I find it relaxing."

"Relaxing? I've seen some of those games my son plays. What's so relaxing about blasting away at zombies for an hour straight?"

"I guess it's a guy thing."

"Whatever. Evan seems different in that way. At least from what his mother says."

"About Evan. He seemed pretty upset about the mother's boyfriend leaving. What's that about?"

Connie glanced at the house, as though trying to peer through the walls to observe the individuals within and perhaps obtain a better grasp on the situation. "I don't see those kids getting much interaction from the grandparents. And they're getting to the age where they want their independence from their mother. I'm guessing Evan was glad to have somebody other than his brother to relate to. A male role model for young boys isn't necessarily a bad thing."

"Depends what type of behavior he's modeling."

Connie made no reply as she opened her car door. Larry continued.

"So this boyfriend.... Ted Myers. Do you think he's responsible for what happened to Aaron?"

"Could be. The mother seems to think so, anyway, so that's some indication. I've seen some messed-up things over the years. It's amazing what people are capable of."

"But why just one of the boys? The hospital said there were no marks on Evan."

"Who knows? Maybe the boyfriend just couldn't relate to Aaron like he does his brother. Maybe he took a shine to one and a disliking to the other. Or maybe it's something else altogether. You never can tell with some of these wackos."

Connie paused, detecting a look of confusion on Larry's face. "Is something bothering you?"

"Just thinking, I guess. I know I should stop in to see the boyfriend. To get his side of the story. But I don't know how to talk to the guy. What do I say? *So, have you been abusing your girlfriend's kids?"*

"No, that definitely isn't the right thing to say. But maybe you don't even need to say anything about it. Just start with a casual approach. Ask him about his connections with the family, and his feelings toward the two boys. Don't say anything accusatory. Just hear him out. You may be able to get an impression of what type of person he is from the responses he gives you."

"I suppose this is easy for you, after all the years you've been doing this?"

"Some parts of it are never easy, Larry. Some things you see in this job you never get used to. But don't let that discourage you. It's great what you're doing here. You can make a real difference in a child's life. I've seen it happen."

"Maybe things will be better for Aaron, now that the boyfriend's out of the house."

"Time will tell. The family has their first counseling session next week with the therapist. Maybe he can get through to Aaron and find out what's been going on in there." As she spoke her eyes were focused once more on the house they had just left, as if attempting to discern the truth about what was going on inside.

Larry glanced at his notes. "Dr. Richard Markham. Have you met him?"

"A couple times. He deals with childhood cases exclusively, so he's had a lot of experience with this type of thing. He's good with kids."

Larry made no reply as Connie placed her purse and notebook on the passenger's seat. Sitting in her car now, the door still partially opened beside her, Connie grabbed her sunglasses off the dashboard and put them on before addressing Larry again. "Let me know if you have any other questions."

"I'll do that. It was nice meeting you, Connie. I hope I don't get to be too much of a pest for you."

"No problem. Email me anytime."

"I'll probably take you up on that."

He stepped to the curb, then watched as she pulled away. Turning to leave, he noticed movement out of the corner of his eye. It came from the family's backyard. As he sauntered to his car he could make out Evan Reed. The boy held a stick, wielding it as though it was a sword. Oblivious to everything around him, he seemed captivated in his play, his imagination no doubt wandering as he immersed himself in whatever make-believe world it was he inhabited.

Larry smiled to himself. He could remember being young himself, not so very long ago, and thinking the world was one big adventure. And as much as he enjoyed his childhood, he recalled wanting more than anything to grow up. Adult life seemed so full of exciting possibilities.

Sometimes, he had to admit, the reality didn't live up to the expectations.

Chapter Ten:

THE SOUND of snoring wafted through the opened doorway. It was dark in the room, the only illumination a nearly insignificant ray of light that sneaked its way through the curtains from the streetlamp outside. The room felt stifling, the oscillating fan in the corner doing little to dispel the heat. It seemed only to rearrange the humid air in the room, causing little comfort.

Mike Franklin snored again and his wife, standing in the doorway looking in at him, smiled at the sound. She'd been hearing the noise for years now. It never bothered her. It was almost comforting, to wake up at night, and hear his heavy breathing coming from the bed next to hers. They had stopped sleeping together following the accident. It was too uncomfortable for him and, with time, she had adjusted to the concept. But it still felt good knowing he was right there, just across the room from her, within easy touching distance if the need arose.

Ruth Franklin retreated from the bedroom, closing the door softly behind her so as not to disturb him. Padding into the living room, slippered feet soundless against the worn carpeting, she sat down in her customary chair, its welcoming embrace comforting her. She kicked her slippers off, her toes wiggling with their new-found freedom. Leaning over to turn on the desktop lamp the pull chord got away from her, making a loud snap as the chain hit against the fixture. It sounded unnaturally loud in the stillness of the night. She grabbed the cord with her hand, stopping the vibration and silencing the disturbance, then glanced in the corner.

Aaron slept soundly, undisturbed by the noise. His blanket only partially covered him. His broken leg lay exposed, the cast reflecting the light as though it glowed from within. It somehow made him look smaller than normal, as if his leg had started to grow and the rest of him had yet to catch up to it. She listened a moment to his steady breathing, a smile gracing her wrinkled features, then turned away.

The hour was late. Upstairs Evan and his mother slept as well.

So she had the house to herself.

Ruth enjoyed these times, when she could lean back and read her Bible, immersing herself into the words that spoke to her from the pages of the book. She took comfort, and inspiration, from the words she found within. They soothed her when she was troubled, and strengthened her when she felt weak.

She hadn't always felt that way. She had been raised Catholic, and she and Mike had been married in a lovely Catholic Church in Adrian Michigan. It was a picturesque country cottage of a place; a relic from a simpler time. A small congregation of relatives, friends, and neighbors had attended their special day. Rain had threatened all morning, managing to not put a damper on the festivities by holding off until later in the evening. She smiled at the recollection, remembering how young they both had been. It felt like ages ago now.

As their life together grew their interests and activities changed as well. Eventually they attended church services less and less frequently, until somewhere along the line they had stopped going altogether. Religion had never played much of a part in their lives. They observed the sacred holidays, and did their best to raise their children according to what they felt was right, but for the most part life went on around them, unperturbed with such things as the Bible and the word of God.

Mike was fifty-seven when he had his accident at the Jeep plant. A maintenance worker, he had been on a ladder, installing some duct work for the ventilation system in the paint department, when he had lost his balance, falling fifteen feet to the hard concrete floor. He had broken his arm and sprained his back.

The arm healed wonderfully, with full freedom of movement restored in no time.

His back had never been the same.

Mike had accepted his disability with a patience and understanding Ruth still marveled at. He suffered through three surgeries without a complaint, never missed a day of rehab, and kept strictly to the exercise routine prescribed by his physician. Refusing to give up on independence, he still managed to do things, though on a much reduced scale from what he had in the past. He was determined not to be intimidated by the restrictions forced upon him. Unable to return to work, saddled with an early retirement from the shop, he continued to do his best to help out around the house, though many of his former activities were denied him now.

Life hadn't come to a stop for him. He had adjusted to the changes and made the most of his situation.

It had been different for his wife.

In many respects it had been much harder for Ruth. For months afterward she cried herself to sleep at night, lamenting the state of affairs and questioning why they had to endure so much. The retirement she had planned in her head for the two of them – the camping trips out west together, the winters vacationing in sunny Florida – was now no more than a dream, a fantasy never to be fulfilled, a reminder instead of what they were missing in life.

She couldn't recall when she started reading the Bible. She had picked it up on a whim, and started leafing through it from boredom more than anything else. Somehow the page opened to a verse from Romans, in The New Testament. She still remembered the words verbatim.

More than that, we rejoice in our sufferings, knowing that suffering produces endurance, and endurance produces character, and character produces hope, and hope does not put us to shame, because God's love has been poured into our hearts through the Holy Spirit who has been given to us.

Even now, a decade and a half later, she found the words inspiring. But then....

Then, the words had called out to her. It was as though her thoughts were laid bare and someone – something – was attuned to her particular needs of the moment. The passage grabbed her as being exactly what she needed; the appropriate words for the struggle she was undergoing.

Since then Ruth had found the Bible to be a source of solace on many occasions. Three years ago, when Laura needed a place to stay and moved into their house, dragging two young boys in tow, the extra work and confusion had seemed hardly a burden at all. Rather, Ruth found it a commitment she undertook willingly.

It had been a difficult time for all of them, but particularly so for Laura. The young woman's relationship with the father of her twins had been a disastrous one. Cal Broker had been abusive to Laura, both physically and mentally, pushing her toward the point of desperation. Ruth had directed her granddaughter toward the good book, hoping Laura could gain strength and understanding through its teachings, but the young woman had resisted the thought from the start. Even now, after living so many years together under the same roof, Laura seemed to regard her grandmother's beliefs as little more than the aimless ramblings of a crazy old woman.

But that didn't matter. *The Lord works in mysterious ways.* One day Laura, and her boys as well, would discover the truth.

Until then Ruth took every opportunity to lecture the twins on the subject.

Evan seemed unfazed by the words. He listened attentively enough, but beyond that showed no interest. He accepted the stories as part of the fantasy world he lived in but regarded them as nothing else.

For Aaron it was another matter. He seemed intrigued by the thought of right and wrong; good versus evil. The power of sin, and the way it corrupted the minds of men, was a concept he struggled to understand. Often the two of them would spend time discussing things, analyzing the words Grandma Ruth read to him from the Bible, deciphering the text as to how it applied to them. Much more introspective than his brother, Aaron seemed to truly want to understand the world around him.

The old woman reflected on this a few moments longer. And then, sitting now in the darkened house, alone but never lonely, Ruth Franklin returned to the book she loved best, immersing herself in the poetic words within, at peace with herself and content with her place in the world.

Chapter Eleven:

AARON LISTENED to the sound of his grandmother's light footsteps as she headed toward her bedroom, followed by the silent closing of the door as she entered the chamber. As usual she had stayed up late, sitting in her chair, reading her Bible.

It comforted him, to know she was there. Just the presence of another person in the room made him feel safer.

Things happened at night.

Bad things.

Most nights he lay in bed, twisting and turning, agonizing over what the nighttime hours would bring. Wondering if he would make it through the night unscathed, or if tonight would be another night to dread. Wondering if the night would again leave him with memories he would strive desperately to forget, but realized he would always remember.

He didn't like sleeping downstairs like this. He felt vulnerable. Normally he would be in his bunk bed, with Evan right above him, which made things feel somewhat safer. He realized it was a false sense of security only. Having his brother in the room wasn't a guarantee of protection.

Nothing had happened since the night of the accident. At least he could be thankful of that. But he knew it was only a matter of time before the old routine repeated itself.

He wished he could get away from it all. He wished he could just leave the agony behind him. But he didn't know how. It was a situation he had to live with and make the best of.

He closed his eyes, feeling alone, and eventually drifted off to sleep.

Chapter Twelve:

HIS SISTER'S couch didn't make for the most comfortable of beds. It was too short for him – he couldn't even stretch his legs and get comfortable – and the cushions were too soft. He preferred a firm mattress. He preferred a bed, period, rather than camping out on someone's living room furniture.

But at least it was a place to stay. Until he figured out what was going on with his life.

Ted Myers finally stood, having abandoned the idea of getting back to sleep, and made his way to the kitchen. The Keurig dispenser was out of water, so he refilled the container and turned the contraption on. Fixing himself a cup of hazelnut blend, the only kind from the selection of specialty coffees Paige had on hand that sounded remotely appetizing, he sat at the kitchen table to stare idly out the window.

The early morning sun streaked rays of light through the trees of the backyard, painting the lawn a mottled display of light and dark. Birds chirped. He spied a robin pecking at the lawn, flying away moments later with a wiggling worm in its beak. A neighbor's dog barked, just once, then fell silent.

The world outside seemed peaceful and idyllic.

It failed to ease his troubled thoughts.

"Good morning, Ted."

He hadn't heard Paige enter the room. He looked her way, watching as she retrieved a cup from the cupboard, but said nothing. She poured her coffee then sat down across from him, staring idly out the window for a moment.

"How'd you sleep last night?" she asked at last.

"It's not the same as sleeping on a bed."

She smiled, an apologetic smile, her eyes crinkled partially shut, cringing as though she had done something wrong. "I'm sorry."

"No. I shouldn't have said anything. It's nice having a place to stay. I appreciate it."

Ted took a sip from his coffee, while Paige continued her backyard vigil.

"Nice morning," she finally commented, as though feeling the need to break the silence.

"Looks like it's going to be a hot one."

She nodded in reply and took her first sip from the morning brew. She seemed to savor the experience; almost like it was worth getting out of bed for. They sat there in silence for several minutes, both of them staring out the window as though in anticipation of something happening, but the view in the backyard remained the same. The birds came and went. The neighbor's dog resumed barking.

Finally another voice intruded.

"I'm taking off," Chris Jackson announced from the doorway. He directed his remark solely at Paige, managing to snub Ted with his attitude.

Paige smiled up at her husband. "Have a good day, honey."

He turned to leave, had only taken a step away, when Paige accosted him. "Wait a minute there, buster. Aren't you forgetting something?"

Chris walked over and presented his wife with a quick kiss on the cheek.

"That's more like it," she remarked, a smile on her face.

He managed a quick "See you tonight" as he walked out of the room. As before, he avoided all contact with his brother-in-law, refusing to even acknowledge Ted's presence. The front door slammed and then he was gone.

Paige placed her coffee cup on the table, leaning closer toward Ted. "I'm sorry about Chris."

"I can only imagine what he must think of me. I suppose I can't blame him. He doesn't know me that well."

"But I do." She reached over, patted him on the hand with sisterly affection. "I know the type of guy you are."

"I would never hurt Laura's kids," he said at last, giving voice to the thoughts troubling him. "Why would I do such a thing? I think her two boys are great."

"I know that. You don't have to convince me."

"I wish I could convince Laura. It's obvious she doesn't believe me."

"Give her time."

Ted rose, walking over to the window to stare out at the backyard.

"I just don't understand what could have happened to Aaron."

"Could they be seeing their father? I thought you said he was a pretty tough character."

"No. He's been out of the picture for years now. Doesn't have any contact with the kids."

"A baby sitter, maybe?"

"I don't think so. The kids are old enough where she doesn't get a sitter anymore. Especially with Laura's grandparents being in the house."

"Well, what about that?"

"About what?"

"The grandparents."

"That's ridiculous."

"Why?"

"To begin with, half the time Mike can't even get out of bed. I can't see him being much of a threat to a healthy nine-year-old."

"Then how about the grandmother?"

"Ruth?" He considered for all of two seconds. "No, I can't see that either."

"Why not? From what you've told me she's pretty wrapped up in that Bible of hers. Maybe she's one of those strict disciplinarians. The *spare the rod, spoil the child* type that wouldn't think twice about hauling off and whacking her grandson."

"No. I just don't see Ruth being like that."

"Well, those marks on the kid came from someone. And until somebody finds out who, Laura's gonna be pretty convinced it was you."

The morning dragged on for Ted. Working second shift at the Jeep plant gave him plenty of opportunity during the day to do things. A few weeks ago he would have been spending time with Laura and her kids. Or maybe watching something on ESPN with Mike. Now he wandered around the house, feeling like a stranger, belonging nowhere.

Paige was unloading the dishwasher when he entered the kitchen.

"Bored?" she asked.

"I suppose so."

"Well, if you're looking for something to do you could always mow the lawn. I'm sure Chris would appreciate not having to get to it after work."

"I'm not *that* bored."

As soon as the words left his lips he felt guilty. He wasn't being fair to Paige. She had let him move in, with no questions asked and no conditions given, and all he did was sit around the house. It hadn't been fair of Laura to kick him out the way she had. But sitting around moping about it wasn't going to change things either.

Ted had just about decided mowing the lawn didn't sound like such a bad idea when the doorbell rang. Paige flashed him an I'm-kind-of-busy look so Ted approached the front door.

A young man, several years younger than Ted, stood on the front doorstep. A lanyard around his neck displayed a plastic identification badge, though from his position inside the house Ted couldn't make out what the sign said. He was casually dressed and carried a notebook and folder in his hands. Ted figured he must be trying to sell something.

"I'm sorry," Ted began, "but we're not interested in buying anything today."

The young man smiled. "That's good. Because I'm not here to sell anything. I'm looking for Ted Myers."

Ted felt instantly defensive. "I'm Ted. What's this about?"

"I'm Larry Kendall." Larry held out his ID patch, displaying his picture and name. "I'm with the CASA office. If you have a few minutes, I'd like to talk to you about Laura Reed and her children."

Ted looked quickly up and down the street, not really certain why, but feeling like he was hiding something and they had come looking for him.

"You're from Children's Services, then." It wasn't a question, but rather a declaration of fact as Ted saw things.

"Not exactly. Do you think I could come in for a few minutes, Ted? I'd like to ask you a few questions and I think we would both feel more comfortable inside, rather than standing out here for all the neighbors to see."

Ted hesitated, weighing his options, when Paige's voice called from the back of the house. "Who is it, Ted?"

Both men stared at one another for a moment before Ted finally relinquished his position. "Come on in."

Larry stepped inside, Ted closing the door behind them, and the two of them walked into the back of the house. Paige was just closing the door on the dishwasher as they entered the kitchen.

"My sister Paige Jackson," he announced to their visitor.

"Larry Kendall." The two shook hands. "I'm here from the CASA office."

"CASA? What's that?" Paige asked.

"I'm a Court Appointed Special Advocate. I'm here concerning Laura Reed's children, Aaron and Evan."

Ted, the sour look still on his face, spoke up. "Like I said. You're from Children's Services."

Paige looked confused as she faced her brother. "I thought you said the caseworker was a woman? Connie, wasn't it?"

"Connie Peters," Larry supplied. "Yes, that's the caseworker from Children's Services. And while she and I work together, our roles are different from one another."

"In what way?" Ted asked.

Larry felt suddenly cornered; he could feel the hostility directed toward him from across the room. In some respects it was understandable. He probably should have called first, to prepare them for his arrival. There was certainly nothing wrong with him stopping in unannounced. As the children's guardian he was permitted to interview the people involved in the allegations at his own convenience. When he was contemplating the visit it had seemed simpler to explain to Ted Myers in person what his role in the case was, rather than trying to talk about it over the phone.

He also wanted to gauge Ted's initial reaction to the visit, in an effort to determine if anything felt unusual or out of place.

In hindsight, he realized now he should have called first.

"There's no reason to feel defensive about me being here," Larry began.

"Who's being defensive?" Ted asked. "Are you trying to say I have something to hide?"

"Certainly not. Could we just sit down for a few minutes, and talk things over?"

Ted glared at him. His sister reached over, rubbing her brother on the shoulder. "It doesn't hurt to talk things over," Paige admitted. She indicated the chairs around the kitchen table. "Please, Larry. Have a seat."

"You can think of me being here to represent the children," Larry began, once the three of them were gathered around the table. "My interest is to insure that they are in a safe place and being taken care of. To do that, I need to first interview the people involved. To reach an understanding of what the children are going through."

"I didn't do anything to Laura's kids."

"I never said you did."

"But you're thinking it."

Before Larry could reply Paige spoke up. "Nobody's thinking that, Ted."

"Yes they are. And who can blame them? Laura and I weren't together that long. I'm a stranger in the house. Who else would they suspect?"

"I'm not here to accuse anyone, Ted. But there's no denying the marks on Aaron's body. Something happened to him. And I don't want to see that happening again. Do you?"

"Of course not." Ted lowered his head, considering his reaction to the affair. In his anger over his rejection from Laura he hadn't stopped to consider what the young boy was going through. Aaron was the one who had been hurt. Physically, and no doubt mentally as well. The only thing hurt for Ted was his feelings. And maybe a bit of his pride.

Paige picked up the conversation. "So what can we do?"

"To be honest, not much. I'll visit the family periodically, as will Connie from Children's Services. We'll be on the lookout for anything out of the ordinary or suspicious."

"So you think something might happen to him again?"

"It's a possibility. Especially since we don't know who was responsible for the previous injuries."

"It wasn't me," Ted reiterated.

"Then who do you think it was?" Larry asked.

"I don't know."

"We were just talking about that this morning," Paige put in. "It doesn't make sense to us."

"Laura does fly off the handle sometimes," Ted admitted. "I've seen her scold the kids from time to time. And threaten them. But I've never seen her hit them. I don't see her being capable of something like that."

"While you were there did Aaron get hurt in any other ways? Any accidents, maybe?"

"Nothing I can think of." He paused a moment, considering the question. "He sprained his ankle one time. I remember that. I think the kids had been playing in the backyard and he fell out of a tree."

"Accidents happen," Paige pointed out.

"They do," Larry admitted. "But so does abuse. Were you there when it happened, Ted?"

A glare crossed Ted's face as he considered the question. If anything his voice was more stern as he continued. "No. I work second shift. At the Jeep plant. So I'm gone most evenings. I think it happened last fall. After school." He took a moment to consider the incident. "Come to think of it, it was shortly after Laura and I met. I hadn't moved in yet. So I wasn't even there at the time."

"Anything else you can think of?"

"No. Afraid not."

"Okay." Larry removed a couple of business cards from his folder, giving one to each of the siblings. "If you think of anything else give me a call. The number on the card is the CASA office, and you can get hold of me through them. Or drop me an email. The address is on the card."

Neither Ted nor his sister bothered to look at the information. They let the cards sit on the table, where Larry had placed them, as the CASA volunteer stood up.

"Thank you for your time."

Ted grunted a noncommittal reply, while Paige rose from her seat. "I'll walk you to the door."

Chapter Thirteen:

MIKE FRANKLIN was having a good day.

That didn't happen very often. The injury to his back limited movement considerably, forcing him to hobble about using a cane. It hadn't been as bad in the years following the accident, but the passage of time – and the lack of physical exertion – had taken its toll on him. On some days a task as simple as walking into the living room sent jolts of pain through him, forcing him to pause and catch his breath from time to time.

He could have taken pain medication – the doctors had offered many times over the years – but he refused to take anything stronger than aspirin. On this point he was adamant. He'd rather suffer with the pain of a sore back than take the chance on becoming addicted to something he was certain he could live without. His viewpoint had earned him the playful nickname *My Stubborn German* from his wife.

It was a trait he couldn't deny.

Grandpa Mike had put on a lot of weight over the years, a consequence of his limited mobility, and it was inevitable that his health would be compromised further because of it. The diabetes had been diagnosed ten years ago, adding additional health issues. With a restricted diet, and Grandma Ruth carefully monitoring his blood sugars, he seemed to have things under control. Even so, it was another complication in an already precarious existence.

The most frustrating thing about it all, as far as he was concerned, was that in the years since his accident his mental faculties had never dulled. He was as intelligent and as sharp as he had been years ago. His mind constantly craved attention. He sought out activities like crossword puzzles and word games, things he could still perform even in his condition.

Or on good days – like today – he worked on a hobby he had been introduced to years ago by his Uncle Walt, when he was not much older than Aaron and Evan. He liked to dazzle the kids by saying he was a philatelist, but they were unimpressed with the fancy sounding term.

They knew it meant stamp collecting.

A table was set up on the far side of his bed with the articles for his hobby. A large leather binder held his prized possessions, the stamps he judged important enough – or interesting enough – to set aside from the rest. The stamp tongs, hinges, and other tools he required were kept close at hand, within reaching distance, to allow him to work from a sitting position with minimal movement. Above his bed, also within easy reach, were some of the catalogs he employed to research his collection.

Working on the stamps allowed his mind to wander free from the other cares in his life. It didn't matter that he was limited in his mobility, because everything could be done from the comfort of his room. He became transfixed, absorbed in his pastime, his hobby allowing him a freedom like nothing else in his life anymore.

"Whatcha doing, Grandpa?"

Mike Franklin turned toward Evan, who stood in the bedroom doorway. He smiled at the boy.

"Come in if you want."

Evan needed no further prompting. Grabbing a folding chair, he moved over beside the work table, staring at the miniature pictures on display. He was fascinated with the various colors and odd shapes in his grandfather's album. Some of them seemed more like tiny paintings, works of art on a small scale, rather than something you would affix to an envelope and send to someone.

"Where are these stamps from, Grandpa?"

"Central America."

Evan's face shone with excitement, as though he had discovered a hidden treasure. "Like the Black Honduras?"

Grandpa Mike laughed, delighted to be sharing the young boy's enthusiasm. "You remembered."

"Of course I remembered. You told me all about it. It's the most famous stamp in the whole world. And there's only one of them!"

"That's what some people claim, Evan."

"Don't you believe them?"

His grandfather shrugged. "Just because they only know of one stamp like it that doesn't mean there aren't others out there. That's part of the fun of stamp collecting. You don't really know what you might find. Or what other people have."

He ran his hand over a page of the album. The plastic felt cool and smooth to his fingertips. "And each collection is unique," he added. "A one of a kind assortment."

He paused a moment, staring up at the ceiling. "Who knows? Maybe, sitting in our attic right now, there's a rare Black Honduras hidden away?" He smiled at his grandson. "Maybe you'll find one some day?"

"That would be great." Excitement gripped Evan now, like it always did when he and Grandpa Mike talked about things. Evan could let his mind wander during their conversations together. Looking at the stamps was like exploring the world. It was like he could travel anywhere on the planet – or anywhere in time – unrestrained by distance. The possibilities seemed endless.

"What would you do, Grandpa? If you found a stamp that rare?"

The old man considered the question carefully before answering. "What would I do? Keep it in my collection, I suppose."

"Not me," Evan exclaimed. "I'd sell it. And buy a boat. Or a motorcycle. Or maybe a big mansion."

"I doubt you'd get a mansion for it."

"But I could get a boat?"

Grandpa Mike chuckled at the notion. "Yeah. You could buy a boat."

Just then Laura walked by, pausing in the doorway. "Evan! Are you bothering your Grandfather?"

"We're just talking, Mom."

"I've told you before, Grandpa needs his rest."

Mike shifted position slightly, to more directly face the doorway. The movement brought a slight pain to his lower back. He took a deep breath, waiting for the spasm to pass, then addressed his granddaughter. "He's not bothering me, Laura."

She looked skeptical. "Are you sure?"

"He's fine, darling."

"We're just talking about stamps, Mom."

"Well, if Grandpa Mike gets too tired you give him a break, Evan. You hear?"

"Yes, Mom."

As she walked away her son's voice resumed, enthusiasm obvious in the way he spoke. "So do you really have stamps from all over the world, Grandpa?"

"Of course I do. Remember those ones I showed you from Australia?"

"They got kangaroos in Australia, don't they?"

"They sure do. I even have some stamps with kangaroos on them."

"Can we look at them?"

"Of course we can."

Their voices faded as Laura walked away.

She could never understand her grandfather being interested in something as stupid as stamps. They were nothing more than little pieces of paper. What could possibly make them so fascinating?

Evan's interest she understood. She realized her son's imagination was unleashed viewing the stamps. In his mind he could travel the world, going anywhere he wanted with a simple turn of a page.

It pleased her that he was so imaginative, but it also worried her. It had been cute when he was smaller. Now, as he was getting older, she felt he should be growing out of these things. It was time to move on in life and learn to be more realistic.

Life wasn't a fantasy.

His brother was proof of that.

As she moved through the living room she observed Aaron sitting in the corner, in front of the television. A video game was turned on but the action on the screen seemed to be paused. Aaron stared at the image as though fascinated with it, the game controller idle in his hands, and made no motion to continue playing.

She moved closer, to the point where she stood beside him, but he still exhibited no reaction, mesmerized as he was with the image in front of him.

Bending down, Laura touched him on the shoulder. "Baby? Are you okay?"

Aaron physically shook, as though awakening from a dream. Instantly his hands started manipulating the controller in his hands, bringing the game on the television back to life. He made no attempt to face his mother.

"I'm okay," he remarked, his voice lacking inflection, the tone hardly a reassuring one.

"Is there anything you want to talk about?"

The young boy shook his head.

For a few seconds she said nothing, uncertain how to react. She wanted to be there for him. But nothing in her experience had taught her how to handle the current problem. Nothing in her upbringing had prepared her for the eventuality she now faced.

Laura turned to walk away then decided against it, opting instead to sit on the floor next to her son.

"Aaron."

The only reply was the beeps and pings from the video game.

"Aaron. Please look at me."

He paused the game then turned to face her, his expression as immobile as a mask.

"If there's anything you want to talk about...?"

"No." He turned once more to face the television. "I'm okay."

"Are you sure? Because –"

He threw the controller to the floor beside him, glaring at his mother. "I said I'm okay! Why don't you believe me? Why is everybody making such a big deal about this? It's not that big of a thing."

"But it is, baby. You're important to me. To all of us. So of course it's a big thing."

"Can't you just forget about it? Can't you just tell those people to stop coming here and leave me alone?"

"We can't do that, Aaron."

He nearly replied but Laura continued, cutting him off. "I know you're a good kid, Aaron. You and Evan both. And I know I've always told you that you have to listen to what grownups tell you. And to do what they say. And I know you try real hard to do that for me. But sometimes...."

She paused, swallowing hard, and forced herself to continue. "But sometimes grownups do things they shouldn't do. It doesn't mean they're bad people. It's just that they make mistakes.

"But if something is wrong – if a grownup tries to hurt you, or make you do things that are bad – then they aren't being good to you. Then you don't have to do what they tell you to do.

"That's not disrespect, Aaron. You have a say in what happens to you. And what happens to your body. You understand?"

She paused, hoping he would respond, but his only reply was a slight nod.

"If a grownup does something wrong to you it's not your fault. And you should tell somebody about it. You should tell *me* about it. Does that make any sense to you?"

He turned away, lowering his head to avoid looking in her direction.

"Because you can always talk to me. About anything. I'm your mother, and I'll always be here for you. Alright?"

He nodded once more.

She waited, giving him a few minutes to reply, hoping she had reached him with her words, but he maintained his silence. Finally she rose and walked away.

Laura paused in the kitchen doorway. The sound of the video game resumed. From Grandpa Mike's room voices continued, her grandfather and Evan finding still more to discuss concerning stamps.

Laura walked into the kitchen, feeling useless and alone, and sat down on a chair. Grandma Ruth looked up from her Bible, studying the young woman's face, but said nothing.

"He still won't say anything about it," Laura confessed. "He still won't confide in me."

"Give him time, Laura. If you push him too hard he may be afraid to say anything at all. *Love is patient, love is kind. It always protects, always trusts, always hopes, always perseveres.* You must prove your love by giving him the time he needs. Aaron will come around. I'm sure of it."

"I wish I had your confidence."

The old woman held out her Bible. "I can show you where to find it."

Laura stared at her for a moment, saying nothing. Then standing up, pushing the chair back with a loud scraping against the floor, she left the room without another word.

Chapter Fourteen:

"HAVE YOU seen my bible?"

It was later in the day, and Laura was rummaging through her purse when her Grandmother asked the question.

"Why would I have your Bible?" Laura replied.

"I didn't ask if you had it. I asked if you'd seen it." Grandma Ruth scratched her head, perplexed with the notion of having misplaced her book. "I always leave it by my easy chair when I'm done with it."

"You sure you didn't leave it in the kitchen? I saw you out there with it earlier."

"I suppose I could check."

She ambled into the next room and, seconds later, called out. "It's not in here."

By this point most of the contents of Laura's purse were spread out on the couch. She moved the items around – discarded tissues, a tube of lipstick, old receipts from things she didn't even remember buying – until finally finding what she was looking for. She shoved her ID badge from the grocery store into an outside pocket of her purse, shoveled the items from the couch back into the bag, and looked over at her sons.

Aaron and Evan sat on the couch, watching some sort of superhero movie on the DVD player. It might have been Spider-Man. Or The Avengers. Laura never could tell them apart. They all looked the same to her.

"Turn that off," she prompted. "And help Grandma Ruth find her Bible."

"Aw, Mom."

"Don't aw Mom me." Laura finished shoving the last few articles into her purse then snapped it shut. "I'm running late for work and don't have time to help her look for it. So you guys can just make yourselves useful."

Evan stood up and moved toward a shelf stacked with books on the side of the room. He looked halfheartedly at the volumes and shook his head. "It's not here."

His mother was at the door by now, ready to depart. "Keep looking. I only have a four hour shift today so I'll be home in time for dinner. You guys be good."

Then she was gone.

Evan moved back toward the couch. Aaron still sat there, having made no attempt to move.

"Where's Grandma's Bible?" Evan asked, in a tone that clearly conveyed the opinion that he expected his brother to have an answer to the query.

Aaron shrugged.

"Where'd you put it, Aaron?"

"What makes you think I put it anywhere?" he shot back at his brother.

"Because you're always doing stupid things like that. Messin' around with other people's stuff. Why don't you leave her book alone?"

Just then Grandma Ruth entered the room, the look of concern on her features having grown in the last few minutes. She seemed at a loss for words, nervousness propelling her forward with no idea what to do next. "Have you boys seen my Bible?"

Aaron, face serious and voice distinct, answered first. "No, Grandma. We haven't seen it."

She rummaged through some newspapers on the floor beside her recliner but the search yielded nothing. "I just don't understand it."

"Maybe you left it in the bedroom," Evan suggested. "I thought I might have seen it in there when I was talking to Grandpa."

Shaking her head, her confusion obvious, she headed for the bedroom.

Evan turned to face his brother. "This isn't funny."

A wicked sort of smile crossed Aaron's lips, as though he was enjoying a secret. "It is sort of funny."

"Where'd you put it, Aaron?"

Aaron knocked on the cast covering his leg, producing a slight hollow sound with the motion. "Well, you know I can't move very far with this thing on my leg. Where do you think I put it?"

Evan looked around, then began moving the pillows and blankets in Aaron's corner of the room. He found nothing. Getting on his hands and knees, he began looking under the furniture. Reaching beneath the couch he felt around until his fingers closed on something familiar. He withdraw his hand, clenching the Bible.

He was just standing up when Grandma Ruth entered the room, the worry on her face evident.

"Here it is, Grandma," Evan reported.

"Thank goodness." She yanked the book away from him, drawing it to her chest as though it was a source of warmth to her. "Where'd you find it?"

"It fell behind the couch," Evan informed her.

"I spotted it first," Aaron added.

Evan glared at his brother but said nothing.

"Thank you boys." She gave them both a quick hug. "I don't think I could have fallen asleep tonight without some reassurance from the good book."

She walked toward the kitchen, carrying her treasure in both hands.

An awkward silence lingered in the room as Evan glared at his brother.

Laura was home from work by four o'clock, in time to have dinner with her family. She had picked up a batch of fried chicken at the grocery store; Grandma Ruth had prepared mashed potatoes and gravy. They ate together in the living room – all of them but Grandpa Mike, who had fallen asleep in bed earlier, his good day having taken a turn for the worse. Not wishing to disturb him, they set some food aside to be warmed later in the microwave.

"The boys found my Bible," Grandma Ruth announced at one point.

"That's good. You better start being more careful where you put it."

"Must be old age creeping up on me."

She delivered the words in jest, though Evan couldn't help but notice a look of concern in the old woman's eyes. She always seemed so unyielding to him, as though she was prepared to take on the entire world if necessary. She was a rock of strength, fortified by her faith in what she believed in.

But for a fleeting instant the rock revealed a crack, a fissure in the stone, a weak point to be manipulated to expose the doubt within.

He felt sorry for her for the first time in his life.

And upset with Aaron for having put her through the ordeal.

Chapter Fifteen:

H<small>E WAS</small> a big man, well over six feet tall, and probably tipped the scales at close to three hundred pounds. He walked with an air of confidence, as though accustomed to having his way in things. His clothes, while not new, were worn with a marked degree of pride, as though his appearance was high on his list of priorities. He wore a gold necklace around his neck, which reflected the glow of the sun's light. He considered it his way of dazzling people with his brilliance.

The man was an intimidating presence as he sauntered onto the porch of the two-story bungalow, the worn planks of the deck squealing in protest as he stepped across to the door. He punched the bell two quick jabs then, after perhaps another half-a-second, rapped on the panel with the palm of his hand.

His actions were neither a lack of patience nor a sign of urgency. It was merely his way of expressing himself. He had long ago discovered he received more satisfying results with a show of bravado than anything else. It had become second nature to him, a part of his life, so deeply ingrained that he never even stopped to think about it anymore.

Laura moved toward the side window, taking a quick peek outside to see who was at the door. For a moment she stared in disbelief.

"Damn it!"

The curse came unbidden, a gut-reaction she felt ashamed of as soon as it left her lips.

The two boys, sitting on the floor watching a movie on the television, both turned to face her. A mischievous grin appeared on Evan's face. "Mom! You said a bad word."

"Never mind what I said." She spun around, flinging the curtain back into place in exasperation. "Evan, go to your room."

"But Mom –"

She pointed to the stairway. "Now!"

Without another word he left the room, wondering what he had done to upset his mother so.

Grandma Ruth rose from the recliner, concern on her face. "What is it, Laura?"

"It's Cal."

The old woman's face acquired a more sour look than usual. "What's he doing here?"

"I don't know. But I don't want him talking to the boys. I don't want him even seeing my kids. Can you help get Aaron into the kitchen?"

"Certainly."

Grandma Ruth moved toward Aaron, who pulled himself to a standing position by clinging to an end table. Having abandoned the crutches days after he came home, he found it easier to hobble into the kitchen without them, especially with his grandmother helping him. Laura bit her lip, watching their slow progress from the room, considering her options.

"I know somebody's in there!" a deep voice called from outside the house. "I can hear you moving around!"

"Just a minute!"

Laura moved toward the door, pausing and waiting the last few seconds it took for Grandma Ruth and Aaron to disappear into the kitchen. Once they were out of the room she stood straighter, brushing against her shirt to be more presentable, as though she was preparing herself for an ordeal to come. The ritual completed, she hooked the safety chain into the slot and opened the door the three inches the chain permitted.

She had a difficult time even looking at the man outside. She had distanced herself from him years ago, hoping to never have anything to do with him again. To see him now, after all the frustration of the last several weeks, was especially trying. It brought back too many painful memories of a life she had hoped to leave behind.

And to think she had once been in love with him. Or that's what she had thought at the age of eighteen, when love seemed something special and sex was a just a game to be played between the two of them.

The game became more serious once she became pregnant. The fun times weren't as fun anymore. The happy-go-lucky boy she was enamored of was unhappy with the role of full time daddy, a position he had never anticipated filling. It began with short words of derision addressed to one another, over time escalating into full-blown shouting matches that could only lead to more trouble between them. The fights became more extreme, with shorter duration between each episode.

The first time he hit her had been a shock, an unexpected blow that hurt her, not so much on a physical level, but as an indication of how much their relationship had deteriorated over the years. The physical altercations intensified, became more frequent, until finally Laura realized living with Cal Broker was no good for her.

Or her kids.

Looking at him now she could only wonder what she had ever seen in him to begin with. He still looked much the same as she remembered, only now she was able to be impartial concerning his appearance, rather than blinded by the infatuation that had first brought them together. She didn't like what she saw.

"Laura!"

He rapped on the panel again, the sound jolting her out of her reminiscing.

"What are you doing here, Cal?" she asked through the crack of the door.

"I came to see how my kids are doing."

"Your kids are doing just fine."

"That's not what I heard. I got a call from some lady at Children's Services saying my son was being abused. Hell of a thing to hear over the phone, don't you think?"

"I don't want to talk about it."

She closed the door in his face, then leaned with her back against the panel, taking a deep breath to calm her nerves.

He actually laughed from his position outside. "I can stand here all day." Then he raised his voice. "Or we can talk about it from here, so the whole goddamn neighborhood knows what's going on!"

Laura spun about, released the safety chain, and flung open the door. "Come on in," she blurted, walking away from him and into the room.

"That's more like it."

He had a smile on his face as he walked into the house, as though he found the whole situation to be comical. He entered casually, like he belonged there, shutting the door with the heel of his foot and calmly looking her over from head to toes.

"You're looking pretty good, Laura. Been keeping yourself in shape?"

Laura felt suddenly vulnerable; intimidated by the very nearness of him. She forced herself to continue. "What do you want, Cal?"

"I want to see my kids."

"They're not here."

"Then where are they?"

"Out."

He smiled again. "So it's just you and me, then. Just like old times."

"My grandmother's in the kitchen." She flung her head back, indicating the direction, but her gaze never wavered from his face. "My grandfather's in the bedroom."

"Is that so? Too bad."

"I don't have anything to say to you, Cal. Why don't you just leave?"

"Because I want to know what's going on with my kids."

"What's it to you?"

"Because they're my kids, damn it, and I have a right to know what's going on with them."

"Your kids are fine, Cal. There's nothing to worry about. The situation...."

She paused, momentarily at a loss for words.

Laura felt suddenly embarrassed with all that had happened lately. She didn't want to explain it to anyone. Especially not to Cal. He had no right to interfere with her life, considering the way he had treated her in the past. She didn't owe him anything.

"Everything's okay now, Cal," she finally announced, surprised at the strength in her tone. She had never been able to talk back to him in the past. It was a satisfying experience to be able to do so now.

"There were some problems," she continued. "But they've been taken care of. The kids are fine."

He stood there a moment, examining her face, as though attempting to judge her sincerity. His next words indicated how unconvinced he was.

"So you think this is it? That you tell me everything's okay and I'm just supposed to take your word for it?"

"You don't have to like it, Cal. You just have to leave my house."

He stepped forward, bridging the gap between them. Laura never flinched, staring him down with a determination strengthened with the fact that she knew she was in the right. She wasn't going to let him push her around anymore.

Eventually he relinquished his position.

"This isn't over with, Laura. You'll be seeing me again."

He stormed out the door, leaving it open in his wake. Laura moved forward, finding a position where she could lean against the door-frame and watch his departure. He never looked back. Climbing into a beat-up Dodge Charger he started the engine to an accompaniment of foul-looking black smoke from the exhaust. A squeal of tires invaded the neighborhood as Cal Broker pulled from the curb.

Laura closed the door. She leaned against it, taking in a deep breath of relief.

The relief passed as she noticed her audience. Evan sat at the bottom of the stairs. Aaron stood in the kitchen entranceway, Grandma Ruth behind him.

Evan spoke first. "That was our father. Wasn't it?"

Laura hesitated with an answer. It was strange to think the children weren't certain who their father was, but having not seen him for over three years their recollections were bound to be obscure at best. She considered Evan's question, wondering how much to tell them, and decided there was no point in hiding what the twins obviously knew.

"Yes. That was your father."

"I don't like him."

Grandma Ruth looked his way. "That's not a good thing to say, Evan Reed. *Do not judge, or you too will be judged.* The man is your father. Whether you like him or not, you still owe him respect. *Honor your father and mother*, as the good book instructs."

"I still don't like him."

He turned and tramped up the stairs, making his feelings obvious to all.

Aaron looked at his mother for several moments, saying nothing, then hobbled back into the room. He sat down in front of the television to continue watching his movie.

"I've got a headache," Laura announced, leaving the room with no additional comments.

Chapter Sixteen:

LARRY KENDALL'S second visit with Aaron and Evan Reed was on a Wednesday morning. Though only required by the CASA office to visit once a month he felt it was important, especially at the beginning of an assignment, to make certain he had a full understanding of what the family was going through. In this instance it was particularly essential, considering he still lacked a clear answer as to what had happened to Aaron Reed.

Another issue influencing his decision to visit the family so soon was the court report he was currently preparing. In less than two weeks Larry would be attending an Adjudication/Disposition Hearing at Juvenile Court. The hearing would consist of two portions.

First would be the Adjudication. This was where Children's Services presented their allegations, attesting to what had brought them into the case and the results of their investigation. Laura Reed would have the opportunity to defend herself at this point. The magistrate would listen to both sides and decide whether there was enough evidence to move forward with the case. The CASA worker was merely an observer during this part of the proceedings, sitting quietly while the evidence was reviewed.

Assuming the magistrate accepted the allegations from the agency – which occurred in most cases – the Disposition portion followed, with a ruling on how best to address the issues and move forward in a manner that would safeguard the children involved. A case plan would have been prepared by then, detailing the steps the parents were expected to follow in order to have their life returned to normal.

This is where Larry would have his opportunity to speak up, and voice any concerns he had regarding the children's situation.

The procedure developed through the CASA office was for each volunteer to submit a formal report a week prior to the hearing. The office staff would look it over, correcting anything that was misleading or inappropriate, and by the day of the hearing the report would already be in the magistrate's hands. In the report Larry would detail the people he had spoken with during his investigation, reviewing the information he had gathered. He would also state any recommendations he had regarding what steps he felt were necessary to insure the well-being of the children under his care, all of which would be considered during the Disposition.

Another prerequisite of the written report – something Larry had inadvertently neglected during his first visit with Aaron and Evan – was to include a photograph of the children involved in the case.

No matter how complete a court report, and how detailed the descriptions of the events involved in the case, it often still read like a page of statistics. It brought to mind faceless people involved in yet another random act, one of the thousands just like it happening across the country. It was easy, over time, to become jaded by such events.

By including a picture of the children it intensified the seriousness of the situation. The fact that kids were involved then became real to anyone reading the report.

Larry also realized he needed more to complete his assessment of the situation. On his first visit he had spoken mostly to the mother. He had met all those residing in the house – save for Mike Franklin, who had been sleeping at the time – and Larry felt he had a basic feeling for some of the family dynamics.

It was time now to fill in some missing details. By observing the family members, talking with them at different times, he intended to get a better idea of what was actually going on in the Reed household. Plus he had yet to speak with the two boys in private. He didn't want them feeling uncomfortable around him. So he had kept his distance.

He hoped, with time, to gain their trust, perhaps even to the point where they would open up to him as a friend.

Larry didn't expect miracles. He was still a stranger to the family, an outsider getting involved in the family's business. So he told himself to be patient, and give it time, and see what would develop.

They were seated once more in the living room. Laura was speaking. "We have a visit tomorrow with the orthopedic doctor."

The words piqued Aaron's interest enough that he turned away from his video games for a moment. "That means I get my cast off. Right?" There was no show of enthusiasm, no sign of excitement, in the way he delivered the words. Rather it was merely a statement of facts, delivered without emotion.

"Don't get your hopes up," his mother cautioned. "It's not certain that you'll be getting the cast off, Aaron."

"But the doctor said four weeks. And it's been four weeks now."

"The doctor said at *least* four weeks. It may be longer than that."

"I'm tired of sitting around."

"You mean you're tired of playing video games?" Larry interjected, a mock tone of disbelief in his question. "I didn't think that was possible?"

"Just tired of sitting around."

"Be patient, baby," his mother advised. "You may still have a few more weeks of wearing that thing."

His face registered disappointment but he said nothing as he returned to his game.

Larry leaned toward Laura, his voice barely above a whisper. "I'd like to talk to your sons – one on one – for a few minutes. Is that alright?"

She hesitated, indecision on her face. "Is that really necessary?"

"I'd like your boys to have an opportunity to speak to me privately in case they have something they'd like to discuss."

"You mean about the marks on Aaron?"

She spoke the words slowly, as though she didn't want to even think about it, let alone discuss the matter. To Laura it was a subject best left alone. All she wanted was for the whole matter to just go away.

As though he could read her mind, and felt it necessary to reinforce his position, Larry spoke up. "Something happened to your son, Laura. Don't you want to make sure it doesn't happen again?"

For several seconds she sat in silence, absorbing his words.

"I don't really need to ask permission," he continued. "I'm empowered by the court to do this. But I don't want you to think of me as an enemy, Laura. I'm here to help your children. To do what's best in their interest. Isn't that what we all want?"

Finally, saying nothing, she stood and walked slowly into the kitchen. Soon her voice mingled with that of her grandmother's, the two women discussing something in the other room.

Larry got up from his seat and moved toward the television, where he was soon sitting cross-legged on the floor next to Aaron.

For a minute or so nothing was said, as the armored figure on the screen moved through the apocalyptic world of the video game. The occasional undead creature that appeared was quickly blasted into oblivion. Taking advantage of the moment, Larry used his cell phone to snap several pictures of Aaron, performing the task as unobtrusively as he could. The youngster either didn't notice or didn't care, the action not affecting him in the least.

"You're pretty good at that," Larry said at last, hoping to begin a conversation.

There was no reply to the compliment.

"That door on your left," Larry prompted. "That's the way out."

Aaron turned to face him. It was the first time Larry had seen the youngster display interest in anything. "You sure?"

"Sure I'm sure. I play this game all the time."

Aaron shrugged, manipulated his character through the designated doorway, and continued the game.

"So how's the leg, Aaron?"

"Okay, I guess. It doesn't hurt or anything. Just makes it hard to get around."

"How's everything else?"

He shrugged in reply.

"Is there anything you want to talk about?"

He shook his head, still saying nothing.

"Because that's what I'm here for, you know. To help you with things."

Aaron turned to face Larry, for an instant only, then focused his attention back on the television. "Nothing to tell," he admitted at last.

Larry felt he should say more but was at a loss how to proceed. He had nothing but good intentions in mind by stopping here today, but when confronted with the prospect of talking about abuse he found he couldn't find the proper words. The boy still seemed distant; as though reluctant to broach the subject. Larry didn't want to alienate himself by making Aaron feel even more uncomfortable.

The CASA worker sat a few more minutes, watching the game, then stood up. "If you change your mind just let me know. Okay?"

The two women stopped talking when Larry entered the kitchen. He felt as though he had caught them conspiring together. They sat in silence as he halted in the doorway, waiting for him to speak.

"He doesn't say much, does he?" Larry asked at last.

"Aaron always has been quiet," Laura replied.

"But don't let that fool you," Grandma Ruth pointed out. "The boy's always thinking. It's amazing how he analyzes things and looks at a problem from every angle before reaching a decision."

"Does he do well in school, then?"

"Not as good as he should," Laura admitted. "I don't know whether he's just lazy. Or has a hard time concentrating. Or just doesn't care." She shrugged. "I know he's not a dummy," she was quick to point out. "I guess it's just not that important to him. He used to do a lot better, but now it's like it doesn't matter to him."

"How about Evan?"

"Evan's grades are better. Especially in something he enjoys, like geography or history. Subjects that fit into his imagination keep his interest longer."

"Has Aaron revealed anything concerning his bruises? Any indication of what happened?"

The two women shook their heads simultaneously. "He just doesn't want to talk about it," his mother admitted.

Ruth picked up on the conversation. "But we've been checking both of them. Every night. Nothing new has shown up since they came home."

"And," Laura was quick to add, "since I kicked Ted out of the house."

"Why would Ted want to hurt Aaron? And why not Evan as well?"

"I don't know. I thought we had a good thing going. He seemed to be happy with everything here. I just don't understand what happened."

"How was he with the boys?"

"He was good," Laura admitted. "He was patient with them. Willing to listen to what they had to say. I actually thought he was a good influence for them."

"Evan seems to miss him a lot."

"Yes. He does."

For a moment Larry thought she had more to say, perhaps further insight into the relationship between Ted and the twins. But nothing else was forthcoming. She seemed lost in her own thoughts.

"I did want to talk to Evan today as well," Larry informed them, after realizing Laura had nothing to add to the conversation.

"I think he went outside," Laura said. "He's probably out front."

Larry turned to leave when Ruth Franklin stood. "My husband would like to speak with you before you go."

"Of course." He hadn't met the grandfather yet – he had been reluctant to force the issue, considering Mike Franklin's medical problems – so this was a good opportunity to follow through on more of his investigation.

Larry stepped aside, allowing the old woman to pass so she could lead the way. They approached a darkened room just off the living room, down a short hallway. Grandma Ruth paused in the doorway.

"Michael? Are you awake?"

"Yes I am." The voice was quiet, like a disembodied soul speaking from the darkness.

"The young man from the CASA office is here. Do you feel up to talking with him?"

"Of course." Larry heard movement, as the old man apparently shifted position in his bed. "Turn the light on, woman. You can't expect the man to sit in the dark."

She mumbled something beneath her breath, but complied with his wishes by switching on a desk lamp.

"He's all yours," she told Larry, walking out of the room and leaving them alone.

Larry entered slowly, reluctant to intrude on his privacy. He could see Mike Franklin now, sitting up in bed, wearing a light t-shirt and a serious expression on his face.

"Well come on in," the old man prompted, his voice gruff. "I don't bite."

"Yes, sir."

Larry entered, spied a folding chair at the end of the bed, and sat down. "I'm Larry Kendall," he announced.

"Mike Franklin. But you already know that, don't you? I suppose you know a lot about Laura and her kids, too."

Larry felt like he'd just received a reprimand, a verbal reminder that he was prying into other people's business. He wasn't certain how to reply. "I mean no disrespect, Mr. Franklin. I'm here because I'm concerned about the children's welfare."

"Of course you are." The man laying on the bed waved with his hand, as though dismissing the issue. "But tell me, Larry. What do you think of this whole business?"

Larry hesitated, considering the question. "I'm not sure what you mean."

"Let's not be bullshitting each other here, Larry. I may not get around much, but I'm not ignorant. I've been hearing the talk. The whispers between Laura and Ruthie when they think I don't hear them. So what's the story with my grandson?"

"He's apparently been mistreated. By someone. Signs of abuse became evident when he was examined at the hospital."

"And who do you think is responsible?"

"Aaron's mother thinks it was her boyfriend. Ted Myers."

"I didn't ask you what Laura thought. I asked you what *you* thought. Aren't you supposed to be looking into all this? Don't you have some opinions of your own?"

"I don't know what to think," Larry admitted, reluctance obvious in his voice. He knew he was supposed to be the authority on the matter. No doubt the family looked to him for advice, assuming he had all the answers. Larry realized that, with time, he would grow more comfortable with his duties, and with more experience he would be better equipped to provide the answers the families he worked with were seeking.

But for now he felt ill-equipped to offer any solutions. So he kept these thoughts to himself, striving to present what he hoped was a professional attitude.

"So far I haven't seen anything out of the ordinary," Larry replied at last.

"Did you talk to Ted?"

"Yes I did?"

"And?"

"He seemed genuinely concerned about what was going on. He of course denied doing anything wrong. But that's to be expected, don't you think?"

Mike Franklin said nothing, apparently considering the information. "Ted's a good kid. I can't see him doing anything like this. I think Laura's wrong."

"Somebody's been mistreating the child. If not Ted, then who?"

"It's the damnedest thing. I don't see how anyone in the family could have done this."

"Well, somebody did. From what the doctors said, and the caseworker from Children's Services, someone has been abusing Aaron. And until we find out who we need to keep a good eye on things."

"Of course you do. Of course you do."

He lapsed into silence then, as though considering what had been said.

"Was there anything else, Mr. Franklin?"

"No. Thank you Larry. You will let me know if you learn anything?"

"Of course."

"This is a hard thing for my granddaughter. You know, things have never been easy for Laura. Ever since she was a child life's been pretty tough on her. Her mother deserted the family when Laura was six. Did you know that?"

"No. I didn't."

"It's true. Stephanie was too attractive for her own good. Billy loved that girl. Gave her everything she ever wanted. They had the two kids – Laura and her older brother, Paul. They should have been a happy family.

"But it wasn't enough for Stephanie. She didn't want to be tied down with two kids and a house. She was too wild for that. I suppose that's a harsh thing to say about your own daughter, but it's true. Billy came home one day and she was gone. Emptied out the bank account, took the car, and high-tailed it out of there. Never even said good-bye to her kids. Ruth and I...."

He hesitated, choking on the words, finally managing a weakhearted epitaph to the narration.

"We never heard from her after that. No idea if she's even alive, or what she's been up to."

"That must have been hard on all of you."

"It was. Billy started drinking after that. Started missing work a lot. Getting behind on his payments. He just couldn't keep it together."

He lapsed into silence. Larry felt a reluctance to say anything, not wanting to intrude on the man's private thoughts. It was one of the things about being a CASA volunteer that disturbed him. He felt like he was prying into people's affairs, forcing them to reveal things about themselves they wished to keep secret. He knew it was important, that the children he represented needed someone watching over them, and to do his job properly he needed to be well-informed. But it still felt wrong at times.

The two sat in continuing silence for several more seconds before Mike Franklin steeled himself to continue.

"Billy sort of drifted away from life after that. Didn't take care of himself. Or the kids. Eventually Ruthie and I had to step in and take the children. It was for their own good." The last sentence was delivered quietly, as though Mike Franklin was thinking out loud, trying to convince himself of the reasons behind what had happened to his family.

His voice resumed its normal gruffness after that, as though committed now to the point. "Somebody had to look after Laura and Paul. And it was pretty obvious their parents weren't going to do it."

"Where's Laura's father now, Mr. Franklin?"

He sighed, taking a deep breath before continuing. "He was killed. In a car crash."

"I'm sorry to hear that."

"It was his own damn fault. Going out drinking all the time. It was bound to catch up to him. Ran into a telephone pole one night."

Larry had no response.

"Laura's been through enough in her life. And now this. She deserves better."

Evan was sitting on the front steps, bouncing a basketball, when Larry walked out of the house. Larry held up his cellphone, hoping to snap a quick photo, but as soon as he did the boy grinned, apparently an automatic reaction to having his picture taken. Larry was hoping for something more spontaneous, rather than a posed shot, but he pushed the button anyway, recording the image.

"Why'd you do that?" Evan asked. "Why'd you take my picture?"

"I need to get pictures of the children I work with. For our files."

"Oh." Evan turned away, as though losing interest, and Larry snapped one more picture.

"You look bored, buddy."

Evan shrugged. "Nothing to do."

"I bet it will be better when Aaron gets his cast off."

He nodded, as though in reply, but Larry was left with the impression the boy wasn't even paying attention to what was being said. He bounced the basketball a few times, his attention devoted to the action. Then, without looking up, he continued. "I miss Ted."

"Did Ted play basketball with you?"

"Yep. And other things, too. He was a lot of fun."

"So you don't think your mother should have asked Ted to leave?"

A slow shake of the head was the answer.

"It sounds like Ted wasn't very nice to your brother –"

Before Larry could say more Evan faced him, shouting out an answer. "Ted didn't do them things!"

Then, as though embarrassed by his display, he looked down once more at the bouncing basketball.

"You sound pretty sure of yourself, Evan. Why do you say Ted didn't do anything to your brother?"

Evan hesitated, as though reluctant to continue. "If I tell you a secret, do you promise not to tell anyone?"

"I can't promise that, Evan. Especially if it has something to do with how your brother got hurt."

Larry could see the strain on Evan's face, as the young boy struggled with the decision on whether to say anything further. So Larry sat in silence, watching as an occasional car would pass by, content to allow the boy to reach his own conclusion.

When it came the words were spoken quietly; barely above a whisper. Larry had to lean closer to catch what was being said.

"Aaron hears voices."

The revelation startled the CASA worker. "What do you mean?"

"Aaron hears voices. Inside his head. Telling him to do things. Bad things. Sometime he'll hide something. Or break something. And sometimes....." The ball stopped bouncing. "Sometimes Aaron hurts himself."

"Are you sure?"

The young boy nodded. "The voices tell him to do bad things. The voices tell him to hurt himself."

"How do you know he hears voices?"

"I've heard him at night. When he thinks I'm asleep. It's like he's talking to someone. But there's nobody there. It's just him talking to himself."

Larry paused, considering Evan's revelation. The whole thing seemed preposterous. Like something out of a bad Stephen King novel.

Evan stood, moving closer to Larry. "Are you going to tell anyone?"

"I don't know. I need to think about it."

"But don't you see? It wasn't Ted that did them things. Ted never should have left here."

Larry considered his alternatives, but for the moment felt confused regarding what to do next. This was something he knew nothing about. But it definitely would bear looking into.

Chapter Seventeen:

THE SOUND from the television in the living room greeted Larry as he walked in the front door, which didn't surprise him a bit. Most evenings his parents liked to relax by unwinding in front of the set. They would find a series on Netflix and watch it straight through – sometimes in a matter of a few weeks, depending on the series – then move on to something else.

He was walking down the hallway toward his bedroom when his mother called out to him. "How was your day, Lawrence?"

He had been hoping to just relax in his room a bit, maybe mull over the things he had heard today, but there was no sneaking by them now that they knew he was home. Which meant he had no choice but to turn direction and head into the living room.

Linda and Jeremy Kendall sat on the couch together, enjoying the closeness of each others company. Jeremy's feet rested comfortably on the ottoman in front of the couch. His hand held a half-empty bottle of beer.

Jeremy took a swig from his bottle before addressing his son. "Been working on your CASA case?"

Larry nodded, then sat down on the rocker across from his parents.

"How's it going?" Linda asked.

"Confusing. You wouldn't think a child abuse case would be so difficult."

Jeremy leaned forward to grab the remote, paused the television program, then faced his son with the stern look he had developed after twenty-five years with The Toledo Police Department. "It's something families are reluctant to talk about, son. Nobody likes to air their dirty laundry in public. Least of all about something like this."

"I suppose. But I heard the weirdest thing today and it got me thinking."

"What was that?" his mother asked.

"I was talking to one of the twins."

"The one that had the accident?"

"No. This was the other one."

"He's the one you said was more talkative. Had all the imagination. Right?"

"That's right. He said his brother hears voices."

His father placed his bottle down on a coaster, his attention firmly established by this point. "What kind of voices?"

"I don't know. Voices. In his head. Telling him to do things."

"Like Schizophrenia?"

"I suppose. That's sort of what it sounded like, anyway. Is that possible in children?

"I don't know." Jeremy leaned back, considering the issue. "Down at the station we see some pretty crazy things. Tuppelo brought this guy in the other day, swore the voices in his head were telling him there were explosives hidden in the hot dogs at Tony Packo's. He laid out a few of the staff and was going after the manager by the time Benji got there to break things up." He shook his head, recollecting the event. "You never know what some people have to deal with."

His wife looked at him in confusion. "But does that happen to kids?"

Jeremy shrugged. "I guess it could. Though I never heard of it."

Linda turned to face her son once more. "So did the brother have anything else to say?"

"He says it wasn't the mother's boyfriend abusing the child. He says his brother was hurting himself."

"With some forms of psychosis," Jeremy explained, "I have heard of people causing self-inflicted injuries."

Linda's hand flew to her mouth in surprise. "But a nine-year-old?"

"I suppose it's possible."

"So you think I should look into it more?" Larry concluded.

"Perhaps. But let's not be missing the more obvious explanation."

"What would that be?"

"Didn't you say one of the kids seemed pretty close to the boyfriend?"

"That's right."

"Was he the one that told you all this?"

"Yeah."

"The same one that has the active imagination?"

Larry paused, piecing together what his father was driving at.

"So you think he's making the whole thing up? Just to try to make the boyfriend look innocent in everything?"

His father shrugged. "Could be."

"It does sound more reasonable," his mother added.

"I suppose it does. So I guess I should drop the whole thing, then?"

"I didn't say that," his father was quick to add. "If I've learned anything from my time on the force it's that you can't jump to conclusions over anything. Nine times out of ten the obvious explanation is the one to go with."

"And the tenth time?"

"Ah, the tenth time." Jeremy grabbed his beer, took a quick swallow, then set the bottle down again. "That tenth one is the one that will bite you every time. You just can't afford to overlook any possibility."

Chapter Eighteen:

LAURA REED sat in the waiting room with the two children, nervous about the coming appointment. She had never seen a family therapist before. Or any kind of therapist, for that matter. It all seemed so foreign to her. She always believed people should take care of themselves. If something good came along you took advantage of it. If something bad happened you made the best of the situation.

Her life was proof of that. Her grandparent's had taken her in after everything happened with her parents. They sheltered her; fed and clothed her. But they hadn't gone through what she had. Even Paul, who was older when it all happened, had weathered the events with seeming ease. Involved as he was with his friends and school life, he had sought out and found other outlets, activities to keep him occupied and help him through the experience.

For her it had been different. She had suffered the intense loneliness of being abandoned by her mother, of waking up one morning and finding she had been deserted by a woman she thought had loved her. Her life had been shattered overnight. As she laid in bed each evening, soaking her pillow with the tears she tried so hard to contain, she couldn't imagine anything worse ever happening.

But life stepped up to the task and burdened her with further hardship. Her father's constant drinking disrupted their lives as he sank further and further into his self-imposed isolation. He distanced himself from life, ignoring his children through his self-imposed exile.

And then one night, one awful night, he never came home at all.

Laura had never felt so alone in her life.

But she had pulled herself through it, facing each day with a combination of sheer determination and the reluctance to give up. It was her battle to fight and she had gotten through it.

Even during her problems with Cal – when he became abusive toward her, and belittled her, and made her life a living nightmare with his demands – she had faced the problem on her own. Had it not been for the two boys she would have left their father much sooner than she had. She felt it was important to keep the family together – for the kids' sake – until the realization finally hit her that they too were suffering with the way things were going.

Leaving Cal was the hardest thing Laura had ever done in her life.

And she never for a second regretted it.

Things were different now. Her life had finally begun to shape up into something she was happy with. The boys were growing older, and required less of her attention, which relieved some of the burden of being a single parent. Her job as a cashier at Kroger wasn't glamorous, but it was a steady income and put food on the table. She had friends there. Working helped to pass the time, and get her out of the house once in a while.

Grandma Ruth and Grandpa Mike certainly contributed to making her life easier. When she had moved in with them she had told herself it was a temporary thing; she would soon be on her own. Now, three years later, they had settled into a routine where they all seemed content with the living arrangements. Grandma Ruth in particular seemed to appreciate having other people around, especially on the days where Grandpa Mike lingered in bed, suffering through his pain. Sometimes Laura could see the old woman's face, beaming with joy, as she watched her grandchildren play. Laura couldn't imagine taking that away from her now.

Even Laura's love life had improved recently. Ted had seemed like the perfect boyfriend; attentive to her needs, helpful around the house, and good with the boys, spending time with them and sharing in raising them. But now, to find he had been abusing Aaron....

Laura pushed the idea from her mind. She didn't want to think about it. She didn't want to believe it. But how else to explain what was going on?

"Miss Reed? Dr. Markham will see you now."

Evan, always anxious for a new experience, jumped from his seat. Aaron was more inclined to linger, prolonging the time before they had to meet the doctor.

The two boys followed their mother as the office assistant led the way through a hallway adorned with bright pictures. They were ushered into an area that seemed more like a living room than an exam room. A comfortable looking couch took up most of the space, with two plain chairs and a desk comprising the rest of the furniture. The pictures on the walls seemed familiar, as though they were part of the same collection as those that were featured in the hallway.

"The doctor will be with you shortly," the assistant advised, then slipped out of the room, closing the door gently behind her, as though afraid of disturbing them.

Laura performed a quick visual scan of the area before sitting down. Some magazines were displayed on the desktop; they looked well worn, as though they had served many previous patients. A plastic box of toys was stacked in one corner, beside a kid-sized table. Bookcases stood on either side of the room's single window, displaying what looked to be medical tomes.

Aaron skimmed over the periodicals, apparently found none to his liking, and took a seat on the couch.

Evan rummaged through the toys until he found a wooden puzzle. It was obviously intended for a younger child but that didn't seem to faze him. Sitting on the floor, as though he was relaxing at home, he assembled the puzzle easily. After perhaps thirty seconds he took it apart, removing each piece in a deliberate manner so it was fully separated from it's neighbor, then placing it carefully back into the box. Once they were all in the container he poured the contents out on the floor and began anew.

Laura, standing in the center of the room, smiled at Aaron.

"I bet it feels good to get your cast off."

"It sure does." He reached forward, scratching at the newly exposed leg. "But it itches. And it still feels sorta funny without it."

"It's only been a couple days. I'm sure you'll get used to it in no time."

It struck her suddenly how curious Aaron looked with his cast removed. Somehow, even with spending every day planted in front of the television, he had managed to develop a tan from the summer sun, his arms and right leg sporting a light brown color while his left leg, having been concealed by the cast, appeared pale and white. It lent him a lopsided sort of look, like things weren't matching up properly, but it was a marked improvement from seeing him wear the cast. At least now he was able to move around in a more normal fashion again.

The door opened, admitting a man in a white lab coat. He looked like he should have been on a basketball court, hanging out with a bunch of college kids. He was tall and skinny; his clothes hung on him. He was younger than Laura had expected a doctor to look, projecting a youthful enthusiasm but not necessarily instilling any sense of confidence. Her concern grew immediately, doubting whether someone so obviously inexperienced could do her, or her family, any good.

"Hello, Laura. I'm Dr. Markham." He presented himself in a friendly manner, acknowledging her with a nod of his head.

"And these are your twins?"

"That's right. This is Aaron." As she introduced them Evan moved from his spot in the corner of the room and took a seat on the couch. "And this is Evan."

"They do look a lot alike, don't they?"

"Not as much as they used to. When they were babies there was no telling who was who."

"Then how did you keep them straight?"

Evan spoke up, apparently anxious to join the conversation. "Safety pins."

"I don't understand," the doctor admitted.

"We wore different colored safety pins on their diapers," Laura explained. "It was the only way we could tell them apart when they were babies."

"I was green," Evan informed him, as though imparting a gem of valuable information.

They all looked at Aaron, expecting a response, and when at last he realized they were waiting for him he managed a meek answer. "I was yellow."

Dr. Markham nodded his head, as though having pondered long and hard on this bit of information. "Well, that's an interesting approach. Though I'm surprised to hear of anyone using cloth diapers. I thought all you could get anymore were disposables?"

"They didn't seem to work out with the boys. The plastic really irritated their skin." As she talked, Laura noticed the therapist leaning back in his chair, getting more comfortable, as though prepared to listen to whatever she had to say. That was when she realized something. She was feeling less apprehensive now about the entire ordeal. She was still nervous, wondering what would happen next. But something about Dr. Markham's manner – an easy-going way of presenting himself, and portraying the impression that he had all the time in the world to talk about whatever Laura wanted to talk about – made her feel more comfortable.

"I'm sorry," she finally blurted out.

"For what?"

"For going on about something as stupid as diapers."

"There's nothing stupid about it, Laura. I'm certain, at one point in your life, you thought you'd be dealing with diapers forever."

"That's for sure. Especially with having two of them at the same time. But we don't need to talk about it. It's not important."

"Why do you say that? I'm certain the twins have played a big part in your life. Why wouldn't talking about them be important?"

"Because that's not why we're here, is it?"

She stopped abruptly, feeling she had ventured into an area she didn't want to discuss. Even though she knew she had to – even though there was no denying the reality of the situation which had brought them here today – she still didn't want to admit to the possibility that someone had been abusing her children. It was unthinkable to her. How could anyone even consider treating kids that way?

"I'm a good mother," she finally blurted out, feeling guilty in spite of herself.

"I'm certain you are."

"And I love my children."

He nodded, allowing her to continue.

"That's why I can't understand why any of this is happening." She felt tears coming on, and forced herself to control the emotions overwhelming her. "How can this be happening?"

Reaching behind him, Dr. Markham retrieved a box of tissues from the top drawer of the desk and offered them to Laura.

"I know this is confusing for you, Laura. As it is for the children. And I don't want to make things any more uncomfortable for any of you than it has to be. But when issues like this come up, they generally don't go away on their own."

"But Ted's gone now. I told him to leave."

"Who is Ted?"

"My boyfriend. At least, he was my boyfriend. But I don't see him anymore."

"And you think he was the cause of Aaron's injuries?"

As he spoke the therapist kept his attention firmly focused on Laura, giving her his undivided attention. Yet at the same time he managed to watch the children out of the corner of his eyes. Evan seemed upset, like he wanted to say something but was afraid to, while Aaron seemed disinterested in what was going on around him, as though it didn't concern him in the least.

Laura continued. "I think it's pretty obvious, don't you? We haven't had any incidents since Ted left the house. That should tell you right there that he was behind it."

"Perhaps. But even if that is the case, there are other issues to be concerned with. Physical scars heal with time. Often emotional scars can fester for a lot longer. They dig deep, and can have long ranging effects down the road that we often don't consider at the moment."

"I guess I never looked at it that way."

"I'm not trying to scare you, Laura. But we need to give this some time. If you'll trust me, I'd like to get to know you and the boys better. That way, maybe we can all reach a better understanding of what happened. And, more importantly, how to prevent it from ever happening again. Okay?"

She nodded.

"How about you boys? Does that sound alright with you if we spend some time together and get to know one another?"

"I guess," Evan replied.

Aaron, like his mother, merely nodded.

"I would like to schedule family appointments, so I can get to know all of you better and observe the way you interact together. Family dynamics are important in a case like this. But I also need to see Aaron by himself."

He focused his attention on the twin.

"I'm not here to intimidate you, Aaron. I want to get to know you better, and understand what's going on in your life. We'll take things as slow as you desire, so you have the opportunity to get comfortable with our time together. You're free to talk about anything you want. But if you'd rather not discuss something that's okay too. Alright?"

He nodded once more.

Dr. Markham offered a reassuring smile to the family.

Laura, hoping for the best but wondering what would happen next, said nothing.

Chapter Nineteen:

THE TONE was subdued on the drive home from the therapist's office. Laura sat in front with her brother, while the twins sat quietly in back.

Paul had dropped them off at the appointment earlier, then had gone to one of the Toledo Metroparks for a short walk while the family had their session. He had been in the parking lot, waiting for them, when they were finished.

The journey began in silence, each of the car's occupants absorbed with their own private thoughts, the steady hum of the car's engine the only sound disturbing the ride.

After an extended period of silence Paul chanced a quick glance at Laura. "Well, Sis? How did it go?"

"Alright, I guess. Though it sort of felt like a waste of time." She turned in her seat to face the kids. "What did you guys think?"

Aaron, staring out the window, said nothing.

"It was okay," Evan said, his tone noncommittal. Then he quickly amended his reply. "Do we have to go see him again?"

"Yes we do. We have another appointment next week."

"Can't I stay home?" Evan pleaded. "This doesn't concern me, anyway."

Laura shifted in her seat, to more directly face her son. "This concerns all of us, Evan. We're a family, and we're in this together."

Neither child remarked on the comment.

Laura straightened up in her seat, staring out the window, as Paul maneuvered his car south onto the Route 75 Expressway. Traffic slowed immediately, merging into a single lane, the bright orange traffic cones on the side of the road barricading the construction work that seemed to have taken over the city during the summer months. Traffic crawled through the area, the cars stacked bumper to bumper.

Eventually Paul felt comfortable enough with the driving, the line of vehicles having settled into a slow but steady pace through the work zone, and he turned to face his sister once again.

"So what did the doctor say about...?" He left the sentence incomplete, motioning with his head toward Aaron in the back seat.

Laura shook her head, refusing to look his direction, her attention devoted to what was going on outside, as though it was the most important thing in the world. She needed something, anything, to take her mind off her troubles. "Not here," she finally offered. "Let's talk about it later."

"Okay."

Paul was five years older than Laura, and had always felt a protective urge toward his little sister. It bothered him, not only to know that she was going through such a difficult time, but the realization that there wasn't anything he could do to help her through it.

His mind drifted back to their childhood years.

He had weathered their family tragedy differently from his sister. After their mother left them he saw Laura's pain, the agony she went through, and had quickly reached the decision that it wasn't for him. As a coping mechanism Paul had built a wall around himself – to keep the pain out – and to insure he never found himself in her position he refused to become attached, to anyone or anything. He lived life on his own terms.

At first there had been lonely times, when he felt he was missing out on something. But soon he began to enjoy his personal freedom, relishing the fact that he made his own decisions and accepted whatever consequences arose as a result of his choices.

He still cared for his sister. He tried to be supportive – offer an occasional lift when the family had to go somewhere, giving her a few dollars from time to time when things got tight – but he knew this was a battle she had to fight on her own.

For the sake of the children he hoped the issue would resolve itself.

The boys disappeared upstairs as soon as they got home, anxious to be away from the scrutiny of the adults.

Laura and Paul headed for the kitchen, where they were pleasantly surprised to find Grandpa Mike sitting at the table with Grandma Ruth. In front of him sat a glass of iced tea.

"I hope that's unsweetened," Laura remarked, indicating the beverage. "You know he's supposed to be watching his sugar."

"Of course it is," Grandma Ruth supplied, as though the very idea of it not being unsweetened was ludicrous.

"As long as it's cold," Grandpa Mike remarked, a smile on his face. He noticed Paul then, and the smile increased in girth. "Well, look who's here! How are you doing, stranger?"

"Hi, Grandpa. You're looking good."

"You just happened to catch me on one of my good days. When I could drag myself out of bed for a change."

"Now, Michael," Grandma Ruth scolded. "You know we each have our cross to bear in life."

"I suppose that's so, Mother. I just wish I could set mine down a bit more often."

He laughed with the comment, as though his disability was a joking matter. He had found over the years there was no sense getting depressed and upset over things. You couldn't change the past. All you could do was move ahead with life the best you could.

Laura gravitated toward him, rubbing the old man affectionately on the shoulder. "You do look good today, Grandpa. It's great to see you up and around."

He waved the matter off, as though it was a trifle. "That's enough gabbing about me. How did your doctor's visit go today?"

She shot him a puzzled look. "I didn't think you knew about that."

"Just because I have a hard time getting around it don't mean I don't see things. Or put two and two together. So what did he have to say say? About Aaron?"

Laura sat, then lifted her head. She could just make out the sound of movement from the bedroom upstairs, as the twins found some activity other than video games to keep them busy. She lowered her voice, as though fearful of her sons overhearing them.

"He didn't say much, really. He wants to see us again in another week. Says he wants to get to know the children. See how they're reacting to things."

"It's a damn waste of time, if you ask me."

"Language, Michael!"

"Don't *language, Michael* me, Mother. This is still my house, and I can say anything I please in my house."

"I don't know." Laura fiddled with her hands, refusing to make eye contact with the others. "Maybe it is a good thing for Aaron to see someone. Just to make sure he's okay."

"Why wouldn't he be okay?" Grandpa Mike asked. "Now that Ted's gone there isn't anything to worry about. We can all go back to how things were before."

Paul spoke up then. "It's not always that easy, Grandpa. For Aaron's sake, we should make certain he doesn't carry any hurt with him."

"Nonsense. People make too much of these things anymore. In my day, when something bad happened, you just made the best of it and moved on."

"Just walk it off, Grandpa?"

"Exactly!" The old man had apparently failed to notice the sarcasm in his grandson's voice as he continued with his line of thinking. "Take my word for it. You keep stirring things up, and making a big issue of things, it's only going to make a bad situation worse.

"Look at me." He set his glass on the table, then held his hands out as though presenting himself to them for review. "You think I want to be the way I am? Of course not. But moping about things doesn't change things. Beating yourself over the head about what should have or shouldn't have happened doesn't change the way things are. Too many people out there crying about things and saying it was their Mommy's fault the way they turned out or expecting the government to hand them everything because life is so tough...."

He stopped suddenly, catching his breath, as though his talking couldn't keep up with his thoughts.

"They need to just get over it," he concluded. "Bad things happen and that's part of life."

Apparently thirsty after his recital Grandpa Mike took a drink from his iced tea, smacking his lips in satisfaction.

No one responded until Laura broke the silence. "I just want to make certain my son is safe."

"He is safe, Laura. We're all looking after him. All he needs now is family."

"He also needs The Lord, Michael," Grandma Ruth admonished. *"So do not fear, for I am with you. I will strengthen you and help you."*

Laura rose from the table, resisting the urge to raise her voice. "Where was your Lord when my son was being abused? Who was looking after Aaron when Ted did those horrible things to him?"

Grandma Ruth rose, approached her granddaughter, and touched her lightly on the arm. "It is not for us to question God. *My thoughts are nothing like your thoughts, says the Lord. And my ways are far beyond anything you could imagine."*

Laura pulled away, took two steps toward the doorway, then paused, turning to face the group. "I don't have to imagine. I saw the marks on my son. I saw the hurt that was done to him. You can't tell me there's a God up in heaven who's content to watch a child be used in that way. If that's the type of God you believe in, then I don't want any part of it."

She stormed out of the room, leaving silence in her wake.

Chapter Twenty:

LARRY STARED at the computer monitor, contemplating whether to call the document complete and send it off to the CASA office. He had spent the previous hour working on the court report, which was due in two days. Everything regarding the case had been filled in to the best of his ability. He had provided a written record of the people involved, as well as summaries of the interviews he had conducted. A history of the allegations was included as well – beginning with Aaron Reed's accident at Broadway Park and detailing the findings at Toledo Hospital – and he felt it presented all the information relavent to the case.

Even so, he realized he had left something out.

No mention was made of the claim that Aaron Reed heard voices.

Larry sat back in his chair, considering what Evan Reed had told him. When it came right down to it all he had was an unsubstantiated statement, and that from a nine-year-old with a vivid imagination.

He planned on looking into the matter, realizing everything he discovered could be important so he shouldn't overlook anything, but he didn't feel justified with including it as part of the official court record. Especially since he had yet to verify the remark.

It was difficult to believe the claims Evan had made. If what the boy said was true – if his brother Aaron was hearing voices and, even more importantly, was injuring himself – it was hard to imagine such things going on in a household full of people. Surely someone would have suspected something before now, or stumbled across an indication that things weren't right with the child.

But nothing he had seen during his visits, or been informed of by the people he interviewed, pointed in such a direction. The only indication he had that something was amiss consisted of a casual remark by an imaginative nine-year-old.

There would be time to pursue the matter later. For now he had other concerns.

He paused to look once again at the cover of the court report he had just completed, paying special attention to the photos taken of the boys earlier in the week. There was no denying they were twins; it could have been multiple pictures of the same child. But there were distinct differences as well, dissimilarities that glared out at him from the images.

He had decided to go with the candid picture of Evan. He had caught the boy staring into space with a dreamy, faraway expression on his face. It seemed to epitomize the boy, and his way of looking at life. Even in repose there was the trace of a smile to him, as though he was satisfied with his life and what it offered to him. It was an uninhibited glimpse into the world of a contented child.

Aaron's picture revealed something different. There was an overall moodiness to the image, like he was distanced from those around him. There was no sign of introspection, or deep-thinking, or indication the child was concentrating on anything. It was a lackluster expression from someone who, to all indications, was simply existing, making his way in the world but not functioning as a part of it.

The young boy seemed so alone. Surrounded by a house filled with family members, he had somehow managed to live a life of isolation. His loneliness was evident in the way he kept to himself. It shone through from the image Larry studied.

There had to be some way to reach the boy. But without fully understanding what he had been through Larry didn't know where to begin.

Chapter Twenty-One:

IT WAS time to get out on his own again. Ted Myers realized that. He just wished the situation prompting his decision had been a different one.

When he moved in with his sister Ted had expected it to be a short stay. He assumed Laura would cool down, and realize the truth of the matter, and call him up to apologize. For the first few days he had even rehearsed in his mind how he would react. Remaining aloof, he would forgive Laura, but not go rushing back to her as though nothing was wrong. He was the injured party here. He had every intention of maintaining some self-respect over the matter.

As the days turned to weeks, the time dragging on at Paige's place as he waited for the call that would restore his life to the way it had been before Aaron's accident, he had opportunity to consider Laura's position. He now understood her anger. A part of him was even pleased with her reaction. The way she stood up for her children proved what a good mother she could be.

It couldn't have been easy for her to ask him to leave. He wasn't conceited about it, but he had been with Laura enough to know that the feelings he felt toward her, the closeness he cherished between them, was reciprocated in her feelings toward him. With that in mind he felt certain she would, given enough time, realize the mistake she had made and come to regret the rash decision she had followed through on. She would call him up and they would do what was necessary to get their lives back on track again, returning their relationship to the way it had been before.

But the call never came. And, with time, Ted accepted the fact that it never would.

By that point the escape he had sought at his sister's – the temporary reprieve he had anticipated – had faded away. He was beginning to feel like a third wheel, an unwanted visitor, a bad penny that simply refused to go away. It wasn't fair to accept her invitation any longer.

Since there was no going back it was time to move forward with his life.

He found himself a one bedroom apartment off Alexis Road. Paige had offered him a dresser and some chairs, furniture he could hardly refuse considering he had nothing of his own to speak of. The day of his move Alan Crenshaw, one of his coworkers at the plant, showed up with his pickup to help him with the items.

It didn't take long to load everything. The belongings looked meager in the back of the truck, hardly enough to be starting a new life with. It epitomized the emptiness he felt since leaving Laura and the boys.

"You don't have to go," Paige advised him, as they stood on the front porch together. "You're welcome to stay as long as you want."

"I know that, Sis. And I appreciate it. But I just don't feel like I belong here."

"I'm sorry about that. I know Chris hasn't been the best through all this."

"No. It's not Chris. It's me. I've been sitting here, waiting for my life to return to normal. As if things would somehow go back to the way they were before. But that's not going to happen. What's done is done."

"Maybe you should call Laura? Maybe she's cooled down by now?"

"No. That wouldn't be fair to her. She has her own life. With her kids. She made a tough decision. I should just bow out and move on without her."

He walked off the porch, taking the three steps to the sidewalk, and turned once more to look at his sister. He felt he should say more but couldn't imagine what it would be.

He climbed in the cab of the pickup and his friend backed out of the driveway.

Alan smiled over at him. "Looks like it's back to the single life for you, Ted. How's it feel to be out on your own again?"

"Great."

He turned to stare out the window, his thoughts somewhere else.

"Just great."

Chapter Twenty-Two:

LARRY KENDALL mounted the stairs to the second floor of the Juvenile Center, glancing at his cellphone as he did so to verify the time. Court was scheduled for the morning, the Adjudication/Disposition Hearing that would determine the next cycle in the lives of Laura Reed and her children. Seeing he had at least ten minutes to spare, and realizing as well that the hearing starting times were often delayed, Larry slowed his stride, taking the steps in a more casual manner.

The Emergency Hearing six weeks earlier had addressed the issue of the child abuse concerning Aaron Reed, but no definite course of action had been determined. Since that time no direct evidence had surfaced regarding what had caused the marks on the young boy's body; no culpable individual had been determined that could be positively identified as the perpetrator of the deed. Laura Reed had accused her boyfriend, Ted Myers, and from all indications he seemed a good candidate for the offender. The fact that no further abuse had been detected since the boyfriend left the house also supported the theory of his guilt.

But that's all it was. A theory. Larry realized the courts didn't depend on hearsay and supposition. The magistrates relied on solid information – provided by Children's Services, or obtained from CASA volunteers like Larry – to make their rulings. When dealing with the cases on their docket they had no intention of tearing families apart unless forced to do so. That's why Aaron's case had gone to Protective Custody, rather than taking the children from their mother. It was the court's way of being supportive to the family unit, yet at the same time maintaining close contact to insure the children were being taken care of.

The frustrating thing, as far as Larry was concerned, was that he feared for the children's safety, wondering if they were truly in a safe environment and away from further harm. Until hard evidence surfaced, or until the child testified regarding what had happened to him, Larry felt uneasy. His job was to protect the children. But it was a difficult task when you were uncertain what to protect them from.

He knew Laura and the kids were seeing a family therapist now on a regular basis. No doubt there would be future visits to come. Like so many things in the system, it seemed to take an overly long time to reach any kind of firm resolution. Larry planned on reaching out to the therapist in a few weeks, talk to him personally if possible, and see if the doctor had any luck getting through to Aaron.

As Larry entered the vast foyer on the second floor he spotted Laura sitting with a twin on either side of her. The boys reminded Larry of a pair of bookends. All three stared into space, their nervousness obvious. Larry made it a point to do his best to break the tension.

"Looks like no more crutches for you, Aaron," he began, as he moved into their field of vision.

Aaron looked toward him but otherwise failed to acknowledge his presence.

"It's been off just over a week now," Laura told him. "But to see him get around you'd think he had never broken his leg at all."

"That's great. And this means you can go swimming now, too. Doesn't it?"

"If we had a pool," Evan supplied, his frustration over the situation obvious from the tone of his voice.

His mother frowned, expressing her disapproval of his words.

"I'm sorry," Larry apologized. "I didn't mean to bring up a sore subject."

She turned toward Evan, reaching for his arm and patting it gently. "That's okay. He just needs to learn that sometimes, in life, you don't get everything you want."

She returned her attention to Larry. "I don't see Connie anywhere. She'll be here, won't she?"

"I'm sure she's just running late."

"How about Emily Landrum?"

Larry considered a moment. "The name doesn't sound familiar to me. Who is she?"

"I guess she's my attorney," Laura replied. "The one that was assigned to me, anyway. I talked to her a couple times on the phone but haven't met her yet."

"Wasn't she at the Emergency Hearing?"

"No. Some guy was there, apparently from the same office. I can't even remember his name, there was so much going on at the time."

"I'm sure. But don't worry about it. I'm certain your attorney be here before the hearing begins."

As they talked Larry noticed a familiar figure walking toward him. Though he had talked with Monica Perry several times on the phone, and recognized the staff attorney from the CASA office after attending several training courses she had presented, he had yet to speak with her on a personal level. He was surprised to see a show of recognition on her face as she drew closer.

"Larry, right?"

"That's right. Hello Monica."

They shook hands, and the attorney turned to face Laura. "So how are you and the boys doing, Laura?"

"Okay, I guess. Nothing much new to report. I'm just glad they didn't take my kids away from me."

"The courts don't like to separate families, Laura. When they do so it is only for the safety and best interest of the children involved."

"My kids are safe where they are."

"I'm glad to hear it. That's why we have Protective Custody in place. So families like yours can continue to function, together and as a unit, while the situation is resolved."

Monica faced Larry once again. "Let's talk a minute. In private."

They walked together to the far side of the room, well out of earshot of the family.

"So, Larry, what are your impressions of the case? You've visited the household, correct?"

He nodded. "Two times."

"And?"

"Nothing wrong as far as I could tell. They seem to be adjusting to things."

"Has the boy said anything to you?" She looked toward the family, her eyes focused on the twins. "Which one was it that showed signs of abuse?"

"Aaron. In the blue t-shirt."

She nodded and Larry continued.

"He hasn't confided anything. He seems pretty quiet. Almost withdrawn. Nothing like his brother. Evan seems to have a lot to say."

"About the situation?"

Larry considered for a moment what Evan had told him the other day. *Sometimes Aaron hurts himself.* Could it be possible? It seemed ridiculous to even consider. Like his father had pointed out, Evan was no doubt saying what he thought would bring his mother's boyfriend back into their lives. And he did have a vivid imagination.

Larry decided now wasn't the proper time to bring up wild speculations.

"Evan doesn't think Ted is responsible for what happened."

"Who's Ted?"

"Ted Myers. The mother's boyfriend. Or make that ex-boyfriend. She threw him out right after the abuse was discovered."

"That's right. I remember the name coming up at the Emergency Hearing. Have you spoken with him yet?"

"I visited with him and his sister. He seems like a decent guy. Claimed he didn't know anything concerning the marks on Aaron or who was responsible."

"And you believed him?"

"He seemed pretty sincere."

She smiled, the type of smile someone displays while watching something adorable. "Isn't that sweet?" Her voice had a sugary flavor to it.

"What is?"

"That you're naive enough to believe what he told you."

Larry felt suddenly defensive. "It sounded like the truth to me."

"I'm sure it did. It always does. After a while you'll lose that innocence, Larry. Once people have lied enough to you, and taken advantage of you one too many times, you start to see things a bit differently."

"Sounds a bit cynical."

"Not cynical. Realistic. Maybe her boyfriend is telling the truth. But until you have more information to back up his claims I'd take everything he told you with a grain of salt."

As they talked two men walked off the stairs and across the vast foyer to sign in at the counter on the side of the room. One of them, dressed in a light gray suit and carrying a briefcase, looked to be an attorney. The other man had a mean look to him. He sported a short beard and mustache, and wore his hair down to his shoulders. Larry could instantly picture him riding away on a Harley.

As they walked past Laura Reed and her children it was obvious to Larry that this was someone she didn't care for. A look of surprise crossed her face first, as though she had never expected to see the individual at the courthouse. This was followed by a look of disdain. That she wanted nothing to do with him was obvious. Even the two boys reacted to the man's presence. They both seemed more nervous than before his arrival, and averted their eyes as though they didn't want to be noticed.

Monica leaned closer toward Larry. "Who's that?"

"I don't know. Never seen him before."

"The attorney with him is Jim Richards. Let me see what he can tell me."

She wandered away. From Larry's position he watched the two lawyers shake hands and then exchange a few words. It didn't take long for Monica to find out what she was looking for, and she returned to Larry with the information.

"That's Cal Broker. The father. Did you know he was going to be here?"

"No idea. I saw his name on the reports but from what Connie had told me Children's Services hadn't been able to locate him."

"Well, they found him."

"I thought he was out of the picture. Hasn't even seen the boys in years."

"Do you know if that was a court ruling?"

"I don't think so. I think Laura just decided to leave and the father didn't bother to stop her. I assumed he had no interest in his children."

"Well, he's interested enough to show up for court."

Just then Connie Peters approached them, greeting them both by name. "Why don't we step in back for a minute?" the caseworker suggested. "Laura's attorney is here already, so we may as well discuss things before we head in to the hearing."

Chapter Twenty-Three:

A SIDE hallway led to a trio of rooms in back which were set aside for preliminary discussions. Jim Richards, the father's attorney, followed them back. Already seated were Mark Anochevsky, the attorney for Children's Services, and the mother's attorney, Emily Landrum.

Seated at one end of the room, a plain Manila folder on the table in front of him, sat a stern looking man in a brown business suit. Judging from the white beard on his chin Larry estimated him to be in his early sixties. He was presented to the group as Dr. Yamal Rahid, but nothing further was disclosed regarding him or the nature of his presence in the group. Connie seemed to recognize him, and accept the fact that he belonged there, but Larry lacked an opportunity to question her regarding it.

After introductions were made all around, and everyone was seated, Mark began the discussion.

"We've been considering the allegations against Laura Reed, and wondering how best to handle this situation. I know Connie has visited several times, and has left with a favorable impression of the family. Miss Reed and her children are currently attending therapy sessions, which I'm sure will be helpful with working through these issues. There's been no indication of foul play or anything unusual since this was first brought to our attention six weeks ago. As of now we see nothing amiss with the current situation. The children appear to be in no immediate danger."

"So what are you saying?" Larry asked, a confused expression on his face. "That everything's okay now?"

"I'm just saying that we see no indications of continued abuse as far as these children are concerned."

"And how do you explain that?"

"Perhaps," Connie Peters broke in, "the mother was correct. That it was the boyfriend all along. With him out of the picture the situation has been resolved."

"Have you investigated the boyfriend?" Monica asked. "Is there anything in his past to indicate he could be a child abuser?"

"We did investigate him," Connie informed the group. "We performed background checks on everyone living in the house."

"And did you find anything?"

"No," Anochevsky admitted. "But there's a first time for everything. Maybe he never had opportunity before. Or maybe he had opportunity but was never discovered. If Aaron Reed hadn't broken his leg at the playground we wouldn't know about this even now."

"So what are your recommendations?" Monica asked.

"We can't prove any wrong doing against any of the family members. And the boy refuses to say anything about the incident."

"I talked to the therapist," Connie added. "He says Aaron is pretty withdrawn. It could be just his nature, or he could be suppressing his emotions because of the abuse he suffered. Dr. Markham feels that, with time, he can reach the boy and do him some good."

"And until then?" Larry asked.

"Children's Services doesn't really have much of a case against the mother. It's difficult to prove she had anything to do with the abuse under the circumstances. What do you suggest we do?"

Jim Richards, the father's attorney, had been silent through the proceedings. At this point he decided to say something. "My client is concerned about the welfare of his children."

"Concerned?" Connie looked astonished over the choice of words. The caseworker took a quick glance through some notes before continuing, as though seeking a pertinent piece of information, though Larry suspected it was more a stalling tactic, to prevent her from saying something she might later regret, than anything else. "From what Laura has told me, the father has had absolutely no contact with the children in almost three years. And now he's concerned?"

"My client's lack of contact with his children is not at issue here," his attorney pointed out. "For whatever the reason, he opted not to maintain a relationship with his children over the last three years. That, however, does not deprive him of the rights of a father. He is entitled to know that his children are safe. And they are being properly taken care of."

"They are being taken care of," Connie stressed. "And we feel they are in a safe place now, with loving people watching over them."

"And can you guarantee another incident won't happen again?"

Anochevsky took over the conversation for Children's Services. "Of course we can't guarantee that, counselor. You know that as well as I do. But we feel the incidents are a thing of the past."

"And what further steps do you propose?"

"We are suggesting the family continue to see a therapist, particularly for Aaron Reed, to help them get through any trauma as a result of the incident."

"What about the Protective Supervision?" Larry asked. "Will that stay in place?"

Mark and Connie looked at one another, as though hesitant to reply. Finally Mark chose to answer the query. "At this point, in light of how things have progressed so far, we

141

question whether it's even necessary."

"If I may interject a moment?"

All eyes turned toward Dr. Rahid, who had been silent through the proceedings. As he talked he removed some papers from his folder. His actions were precise, with a deliberateness of motion, as though he was performing a task that required the utmost care and attention.

His voice matched his manner, the words delivered with perfect diction. "I examined Aaron Reed in the emergency room at Toledo Hospital. I conferred with Dr. Lois Tyrone, the physician on duty that day, as well as with the mother, to reach an understanding of what had transpired.

"I have also delved deeper into the boy's medical history. In the previous two years Aaron Reed has had multiple emergency visits, both with his pediatrician and at the hospital. An abrasion on his arm." He placed a paper of written information neatly beside him. "This resulted from falling off his bicycle. A twisted ankle." Another page joined the first. "Apparently he fell from a tree, though conveniently no one was around to witness the accident. A dislocated finger." He continued with his motion, adding to the pile once again.

Mark Anochevsky spoke up, interrupting whatever else the specialist had to say. "What's your point, Dr. Rahid?"

"It seems to me this is suspicious behavior, this continuous string of accidents the child has experienced. It makes me question what is actually occurring in his household."

"Children fall," Connie Peters put in. "They have accidents."

"Yes they do. And one of these incidents would hardly be cause for alarm. Two may perhaps be construed as an unlikely coincidence. But with so many...?"

He paused, taking time to remove some pictures from the folder, black and white images on glossy paper. He spread them out on the table, fanning them so all present could see. They had been taken at Toledo Hospital the day Aaron fell from the jungle gym, breaking his leg.

Larry hadn't seen the marks on Aaron Reed's young body. His involvement came later, after much of the healing had occurred. Seeing them now, for the first time, brought home to the CASA worker the seriousness of the injuries. The absence of color in the pictures seemed to highlight the damage, the torn flesh presented with a harsh realism.

"These were no accident," Dr. Rahid continued. "If you look closely you'll notice that there are two series of bruises, delivered with at least several days, perhaps even weeks, duration between the events. This was no isolated incident. This was a recurring nightmare that young child has had to contend with."

He waved his hand above the pictures, imploring those gathered around the table to take a closer look.

No one seemed interested in accepting the offer.

"No one is disputing the allegations," the attorney for Children's Services finally remarked.

"Perhaps that is true," Dr. Rahid conceded. "But what you don't seem to be acknowledging is that these were not isolated incidents. I contend this has been going on for some time now. Years, perhaps."

No one replied, each no doubt struggling in their mind to understand the ramifications of the doctor's announcement.

Connie Peters recovered first. "But you're talking of the past, doctor. It's regrettable that we were unaware of this sooner. But now that the boyfriend is out of the house –"

Dr. Rahid held up a single finger, beckoning for silence. "Ah! The boyfriend. How long has the boy's mother been seeing this boyfriend?"

"I don't know for sure," Connie replied. She looked across the table at Larry.

"It seems like she mentioned something about that," he said. "When we visited a few weeks ago. I'm thinking it was around six months, maybe."

Connie nodded her head. "That sounds about right."

Dr. Rahid reached for the folder, waving the papers in the air for emphasis. "Yet these accidents have been going on for several years now. What does that tell you?"

Larry, feeling uncomfortable with where the conversation was headed, shifted in his seat. Monica, beside him, noticed the movement.

"Do you have more to say, Larry?"

"I just don't have a good feeling about any of this. Perhaps Dr. Rahid is right. That there's more going on then we realize. I think things should continue as they are for a while longer."

"I agree," Monica added, then turned toward the representatives from Children's Services. "I think it's in the best interest of the children for Protective Custody to continue until the findings on this case become more definitive. It's far too early to say we've reached a conclusion to this case."

Anochevsky nodded his head slightly, as though in agreement. "I see." He turned toward Cal Broker's attorney. "Mr. Richards. Would this be agreeable to your client?"

"I believe so, yes."

"Very well, then. We will recommend to the court that Protective Supervision for Aaron and Evan Reed continue until further notice, or until the parties involved agree to closing the case."

Laura Reed's attorney, Emily Landrum, spoke up. "Considering the mother's role in all this – or, more correctly, her lack of involvement in these events – I have a problem with some of the language in the documents being filed today. It concerns something on page 2 of the court report." As she spoke the individuals around the table reached for a copy of the written allegations as presented by Children's Services. "Paragraph 3 states *Laura Reed was neglectful in allowing her child to be abused by unknown persons.*"

"You can hardly refute that," Anochevsky replied. "It's obvious from the findings at the hospital, and from what Dr.

Rahid has so clearly pointed out to us, that the child was abused."

"I'm not denying the allegations. I just don't like the word *neglectful*. It implies my client was aware of the situation and allowed it to occur. It makes her sound responsible for what happened."

"What do you suggest?"

"I think the sentence should be stricken from the record. The child's situation is explained in adequate detail and, as you pointed out, there's no denying something happened. I just don't think it's fair to blame my client for a situation she had no control over."

"I disagree," Connie remarked. "As the mother she should be aware of what's going on with her children."

"Do you have children, Miss Peters?"

"Yes I do. A fifteen-year-old son. And I keep an eye on what's happening with him all the time."

"I'm sure you do. And I'm sure you're a good mother. Just like I'm sure Laura Reed is a good mother. But you can't watch them every second of every day. Especially at that age. I think it's unrealistic to expect such a thing."

"I know what's going on with my child. I know he's safe."

"I hope for your sake, Miss Peters, that those words don't come back to haunt you."

"If I can say something?" Larry interrupted. "From what I've seen Laura Reed is an attentive mother who cares for her children. I certainly wouldn't call her neglectful toward the two boys. It's unfortunate what happened to Aaron, but I don't think you can blame the mother. The fact that she asked the boyfriend to leave, and has had no contact with him since then, shows she has her children's best interest at heart."

Monica Perry added her opinion to the conversation. "I have no problem with striking the sentence regarding neglect from the record."

Mark Anochevsky made a bold line across his page. "Consider it removed. Anything else?"

No one spoke up.

"Very well. I believe the magistrate is waiting for us."

Chapter Twenty-Four:

THE HEARING proceeded as Larry had anticipated, with no new revelations in the court room. The magistrate approved the extension of Protective Custody for the children, which seemed the most pressing issue as far as the CASA volunteer was concerned. Now he could concentrate on getting to know the children better in an effort to more fully understand their situation at home.

After spending a couple more minutes with Monica Perry, discussing the particulars of the case, he took his leave.

Heading downstairs he spied Aaron and Evan standing inside the front door of the Juvenile Court Building, just beyond the security gate. They stared out the glass-paneled entrance-way, their attention focused on something outside of Larry's line of sight.

"Is everything okay, guys?"

Evan answered. "Mom told us to wait inside." Then, following a brief pause in which Larry remained silent, Evan continued. "She's talking to our Dad."

Not sure how to react – uncertain whether he should even become involved – he stepped outside from the air-conditioned comfort of the building. The heat and humidity struck him with a suddenness that nearly took his breath away. It wasn't even lunchtime, yet the temperature was well into the high eighties already. The heatwave that gripped the area still lingered. Larry found himself momentarily missing the cold days of winter.

He was considering heading right, toward his parked car, when he heard a voice from the other direction, raised in anger, that caught his attention. It was Laura Reed. He turned around as unobtrusively as possible and spotted her speaking with Cal Broker, who had confronted her just outside the three-story red-bricked structure on Washington Street that housed the Juvenile Court. They stood inches away from each other, like sparring partners about to go at it.

"Don't you dare tell me how to raise my children," Laura was saying, the irritation in her voice obvious.

"Apparently somebody's got to. Doesn't sound like you're doing a very good job of things."

"I do a great job. They know they're loved and taken care of. My children do just fine."

"What's with this *my* children crap? Those kids are mine too, you know. As the father I have rights."

"You don't have any rights. You walked out on any rights you had three years ago when we split up."

"I didn't walk out on you, Laura. You left me. Or don't you remember how you took my children away from me?"

"That's not the way it was, Cal, and you know it. I had to get away from you. I had to get away from us. What other choice did I have?"

"You can spin it any way you want, Laura. It still wasn't right. And now I find out you're abusing them –"

"I am not abusing them," she interrupted. It was obvious, from the expression on her face and the tone of her voice, that she was struggling to control her anger. "I love my children."

"You've got a hell of a way to show it. I want to be sure those kids are taken care of. And if you can't do it, then it looks like maybe it's up to me."

"You're a fine one to speak. You haven't even seen them in three years. No Christmas presents. No birthday cards. You sure are a fine example of a father figure."

"Did you ever think that maybe I stayed away for their sake?"

She stopped, taken aback with his words, allowing herself a few moments to collect her thoughts. "And what's that supposed to mean, Cal?"

"I wasn't ready to be a father when we had the kids. I know now I had a lot of growing up to do. And after you left, and I realized how stupid I had been about everything, I wanted to see them. And be part of their life. But I figured they were better off without me."

"That was mighty noble of you, Cal."

He gave a halfhearted chuckle. "You can be as sarcastic as you want, Laura, but what I'm telling you is the truth. I figured Aaron and Evan belonged with their mother. That was what was best for them. Me forcing myself back into their lives would only make things more confusing for them. So I just decided to let things be."

"Then why are you even here? How come all of a sudden you've decided to be a father?"

"Because the situation is different now, don't you think? I was okay staying away, knowing the boys were being taken care of. But with what's been going on lately I just don't know."

Larry could detect the signs of an inner struggle going on with Laura. He sympathized with her. No doubt she wanted to lash out, but she feared such a reaction would only make the situation worse. He wondered too if anything Cal Broker was saying was true, or whether it was all just a string of lies fabricated so he could get his own way.

When Laura resumed her voice was more calm; the tone more relaxed. She spoke slowly, enunciating each word carefully, as though it was an effort to keep her emotions in check.

"I'm glad you're concerned about your kids, Cal. I really am. I only wish it had come about under different circumstances. But, maybe, with all the bad, this will be a good thing. If it brings you all back together again."

For a few seconds the boys' father said nothing. Then, in a tone no different from his earlier outbursts, he continued. "That's bullshit, Laura, and you know it. You just want me feeling sorry for you. And thinking what a great mother you are. But it's not gonna work. I know you better than that. I know what you're really like."

"You don't know shit." Her initial anger had returned with the words. "I don't care what you say, you're not going to have my children. Not if I can help it."

"Then it's a good thing for me that it's not your decision. I've waited this long. I can be patient. And we'll see what the court decides. Just because you're the mother doesn't give you the right to do whatever you want to our children."

"They're not *our* children." She practically spat the words out. "They're *my* children. I'm the one who raised them. I'm the one who's taken care of them all these years."

"The truth will come out, Laura. It's gonna come crashing down on you one of these days. And guess who's gonna be there to pick up the pieces?"

He stepped closer, throwing his chest out as he pointed at himself with a beefy thumb. "Me, that's who. And I'm not gonna forget the way you talked to me. All highfalutin' like. Like you're so much better than me."

He turned and walked away, toward where Larry stood, nearly bumping into the college student as he walked past.

Laura, aware of the CASA volunteer's presence for the first time, lowered her head as he drew closer.

"I'm sorry you had to see that."

"I'm sure it wasn't easy for you, Laura." Larry looked around, feeling suddenly conspicuous standing on the sidewalk in front of the court.

Having watched their father depart the twins must have assumed it was okay to come outside. Aaron and Evan sauntered toward their mother. Larry offered a smile but neither boy seemed very responsive.

"Can he really do that?" Laura asked. "Can Cal take my children away?"

"He would have to show definite cause for something like that. The Court is always reluctant to remove children from their mother. That and the fact he's been out of their lives for so long doesn't paint him as a sympathetic father figure."

"But it's possible?"

He considered what to say. "He is the father. And, as such, is entitled to a say in things."

She drooped her head, as though defeated already.

"I wouldn't worry about it. Just keep taking care of your boys. Keep an eye out for anything out of the ordinary. As long as things stay good at home you'll have nothing to worry about."

She nodded, as though agreeing with the sense of what he said, but it was obvious the doubt remained.

"I'll probably stop by in a few weeks," Larry continued. "To see how things are going. Okay?"

She made no reply.

As Larry turned to leave Evan give him a meek "Good-bye." Aaron offered a weak wave.

It was a start.

Chapter Twenty-Five:

T HE NIGHT was quiet; the house dark. Even so, Aaron was glad to be back in his familiar room again. He had never appreciated his freedom of movement, his mobility, until, now that it had been denied him, he realized what it was like to be without it. He still took small steps whenever he walked anywhere, gingerly, careful not to rush things for fear of damaging himself once again. But he could now make it up the stairs unassisted, so it had been decided to return the house to a sense of normalcy. No more sleeping on the floor of the living room.

It felt comforting to see the blue walls of his bedroom again; the twin dressers on the side of the room, the Teenage Mutant Ninja Turtles poster on the far wall, the collection of die-cast cars and plastic guns and mismatched Legos that filled the toy box. It felt like being home again, like he was back where he belonged and not on display for the entire family and a legion of strangers to gawk at.

He could hear Evan in the bunk above him, his brother's gentle breathing the only sound in the room. The creatures of the night – crickets or frogs or whatever it was that came to life when the sun went down – spoke through the open window, their melody a persistent buzz of sound that overpowered everything else. The full moon outside lit up the room, casting a cool glow over the familiar surroundings.

It was a tranquil light, cool and soothing, but for Aaron there was no comfort to be found.

Aaron closed his eyes, trying to fall asleep, but his skin felt clammy and wet, making the chore a difficult one. The sheets clung to him, sticking to the sweat that coated his arms and legs. It was a warm evening, the temperatures of the day failing to diminish with the setting of the sun, but it wasn't the heat alone that caused him so much discomfort.

His mind drifted back to the day of the accident, to the events leading up to the ambulance ride to Toledo Hospital. His mind drifted back to the voices that, like so many times in the past, had once again goaded him.

He had never expected to hear them that day. One minute he was enjoying the morning, thinking of little other than the coming trip to the zoo. It was a nice diversion, stopping at the playground. He relished the idea of moving around; the challenge of maneuvering through the metal bars that comprised the jungle gym appealed to him.

Then suddenly, as he was balanced precariously near the top of the metal structure, the voices made their presence known to him.

You shall go higher. You shall ascend to the heavens.
I think this is high enough.
There is naught to be fearful of.
What if I lose my balance?
You shall not lose your balance. Trust in yourself.
What if I fall?
You are born to suffer. Accept what fate has in store for you. Embrace the pain.
I'm afraid.
What right have you to be afraid? Was Daniel afraid when cast into the den of lions?
But I'm not Daniel. I'm just a boy.
You are a sinner. Like everyone else. To overcome your sins you must overcome your fears.

I think this is high enough.

Stand up!

Why?

To prove you can do it. To prove you can overcome your fears. To be worthy you must prove yourself.

But I don't understand this. Why do you tell me these things?

Because God does not abide sinners. He does not abide the weak. You must prove your worth to stand at the side of God in heaven. You must earn his love through your actions as well as through your thoughts. You must be prepared to sacrifice yourself if need be. You must show him you are worthy of his affection.

How? How can I do that?

Stand. Stand now and reach with your arms to the heavens above. Stand now and show how worthy you are to bask in his glory.

But I'm afraid.

Stand now!

It was the last thing he remembered before falling to the ground and breaking his leg.

The voices had returned only once since the incident at the park, and again the occurrence was a surprise to him. He hadn't heard from them in so long that he was beginning to think he had imagined the whole thing. Their absence strengthened him, and made him more aware of the reality surrounding him. His mother, his grandparents, the people around him – that was what was real. The things he could touch with his hands – and see with his eyes – those were the things that mattered in life.

But with the renewal of the voices came the return of doubt and confusion.

Where did they come from?

How did they know so much about him?

Were they sent to protect him, or to torture him?

And rising above all the other queries was the most haunting question of all.

How could he deny something that felt so real?

With their usual persistence the voices prodded, and goaded, and encouraged him to do things he normally wouldn't have considered.

They changed him.

They transformed him.

They made him into someone he no longer recognized, a stranger he did not care for.

The old woman must be taught a lesson.

Why would you say that?

Because she notices too much. She perceives things the others do not. She is more aware of what occurs around her than the rest. If she begins to suspect what is happening there may be complications.

But she helps me. She's good to me.

She must be taught a lesson.

I can't hurt her. I just can't.

It does not require a physical hurt. There are other considerations. Other ways to achieve the goal. What does she prize most? What that she possesses is she most enamored of?

I don't understand. What do you want from me?

You don't understand because you are weak, and must be shown the way. It is her book that she most treasures. Her Bible. You must destroy it.

No. I can't do that.

Then you must remove it from her sight. You must deny her the pleasure she seeks from the words within.

What must I do?

You will take it away when she is not observing you. Hide it from her sight. Remove it from her presence. This is what you should do and this is what you will do.

Evan had realized the truth. Somehow he had surmised that Aaron had taken Grandma Ruth's Bible. He didn't mention it again. He never accused Aaron of any wrongdoing. But every time Aaron looked at his brother he could feel the weight of Evan's stare. It made him promise not to listen to the voices anymore. It made him feel like he could resist their promptings.

But he knew it was all in vain. He knew the voices would return. And he knew he would be too weak to do anything but submit to their wishes.

The way he always did.

Chapter Twenty-Six:

LARRY FOUND himself spending his free time online. There was nothing unusual in that, because his computer had long been a gateway for him, a conduit to access information as well as a source of entertainment. But recently he had abandoned the indiscriminate roaming of the past, those times when he would get distracted by a random pop-up and pursue it regardless of how meaningless or nonsensical it became. His searches were more defined now, with a set goal in mind.

Childhood-Onset Schizophrenia, or COS, was the topic he found himself investigating.

Evan had told Larry his brother heard voices; voices that sometimes instructed the youngster to hurt himself. It seemed like something out of a bad movie. Surely those things didn't occur in real life?

But before he could justify dismissing the allegations he felt he should consider the possibilities. And the deeper he delved into the subject the more confused he became.

Schizophrenia was a common enough topic. Larry had taken courses at the University of Toledo concerning mental illness, as part of his training to become a social worker. The classes were of a general nature, discussing a wide assortment of mental ailments, including such things as anxiety and depression, and how these disabilities affected the people coping with them. Schizophrenia was only one of the mental illnesses they had talked about.

Whenever Larry had heard it spoken of in the past it was always in reference to people with split-personalities. It reminded him of the old Dr. Jekyll and Mr. Hyde stories; the good versus evil of people's identities.

But, according to the online information he reviewed, this was only part of the explanation, and in many instances a small part only. More correctly, the term dealt with a severe brain disorder, one in which the person involved has a difficult time distinguishing between reality and fantasy. This can manifest itself in many ways, affecting a person's thoughts through delusions and their perception of the world around them through hallucinations.

Or, in the case of many schizophrenics, by the hearing of voices.

Though generally associated with people later in life – it often developed in men during their mid-twenties – it was known to occur as well in children. Unfortunately, in these instances the illness was often not recognized as such. Many of the symptoms involved – moodiness, change in personality, failure to relate well to others – were common enough traits for adolescents going through puberty.

Which meant the illness often progressed, undetected and unsuspected, for a long time before being diagnosed properly.

For kids under the age of fifteen Childhood Onset Schizophrenia was estimated to show up in perhaps one out of every 40,000 children. Certainly not very common, but not outside the realm of possibilities either.

As he continued his online research Larry considered the symptoms discussed, realizing that not all of them would be manifested in every case. But enough reminded him of Aaron Reed to make him question things.

Apparently children suffering with COS were often withdrawn, preferring to keep to themselves. He had as yet had little interaction with Aaron. Even when he attempted to communicate with the child on his own level, during the course of the video game, the boy seemed shy and somewhat aloof, as though uncomfortable with expressing himself. This was in marked contrast with his brother, who seemed friendly and outgoing.

Though maybe it was just the contrast between the two siblings that gave Aaron the impression of being more withdrawn. Maybe, when taken on his own, he wasn't that different from other nine-year-olds. Larry had so little experience dealing with children that age that he couldn't say for certain what was normal.

Showing little emotion and speaking rarely were also cited as symptoms of the illness, along with a tendency to exhibit little or no eye contact with others. Larry had already witnessed these traits, during his visits with the family. Aaron had resisted Larry's attempts to be engaged in conversation, exhibiting little interest in those around him. He had constantly kept to himself.

Other points caught Larry's interest. An inability to make friends was cited, along with failure at school. Having only seen the children during summer break these points were difficult to verify one way or the other, though they presented Larry with some points to bring up with Laura Reed the next time he saw her.

It would be interesting to learn more about Aaron's behavior, particularly whether it had changed much recently.

But what Larry found himself returning to, time and again during his research, was the issue of hearing voices. More often than not the voices were known to say bad things, injuring the child's self-esteem and confusing them concerning what was appropriate behavior. Some cases resulted in the child actually doing physical harm to himself, or to others, due to his illusions.

Larry hadn't seen the marks on the young boy's body at Toledo Hospital, though the pictures Dr. Rahid had presented before the Adjudication/Disposition Hearing had given an extremely graphic indication of what the boy had experienced. He had read the reports, and talked to Connie Peters, so he had an understanding of what was at stake. Still, he felt there was more research to be done before reaching a conclusion.

And part of that research was reaching out to the people who could gave him the answers he sought.

Rising above the continuous clatter of the Emergency Room, a voice issued from the PA system. "Dr. Tyrone. Please report to the nursing station for an outside phone call."

Dr. Lois Tyrone heard the page but didn't let it faze her. She had learned early in her career that, even in an emergency situation, the best thing to do was to remain calm and collected. You finished one chore before rushing into another. As much as people liked to praise the value of multi-tasking, there were instances where it just wasn't the proper procedure to employ.

She had three more stitches to complete on the wound she was suturing and could hardly leave now.

The phone call would have to wait.

"Do you want me to finish up for you?" the assisting nurse asked.

"No sense in that, Eileen. I'm almost done."

With professional ease she continued the task, making certain not to hurry through the procedure, performing the routine as though it was the most important thing in the world and required her undivided attention. Slipping the silk thread through the final loop she pulled tightly, the precisely spaced knot identical to the seven others along the length of the wound. It was a sense of pride with her to always do her best, no matter the situation, and she was pleased with her results. Chances were good there wouldn't even be a scar.

"You can finish up now, Eileen. Make certain he gets a written sheet of care instructions to take home with him."

"Yes, Doctor."

Dr. Tyrone left the cubicle, stripping off her rubber gloves as she scurried down the hallway, and deposited the soiled articles in a waste bin set aside for bio-hazardous material.

"This better be important," she mumbled to herself as she approached the front desk.

She took a deep breath before retrieving the receiver handed to her. Feeling more controlled, she presented her most professional tone to the caller. "Dr. Lois Tyrone. May I help you?"

"Hello, Dr. Tyrone. My name's Larry Kendall. I'm a CASA volunteer through Lucas County Juvenile Court."

"What is this about, Mr. Kendall?'

"It concerns a child you treated about six week ago."

"I've seen a lot of children in the past six weeks, Mr. Kendall."

"I'm sure you have. But I'm hoping you'll remember this one. His name is Aaron Reed?"

"Are you related to Aaron Reed?"

"No I'm not, but –"

"Then I suggest you talk to the child's parents." She didn't have time to waste on this kind of nonsense, a fact which clearly showed in her present tone of voice. "There's nothing I can tell you."

"Please bear with me a moment longer, doctor. The child came to the hospital with a broken leg. He had fallen off some playground equipment. While you were examining him you detected other marks. Indications of possible abuse."

He paused, allowing her to respond, but Dr. Tyrone said nothing. Instead she found herself reviewing in her mind the circumstances of the case. She did remember the incident.

"You called Children's Services," the voice from the other end continued.

"I recall the circumstances."

"Good. The family has been under observation since then. To insure that the children are safe. I've been appointed the guardian of the children and I need to determine what actually happened to Aaron."

"Has something else happened to the child? Are there more injuries?"

"No. Nothing like that."

"Then why are you calling me? What's so important that you had to interrupt me during my shift? There are people here I should be treating, right now, rather than talking on the phone about something that happened weeks ago."

"Some new information has surfaced. Regarding the marks on the child. I need your input regarding it."

"This is very unorthodox, Mr...." She stopped, having forgotten his name.

"Kendall. Larry Kendall."

"I appreciate what you're doing here, Mr. Kendall. And I'm sure you have the child's best interest at heart. But you're asking me to divulge private information concerning a patient."

"I understand your reluctance. And I certainly don't want you to do something you're uncomfortable with. If it eases your mind any, I have a Court Order issued from Lucas County that allows me access to any information I deem necessary concerning the child's welfare – including medical records – with no parental approval required.

"Is there an email I can reach you at? Or a fax number? I could send you a copy of my credentials, so you can verify who I am, and a copy of the document. Then, at your convenience, you could call me back to discuss the matter. I promise it will only take five minutes of your time."

She deliberated for all of three seconds, then handed the phone to one of the clerks at the desk. "Please take down this gentleman's information and give him our fax number. He'll be sending something over and I want to see it when it gets here."

"Very good, Dr. Tyrone."

She took two steps away from the desk, turned on her heels, and retreated to her previous position. "And pull the file for Aaron Reed and bring it to my desk." She pointed to the phone. "He can get you the child's information."

She turned again and it was back to work.

Chapter Twenty-Seven:

"Is THE devil real, Grandma?"

Ruth Franklin lifted her gaze from the Bible in her hands to look toward Aaron, who stood in front of her, an intense look of confusion on his features.

She replied immediately, having no doubt in her mind as to the answer. "Of course the devil is real. He's all around us. The good book tells us *be watchful. Your adversary the devil prowls around like a roaring lion, seeking someone to devour.*"

The answer brought a reaction from the child she hadn't anticipated. A sudden laugh, combined with a smirk, enveloped him. His eyes held a faraway look as he chuckled, as though in contemplation of a humorous anecdote.

"The devil is no laughing matter, Aaron."

"I know, Grandma."

He sobered up, instantly, as though his previous reaction had never occurred. His voice took on a distant cadence. "Is the devil all-powerful?"

"Of course not." The suggestion seemed abhorrent to her. "Only God is all-powerful. Only God has control of our destinies."

"But the devil tries to take control, doesn't he? He tempts us to do wrong."

"Everyone does wrong from time to time. That's what makes us human. Sin is but a part of life. *For all have sinned and fall short of the glory of God."*

"Then there's no way to get around the devil, is there? If the devil controls sin, and all men sin, then the devil must control all men. He must be more powerful than God."

The concept confused Aaron. None of it made sense to him. The voices that spoke to him – was it the devil, leading him astray? Forcing him to do things he shouldn't do? Or was it God testing him? Did he fall short because he couldn't live up to the expectations the voices presented to him? Was he a failure in the eyes of God?

"I believe the devil is all around us," he admitted at last, though he didn't fully understand the ramifications of the statement.

"Of course the devil is all around us," Grandma Ruth informed him. "He seeks our souls. He strives to draw us away from righteousness. He tempts us with illicit favors and promises he can never fulfill."

"Then how do we fight him? How do we beat him?"

"By trusting in The Lord. *Resist the devil and he will flee you.* You must stand strong, Aaron. You must have faith."

"But I'm not strong enough. I'm just a little boy."

"You must always remember the words of Jesus. *Let the children come to me, and do not hinder them, for to such belongs the kingdom of God.* You need never fear. Jesus has a place in heaven for you, Aaron."

The young boy had no reaction to the words. He wanted to believe in Jesus. He wanted to believe there was a location called heaven, where a place had been set aside for him to love and be loved. But it was all so foreign from what he knew. Too many bad experiences, too many sleepless nights, too much pain had left him numb to anything but the feeling he needed to escape from it all.

Nobody else understood. They were all different. None of them could see things the way he saw things. None of them heard the things he heard.

It used to be a comfort to him, listening to Grandma Ruth, as she read from the Bible and praised the deeds of that glorious past. But now it seemed merely empty words. It didn't have anything to do with him. It couldn't change things. It couldn't alter his life.

It couldn't prevent the voices from returning again.

Ruth Franklin stared at her grandson. Though she didn't understand what he was going through she could feel his sorrow. She was aware of his pain.

"Have faith, Aaron," she admonished. "God has something in mind for you. I'm sure of it."

He made no reply, only turning to walk away, and she resumed her favorite pastime.

Chapter Twenty-Eight:

Moments LATER Laura entered. She approached the coffee table in the center of the room and sat on the edge, facing her Grandmother. "Why do you tell him those things?"

Grandma Ruth set her Bible down, regarding her granddaughter with a stern look. "What things?"

"Those stories. About devils and demons and all that nonsense."

"They aren't stories, Laura. And they certainly aren't nonsense. They're the word of God."

"I don't care what you call them. You have no business talking to Aaron about it."

"The child seeks understanding. He wants to know the truth about the world and his place in it. Who am I to deny him?"

"But he doesn't understand!"

Her voice had risen in anger by now, and she found herself yelling at her grandmother. Laura made a conscious effort to regain control, taking a deep breath to steady herself.

"Don't you see?" Laura shifted position as she continued, feeling uncomfortable talking to her Grandmother about these matters but knowing something had to be said. "He thinks it's all real."

"It is real, Laura."

"But the devil? You make it sound like some kind of demon is going to sweep out of the sky and carry Aaron away. Like he's living in one of those ridiculous superhero movies he watches. Don't you think the boy is dealing with enough now without adding to his burden?"

"He's questioning things in his life, Laura. He's trying to understand why he has to suffer the way he does. He's searching for peace, and it can be found in the words of the Bible. *Therefore, since Christ suffered in his body, arm yourselves also with the same attitude, because whoever suffers in the body is done with sin.* It's salvation he's seeking and the good book can lead him to it."

Laura rose to her feet, her voice once more elevated. "It doesn't help! It doesn't ease the pain of what he's going through. Can't you see that?"

"How do you know it doesn't help? The fact that he's asking questions shows he's interested. It shows he wants to believe."

"All it shows is that he's a troubled child searching for answers. But what you're telling him.... The things you're exposing him to.... It's not what he needs, Grandma. Please don't talk to him about this anymore. I want you to just stop talking to him about this."

For a full twenty seconds they stared at one another, each reluctant to hurt the other but each just as determined their point of view was correct. Ruth Franklin broke the silence.

"When did you stop believing, Laura?"

"I never believed," Laura immediately retorted. "Not the way you do. And you didn't, either. Not when you were my age."

"I didn't know any better then. But now that I know I understand. God has plans for us all."

"I don't believe that, Grandma." She stood, walked several steps away, then turned to face the older woman once again.

Laura trembled with emotion, striving in vain to control herself. "I can't believe that, Grandma. Because if I do, what does it say about what God thinks of me?"

"God loves you, Laura. He loves each of us."

"Does he?"

"Of course he does. *For God so loved the world that he gave his one and only Son, that whoever believes in him shall not perish but have eternal life.* Eternal life, Laura. That is God's promise to us. That is his gift to us."

"What about our life here on earth, Grandma? Doesn't he care about us now?"

"Of course he cares about you, Laura. You have to believe that."

"Sure he does. He loves me so much he took my mother from me when I was six years old. He loves me so much he took my father away when I was ten."

"Your father is in a better place now. I'm sure of it."

"What about my place? What about where I'm at? In an abusive relationship with Cal for five years? Was that a better place? How about Aaron? How about an innocent child that is abused and mistreated? Is that living in a better place?"

Laura turned, stepped away, and stopped. For several seconds nothing was said. When she resumed her voice was garbled, the tears making the words indistinct.

"I'm glad you have your faith, Grandma. I know it's helped you through a lot of bad. With what Grandpa Mike went through and everything. I know it's important to you."

She turned, the moisture in her eyes reflecting the dim light of the room.

"But it's not my faith. And it's not my children's faith."

She turned to walk from the room, then halted again. Her voice, resuming, was barely above a whisper, as though she was reluctant to say the words.

"I don't want you talking to the kids about this again. Understand?"

Ruth Franklin's hands trembled. She stroked her Bible, as though seeking solace from the closeness of the book. Finally she closed her eyes, bowed her head, and nodded a meek acceptance to her granddaughter's words.

"As you wish," the old woman replied.

Chapter Twenty-Nine:

W AITING FOR the callback from the doctor at Toledo Hospital – wondering if she would even bother to get back to him – Larry felt apprehensive. He hoped she would have some good information for him, something that would explain Aaron's behavior in a way that made more sense than the theory he found himself advocating. All the online information pointed to the possibility of what Larry suspected. Perhaps the young boy was experiencing symptoms of mental illness, to the point where he was having a difficult time judging between reality and delusion. It certainly was within the realm of possibility.

But was it probable? His research so far indicated that Schizophrenia in children usually developed around the age of twelve. Certainly there were exceptions to this rule. Several sites mentioned children as young as six having been diagnosed with the illness. Aaron Reed could be one of these rare instances, the exception to the rule, when things don't progress in a normal fashion.

Larry paused, pondering over his word choice. What was normal about mental illness? There was nothing normal about it. Hallucinations, delusions, hearing voices, these were all things Larry had never considered before. Nothing in his personal experience had prepared him for these possibilities. He couldn't imagine living in a world where it was impossible to distinguish between truth and fantasy; where the line between what was real and what was imagined became blurred.

He sat in silence, staring at the four walls of his bedroom, contemplating what he should do next. He finally decided to make another phone call.

"Connie Peters here."

"Hello, Connie. This is Larry Kendall. From the CASA office."

"Hello, Larry. How can I help you?"

"I've been thinking about Aaron Reed. About what he's going though. I'm just trying to make sense of it all."

"I know what you mean. This is a great job. As a caseworker I have the opportunity to do a lot of good for a lot of people. It can be extremely rewarding at times. But sometimes you get a case, like this one, and you wonder about the futility of it all. There's a lot of bad out there, Larry. The things people do to their children...."

She paused, the silence on the line saying more than her words ever could.

"You never get used to seeing it," she concluded.

"What do you think happened to Aaron?"

"We may never know, unless another incident occurs, and I certainly hope that doesn't happen. It seems to me that Laura was right. About the boyfriend."

"So you think he was responsible?"

"It looks that way. Don't you agree?"

"I guess I just have my doubts. I was thinking about what Dr. Rahid said. About the other accidents."

"What about them?"

"If the boyfriend has only been around for six months he couldn't have been responsible for anything before then. There has to be another explanation for what's been going on."

"You're over thinking things, Larry. If I had to bet on it, I would say those previous accidents were simply that. Accidents. Plain and simple."

"So you don't suspect abuse or.... Or, maybe something else?"

"We're talking two young boys, Larry. They get wild. Rambunctious. Play a bit too rough at times. Things are bound to happen."

"I suppose you're right."

His tone lacked the conviction evident in his words, but the caseworker failed to notice.

"I have a good feeling about this, Larry. I really do. Laura is very involved with her children. I think she cares for them a lot. And having the grandparents in the house is another plus. She doesn't have to raise the kids by herself while trying to work a job to make ends meet. That can be a rough burden for someone to handle alone."

"So what happens now?"

"We continue to monitor things, of course. But from what we've seen so far I suspect this case won't run full length in the courts. As long as there are no more incidents, and nothing unexpected pops up, I think Laura and her kids will do just fine."

"I hope you're right."

"So was there anything else?"

"No, Connie. Thanks."

"No problem. Glad I could help."

Chapter Thirty:

AARON UNDERSTOOD enough to realize the voices he heard weren't normal. But they were all he knew, having no frame of reference to compare them to. And so he attempted to rationalize what he was going through; to find a logical reason that would make sense to him and explain what he was experiencing.

Perhaps it was just an increased awareness on his part that allowed him to hear the voices. Maybe he was more perceptive than the others around him, allowing him access to sensations they missed. Maybe he was the normal one, and everyone else was strange.

As soon as such thoughts entered his head he dismissed them. He knew he was different. There was no denying the truth.

But he refused to believe that meant there was something wrong with him. God wouldn't allow that. His grandmother told him that. God was looking after him. And protecting him.

Aaron lay in bed, resting on top of the sheets on a sweltering summer's night, longing to fall to sleep and so escape the confusing thoughts he wrestled with. Presently his brother leaned down from the top bunk, a serious expression on Evan's face.

"Why do you do it?" Evan asked.

"Do what?"

"The bad things you do. Like hiding Grandma Ruth's Bible the other day."

"What's it matter to you what I do?"

"It doesn't matter. I guess. I just don't understand it, that's all."

"What's to understand?"

Aaron rolled over to face his brother, propping himself up on one elbow. "Haven't you ever wanted to do something bad? Something you know you're not supposed to do? Just to see what it feels like?"

"No. I haven't." His words came slowly, as though he had to consider them first. It didn't make for a very convincing rebuttal.

"I don't believe you." Aaron's tone was taunting, mocking his brother. "I think you want to do bad things too."

"So what if I do? Maybe I think of things," Evan admitted. "Things I shouldn't do. Once in a while. But I don't do them."

No reply came, and for several long seconds silence gripped the room.

"Don't you ever hear a little voice in your head?" Aaron asked the question slowly, realizing he was treading on dangerous ground by revealing too much information, but he was desperate to hear what his brother would say. After all, they were twins, and who could be closer to him than a twin? Who else could better understand what he was going through?

"A little voice in your head," Aaron repeated, "telling you to do things?"

The response was immediate.

"No."

Evan's face suddenly disappeared, as he withdrew from the awkward position of leaning over the side of his bed to lay down on his mattress in the top bunk. For several seconds no words were spoken, the silence of the night dragging on between them.

Movement sounded from above, and Evan's face came into view once more.

"Do you, Aaron?"

"Do I what?"

"Do you hear voices?"

"No. Of course not." Aaron rolled over, turning from his brother to face the wall. "No. I was just joking around. Just wanted to hear what you'd say."

And so he lay there, pressed up against the wall, hoping for sleep's release, until eventually the soft breathing from the bunk above told him his brother was asleep.

Why did you seek your brother's counsel?

Because I'm confused. I don't understand what's going on. None of this makes sense to me.

It is not for you to understand. You need only to obey.

But why are you here?

To guide you in the important ways. To lead you to the true light. To teach you right from wrong.

I know right from wrong. My mother tells me. Grandma Ruth tells me.

They do not know. They can not show you the proper path to salvation. The true path. You must heed the instructions delivered to you.

I don't want to. I want you to leave me alone.

You cannot deny the truth. You have been so informed in the past. To deny what you hear means you must be punished.

I don't want to be punished.

Such things are beyond your control.

Can't you just leave me alone?

You must be punished.

Please stop.

Not until you are punished.

I don't want to be punished.

You must be punished.

The voices were relentless.

Though they were often absent for a long time, filling Aaron with the false hope that perhaps he was finished with them after all, when they returned it was as though they had never departed. They resumed where they had left off, barraging Aaron with accusations that weren't true and questions he failed to comprehend.

They could not be reasoned with. He knew that. Because in the past he had attempted to reach them, imploring them to let him be. But they would not listen. They were never satisfied. No matter how hard he struggled, how hard he resisted, there was only one way to make the voices go away.

By appeasing them.

By punishing himself.

By inflicting damage.

With pins and needles.

With a belt across the side.

With a rope tied tightly around the throat.

Whatever was at hand could be used to inflict pain on himself. He had learned that over the years.

Only then would the voices leave him alone.

Only then would the voices give him peace.

Chapter Thirty-One:

IT WAS late when the call came through; approaching midnight. Larry rolled over, the sound instantly awakening him, but it took a few seconds for his mind to register what the noise was. He reached for the cellphone from the table at the head of his bed.

"Hello. This is Larry."

"Hello, Mr. Kendall. This is Dr. Tyrone. From Toledo Hospital."

"Dr. Tyrone." It took him a moment to register the name. His mind, reacting slower than his body, was beginning to function by now, recovering from his sleep-induced lethargy, and it all came back to him. "Thank you for calling me," he managed, as he sat upright in bed.

Her voice continued in an apologetic tone. "I was just finishing my shift and I was afraid if I didn't call you now I would forget all about it."

"Then I'm glad you got hold of me. You received the document I faxed you?"

"Yes I did. You understand, of course, that we have to be careful who we divulge patient information to."

"Of course."

The papers sent to the hospital had been prepared by the Juvenile Center when Larry was first assigned the case of the twin boys. The form spelled out his legal rights as the guardian of the children, allowing him access to any medical records, school reports, or similar information he deemed appropriate in his investigation. It was a valuable tool when dealing with bureaucracy, especially with all the privacy stipulations in effect, well-intentioned safeguards put in place to protect people.

But the CASA volunteer's job was to protect as well. The children they represented were often at their most vulnerable, neglected or abused, many times separated from the only home they knew. To properly provide for them the CASA guardians needed to be as well-informed as possible.

You couldn't always rely on family members to provide accurate – or even truthful – information. Sometimes you had to talk with others.

Such as the physicians who dealt with the children on a one-to-one basis.

"So I understand you're the guardian for Aaron Reed and his brother?" Dr Tyrone was saying.

"That's correct."

"How are they doing?"

"The boys are still at home. They were allowed to remain in Protective Custody with their mother."

"Any other incidents?"

"None."

"Then what is it you needed to know? I felt a sense of urgency when you contacted me earlier."

"I'm just trying to understand what's actually going on here. You treated Aaron when he arrived at the hospital?"

"That's right."

"And you saw some suspicious marks on him?"

"Suspicious is hardly the word I would use."

"Why do you say that?"

"There was no doubt in my mind as to the meaning of the marks on the young man. From the nature of the bruises on his abdomen, I can't see any way they could have happened accidentally."

"And you're sure about that?"

"Sure enough that I felt justified in calling Children's Services. Why do you ask?"

"Because I was just wondering...." He paused, almost embarrassed to continue. Thinking about it now, ready to voice his conjectures to an authority that could easily discredit his thinking, it all seemed ridiculous. But he had come this far. There was no turning back now.

"Could the marks you witnessed on Aaron Reed have been self-inflicted?"

"What do you mean?"

"Could Aaron have done them to himself in some manner? Were they necessarily caused by someone else?"

Silence answered him. He waited, wondering what the doctor was thinking and how she was going to react to his line of questioning. Would she dismiss him outright, and chastise him for wasting her time?

He didn't have to wait long to get an answer.

Her words, when she began anew, were delivered in a slow, precise manner. She seemed to be considering the possibility in her mind, examining what she knew about the incident, and attempting to reason whether there was anything of truth behind Larry's questioning. "Why would you ask that, Mr. Kendall? Is there a particular reason you bring this up?"

"It was something Evan said. That's Aaron's brother. You examined him the day at the hospital as well, correct?"

"Yes I did."

"And found no signs of abuse?"

"That's true, though it hardly signifies anything. Often a predator will single out an individual child to prey on. For whatever reason, they often see one child as more of a threat to them. It's hard to explain, and harder to understand, but it's not that unusual. Especially if the abuser took a particular liking to one of the children."

"But setting aside the idea of someone abusing the child. Could the marks have been self-inflicted?"

For several long seconds nothing was said. Larry thought he detected the sound of papers rustling from the doctor's location, as though she had information in front of her and was reviewing the files she had on hand.

"Yes," she said at last. "I can see where Aaron could have done this to himself, using a belt, or some sort of strap. The marks all appeared to be on the left side of the body, which would be consistent for a right handed person. Do you know if he's right handed, Mr. Kendall?"

"I never really noticed. Sorry."

"Well, most people are, so let's assume it. Though the idea of a child doing this to himself seems a bit...." She paused, struggling to find the right word.

"Preposterous?" Larry suggested.

"Exactly. So what leads you to believe this is a possibility?"

"I've been researching COS on line. Childhood-Onset Schizophrenia."

"I know what COS is, Mr. Kendall."

"Aaron's brother told me that Aaron hears voices. And the voices tell him to do bad things."

"So you're assuming delusions?"

"I'm just considering the possibilities. I don't know the child that well. I've only visited with him a couple times. But he does seem withdrawn. And isolated."

"If what you're saying is true, then it's important that he gets treatment. And soon. Particularly if he has already progressed to the point of doing personal damage to himself."

"So you think this could be what's happening?"

"I didn't say that. I'm not about to attempt a diagnoses of this sort after only seeing the child for a few minutes, and that nearly six weeks ago. And I have to tell you, this sort of condition is rare for someone his age."

"But not unheard of?"

She paused a moment to collect her thoughts. "It isn't beyond the realm of possibilities."

"So what do I do? How do I proceed?"

"Is the child in therapy now?"

"Yes he is. He's seeing Dr. Markham."

"Richard Markham. Yes, I know him. He's in good hands, Mr. Kendall. I suggest you contact Richard and tell him exactly what you told me."

"Do you think he'll believe me?"

"I don't know. But I do know he'll take seriously anything you tell him."

"Thank you. I'll definitely do that."

"Was there anything else, Mr. Kendall?"

"No doctor. Thank you for calling me back. I appreciate it."

"Whatever you do, don't delay on this. If Aaron Reed is developing COS the sooner he's treated the better. There's no telling where this could lead to."

At that point the line went dead.

Larry set his phone down, lay back in bed, and stared up at the ceiling. There was no returning to sleep that night.

He felt an incredible burden had been placed on his shoulders; a responsibility he wasn't certain he was able to accept. He had known his chosen work was important. He knew there were children out there, depending on him, and realized the decisions made in their behalf could affect them for the rest of their lives.

He had always assumed everything would be cut and dry. It was either right, or it was wrong. When he had first read the email from the CASA office, requesting someone to take the case of the twin boys, everything seemed so simple. Someone was abusing the child and it had to stop. Remove the abuser and the problem would go away.

But as he delved deeper into Aaron Reed's life he encountered other factors he had never considered before, factors that contaminated the issues and turned them a murky gray. What did he know about Schizophrenia? How could he be expected to make an informed decision when he lacked the background to fully explain what was occurring?

Was he truly being a help to the family, a guardian to the children, or was his work becoming more of a hindrance? Was he losing perspective, allowing himself to be misguided by a few simple sentences from a nine-year-old boy?

After agonizing over the issue further Larry crawled out from beneath the sheets and pulled his laptop onto the bed. Moments later he was scouring the online information, searching again for clues that would point him in the correct direction.

Keith Julius

Chapter Thirty-Two:

"I'M HUNGRY. Don't we have anything to eat around here?"

Laura looked up from the collection of bills on the table in front of her, relieved to take her mind off them for a minute but in no mood to deal with a complaining child. "How can you be hungry, Evan? We just had dinner an hour ago."

He shrugged, smiling in an impish sort of way. "I guess I'm just a growing boy."

She reached out, ruffling his hair. "Well, you might have to stop growing for now because I don't get paid for two more days. I'll go to the grocery store then."

He nearly said more, but seeing the distraught look on his mother's face gave him reason to pause and consider. She always got this way when she was paying the bills. It didn't make sense to him. All you had to do was write out a check, put in in an envelope, and you were done with it. What was so hard about that?

Still, it was obvious she didn't want to be bothered right now. So without another word he left the kitchen and Laura returned to her paperwork.

There never seemed to be enough money to go around. By the time she paid the cellphone bill and some money toward her charge card – the minimum amount due, which was all she could afford – there wasn't much left. School wasn't too far away and she knew the twins were growing out of everything they owned. Which meant more money going out.

Besides her own bills Laura always tried to help with her grandparents' accounts; she even handled the paperwork for them. She had taken over the chore shortly after moving in with the kids three years earlier, as a way to atone for the extra confusion she brought to their lives. Though the house was paid for, her grandparents had taken out a home equity loan shortly before Grandpa Mike's accident to pay for a new roof and some other needed renovations, never realizing they would be feeling a drop in their income due to his disability.

At least they still had a roof over their heads.

For now, anyway.

Things had been easier when Ted was living with them. He helped out with the bills, on occasion giving her grandparents money when things got particularly tight. They had felt awkward about it at first – that was obvious from their initial hesitancy – but with time they came to rely on the extra to see them through.

Occasionally Ted would take Laura and the kids out to dinner, which was always a special treat for them, or he'd pick up some groceries during the week. His income had made things more comfortable for all of them, providing some of the luxuries they would have otherwise been denied. Laura missed those extras, especially considering how stressful things had been in the last month and a half.

As soon as the thought crossed her mind she felt guilty about it. There was of course more to Ted's absence than a loss of income. She missed having someone her own age to talk to and do things with, even if it just meant going for a walk together on the weekends.

And of course it was much more lonely at night, something she considered every time she crawled into her bed alone.

She tried to ignore those thoughts. She had done the right thing by telling Ted to leave. The lack of any problems since his departure bore that out. Aaron had recovered from his broken leg and had shown no more signs of mistreatment since then. At least that was one aspect of her life that was looking better.

"What are you up to there, Laura?"

She looked up to see Grandpa Mike standing in the doorway, pausing for a much needed breath. Laura was surprised she hadn't heard him approaching. With the clip-clop of his cane and the heavy breathing that developed each time he exerted himself he generally announced his presence ahead of time. He rested against the door frame for a few seconds before entering the kitchen.

"Hi, Grandpa."

Laura rose to her feet, pulling a chair out from the table to make it easier for him to sit. He always seemed to move in slow motion, positioning his body just so, carefully aligning himself with the seat of the chair before completing the procedure. Sometimes she wanted to push him into action; to cajole him into moving faster. She would then instantly regret her lack of patience. It couldn't be easy for him, struggling with his disability on a daily basis. The least she could do was to be understanding about it.

Once settled into position the old man rested his cane on the floor beside him and his hands on the table in front of him. "Looks like you've got your hands full there."

"Bills. They seem to never end."

"And they never do. At least, not in my experience."

"Why does life have to be so tough all the time? Why can't I ever catch a break?"

"Everybody feels that way from time to time, darling. Don't let it discourage you."

"But it does, Grandpa. I feel like I can never get ahead. I'm almost afraid when things start going better. It just means something bad is bound to happen."

"You're thinking about Ted now, aren't you?"

She nodded.

"Who knows? Maybe things will work out after all," he suggested.

"I don't know how you manage to stay so optimistic all the time."

He leaned closer, a twinkle in his eyes and a smile on his lips. "Comes from living with your grandmother all these years. She's taken all the fight out of me."

He then sat back, his voice becoming more serious. "I heard you and Ruthie had a bit of a tiff the other day."

"Yeah. We did."

"Don't be so hard on her, darling. She means well."

"I know she does. And I appreciate everything she's done for me." Laura reached over, patting Grandpa Mike affectionately on the hand. "Everything you've *both* done for me. But I have to raise my kids the way I think is best."

"And you should."

She smiled, encouraged by his words.

"But it doesn't hurt to have a more positive attitude about things." He brought his hand up to his face, stroking his chin as though deep in thought. "You know the old saying? About whether the glass is half full or half empty? I definitely see you as a half empty person, darling. And that sort of thinking doesn't get you anywhere."

"I suppose you're right. I need to be more of a half full person." She smiled at him, comforted with his closeness. "Like you."

"On the contrary. I see the glass as completely full. It's just half water and half air. Just because you can't see it doesn't mean there isn't something there. Just like life. It's all there, it's just sometimes we don't take the time to see what's right there in front of us. It's up to you to decide how to use the opportunities you're given."

She stood and walked over to his side. Reaching out, she wrapped her arms around his shoulder, giving him a hug. "I never knew you were such a philosopher, Gramps."

"Like I said. It comes from living with your grandmother for so many years."

Chapter Thirty-Three:

"MISS REED? Dr. Markham will see you now."

Laura set her magazine down on the couch cushion beside her and stood up.

"Come on, boys. Let's get this over with."

The nurse standing in the doorway remained where she was, blocking entrance to the suite of medical rooms in back.

"Actually, Miss Reed, the doctor would like to talk to you for a few minutes first without the children present."

"Is there a problem?"

"I'm sure everything is just fine. The children can stay in the waiting room and I'll come get them when the doctor is ready."

Laura faced the twins, concern on her face.

"You boys sit quietly and behave. Understand?"

Evan responded. "Yes, Mother." He dragged the words out, like it was ridiculous to even consider them not behaving.

Laura smiled, her mood momentarily lightened, and followed the nurse through the door.

Dr. Richard Markham pondered over what to say to Laura Reed. He knew from experience it was never easy, telling a parent there was the suspicion of mental illness concerning their children.

The immediate response seemed to be denial. No parent could ever believe there was something wrong with their child. It just wasn't a possibility.

Which meant they would talk things over, examining the symptoms and how they related to the child. He'd seen it many times: the growing understanding of the issues involved, the dawning awareness of how things related to their son or daughter, and the eventual acceptance that there could be a problem.

What followed next was invariably the self-recrimination, with the parent accepting the responsibility of what was going on as though they were the cause of everything. He had heard it all over the years. I babied him too much when he was little. I should have stopped breast-feeding him sooner. I didn't pay enough attention to him when he was younger. Or, conversely, I never allowed him his independence, never gave him the room to grow that he needed.

His reply to them all was the same.

It's not your fault.

The hard truth of the matter, a fact many people refused to accept, was that mental illness happened. It was as simple as that. Regardless of how involved the parents were, or how informed they were, or how carefully they safeguarded the children in their care, sometimes there was no preventing what was going to occur.

Plenty of research had been done on the subject, and plenty of theories thrown about and discussed. But the truth of the matter remained elusive. Often there was no discernible explanation to what caused the illness. Like so many things in life there was no rhyme or reason to explain why some people became mentally ill.

Much of the discussion involved genes and predisposition to an ailment. It could have been hereditary, picked up from distant cousin Tommy or something that your great-grandmother once had, an unwelcomed inherited trait that manifested itself from time to time. An overwhelming amount of data did support the theory that family ties could indeed determine whether someone would develop signs of a particular mental illness.

Or, just as likely, there was nothing in the family history that indicated such a disposition, no clue from the past that may have forewarned what was to come.

There was just no easy answer to say what caused the problem.

Many assumed child-rearing techniques were responsible for a child's behavior, and to a certain extent that was true. But child behavior and mental illness were two separate issues. One had only to examine two siblings, raised under nearly identical conditions, each developing different personalities and individual likes and interests, to realize there was more to it than environment. And while parents could certainly influence behavior, whether positively combating issues or having an adverse effect due to negative influences, in many cases even the best-intentioned were helpless in the situation.

There was often no explanation as to why one child developed a mental illness and another did not. It was one of the frustrations of dealing with these diseases. It's difficult to find a cure when you can't explain what's causing the problem.

Dr. Markham had suspected there was something different with Aaron during their first meeting. The child had seemed much too withdrawn, distanced from what was happening around him. Some of this could be attributed as a reaction from the abuse he had received. But other telltale signs, that should have been observable in an abused child, were absent.

He had seemed at ease in the unfamiliar surroundings of the doctor's office. Abused children were often nervous in strange settings. They seemed in an ever-ready state of alertness, as though fearful of something that might happen to them, but this was something Aaron Reed showed no indication of. He seemed comfortable with his mother and brother in the same room. Not overly close, but certainly not afraid.

There were many possibilities for Dr. Markham to consider, but his focus had narrowed as a result of the phone call he had received several days earlier. Larry Kendall, the CASA volunteer assigned as guardian to the children, had presented him with some interesting food for thought.

"I'm concerned about your son, Miss Reed."

"I appreciate that, Dr. Markham. But I really think the worse is over."

"Why do you say that?"

"I just feel things have returned pretty much to normal. Aaron's leg is healed. There have been no other incidents. And I don't expect to see any."

She hesitated, as though reluctant to continue.

"Anything you tell me, Miss Reed, will be held in the strictest of confidence."

"I know. It's just that....." She faced the floor for a moment, fiddling with her hands, collecting her thoughts. "It must have been Ted."

"Your boyfriend?"

She nodded slowly, as though in acceptance of the fact but reluctant to admit it. "It had to be him. I asked him to leave, right after this all happened, and things seem okay now. At first I was angry with him. For doing something like this to my son. But now when I think about it...."

She paused once again. The doctor remained silent, knowing Laura would continue when she felt ready.

"It hurts to think he could have deceived me so much. I thought he cared about me. And my children. Then to find out he would do something like this –"

"Are you certain it was Ted that abused your son?"

"It had to be. There's nobody else."

"Has Aaron's personality altered much lately?"

The change in topic startled her. "What do you mean?"

"The way he is. Quiet. Withdrawn. Has he always been like that? Or are these changes that have manifested themselves only recently?"

She considered a moment. "He seems a bit more withdrawn, I suppose. He doesn't want to talk about things. We used to get along pretty good, but anymore the only one he seems to talk to is Grandma Ruth. He even seems more distanced from his brother lately."

"And how long has this been going on?"

"I don't know. Does it matter?"

"It could. Was he like this before the accident that sent him to the hospital?"

"I suppose. He might have been. It's just sometimes you get so busy you don't notice these things right away."

"I can appreciate that, Laura."

"Anyway, if he did change, it was probably because of Ted. And what was going on. Don't you think?"

"Perhaps." Dr. Markham leaned back in his chair. The movement seemed to put an end to the line of conversation, preparing him to move on to other topics. "What do Aaron and his Grandmother talk about?"

She considered a moment. "Well, this is probably going to sound funny. But they talk about the Bible."

"There's nothing funny about that, Laura. Children are often drawn to the epic adventures found within the pages of the Bible. The struggle between good and evil. Right and wrong. These are universal stories, handed down from generation to generation, that appeal to people of all ages and backgrounds. How can children not be interested?"

"I suppose. I just think Grandma Ruth makes too much of it sometimes."

"Why do you say that?"

"Because she never used to be this way. She used to be more...."

She paused, searching in her mind for the proper word.

"Normal?" the therapist supplied.

Her guilty look betrayed the fact that she was indeed looking for the word normal. "I'm sorry, That's not a very nice thing for me to think, is it?"

"Often, when people get involved with something to the extent that everything else becomes left behind, their passion for the subject does seem abnormal to an outsider."

"I suppose that's it."

"Does Aaron believe? The way your grandmother does?"

"No." She shook her head. "I don't think so. I think he just questions things because he's trying so hard to understand."

"What is it that he's trying to understand?"

"I don't know. He's a nine-year-old, for goodness sake. There's a whole world out there he has yet to discover. And he's curious about things. You know? I don't think that's so unusual. Do you?"

"Of course not. But a lot of times it depends on how he channels that information."

"I don't understand."

"When I first met your son I felt he was withdrawn. More withdrawn than normal for his age."

"Well, that's pretty understandable, don't you think? Considering what he's been through lately."

"But what has he been through, Laura? What's really going on here?"

"The abuse, obviously. Whatever it was that Ted did to him."

"Perhaps." Dr. Markham rose from his seat, paced to the other side of the room, then turned to face Laura. "I'm concerned there may be more involved here than I originally suspected."

"You're scaring me, doctor. What are you trying to tell me? What's wrong with my son?"

"I don't know yet. But, with your permission, I intend to find out. I think the family sessions are good, but I would like to have more individual time with Aaron. So I can get to know him better."

"Of course. Whatever it takes. I just want my son to be happy again. I just want this whole nightmare to be over with so we can get on with our lives again."

She was in tears by now, her words choked with emotion.

"I just want to be able to go to sleep at night, not worrying about my kids. And wake up in the morning and know they're alright. Is that too much to ask?"

Dr Markham wanted to offer her comfort; to tell her everything was going to be fine. But he couldn't lie to her. And, until he had a better understanding of the situation, he couldn't promise her everything was going to be alright.

Chapter Thirty-Four:

*W*E HAVE *been betrayed.*

No. It's not like that.

Do not intensify your shame through denial. Your ways are known to us. You have been found unworthy of our trust. A punishment is at hand.

Please. Don't make me hurt myself again. I promise it won't happen again.

We shall not allow it to happen again. Of that you can be certain.

I don't understand.

That, then, is your fault. Your lack of understanding shall be your ultimate downfall. But it is not you alone who must suffer. Others must pay the cost for your indiscretion. Others will pay the cost for your indiscretion.

What others? What do you mean?

You shall be the catalyst. You the spark that ignites the conflagration that cleanses your soul of wrongdoing.

What are you trying to tell me?

A scourge is at hand. To cleanse the wrong you have perpetrated reparations must be had. We must be appeased.

But I didn't do anything wrong!

You revealed us to the physician. You disclosed to the man of medicine your innermost secrets, that which should never have been revealed. You lifted the veil which shields us from discernment.

I couldn't help it.

It does not matter. You have erred. The time for atonement is at hand.

What can I do? What should I do?

You must obey our instructions. You must perform the task set before you. You must not hesitate and you must not shirk. Nothing less will suffice.

And if I don't?

Then you risk your soul and salvation.

Yes. I understand. Now I understand. Tell me what I must do.

Chapter Thirty-Five:

T ED MYERS left work, got in his car, and headed nowhere.

His shift had ended at midnight, and at such an hour there wasn't much choice of where to go. A lot of the guys hit the bars after work, unwinding and relaxing with a few drinks before heading home. That idea never appealed to Ted.

There were all night restaurants, or doughnut shops, or even grocery stores, places he could stop to at least share some time with other people. But sitting alone nursing a coffee and munching on stale pastries wasn't his idea of a good time. Neither was meandering past shelves of cereal boxes or canned fruit. Browsing the grocery aisles could hardly qualify as a productive way to spend his time.

He could have just headed home, back to his apartment, back to the empty rooms that held his meager belongings, but he knew there wasn't much to go home to. A television and two mismatched chairs from his sister occupied the living room. The dresser Paige had given him now had a companion piece, a full-sized bed he had picked up at Value City.

Besides his clothes it was all he had in the world, all he had bothered to accumulate for himself over the years.

He wasn't comfortable at the apartment. It still felt like a stranger's place, a transient stop while he waited for something better to come along.

It wasn't the same.

It wasn't the same as heading home to Laura.

Some nights she would wait up for him, and they would share a few minutes together before calling it a day. She would tell him about her shift at the grocery store, and he would complain about his frustrations at the plant, neither one of them fully appreciating what the other had to go through. But at least they each had someone to share things with. Someone to talk to. Someone to confide in.

But not anymore.

So on most nights, after leaving work, he would just drive, nowhere in particular. Just somewhere to clear his head and try to forget what he was missing.

A favorite route was to travel The Trail from downtown, under the Route 75 interchange and past the zoo. Often he would lose track of time and find himself in Waterville, the sleepy little town seeming more deserted than ever in the early hours of the morning. Once he even made it as far as Defiance before turning around and heading home.

But on some nights, like this one, he would take the accustomed turn off The Trail onto Locust Street, slowing down past the row of familiar houses he had traveled by so many times in the previous six months. He pulled to the curb across from the two-story bungalow, shutting off the engine and sitting in the dark, basking in the solitude surrounding him. The night air felt warm through the open window of his car as he listened to the melody of the neighborhood crickets, chirping their endless lament to the night.

He looked up toward the second floor of the house across the street, watching the slight movement of the sheer curtains as they shifted ever-so-gently from the breeze drifting into the room. He could almost picture Laura, on the other side of the curtains, laying on the bed and sound asleep. She invariably slept on her left side, arm tucked under the pillow, as close to the edge of the bed as she could manage, as though ready to launch herself from the room at a moment's notice. Even in repose she seemed to never relax, a high-strung personality who had never learned to take things easy.

As he observed the structure a light switched on in the back of the house, on the first floor. Knowing the layout of the place, he realized it meant someone was in the kitchen. He couldn't help wondering if maybe it was Laura. Perhaps she had stepped downstairs for a bite to eat. She did that sometimes, especially on the nights she waited up for him. Many a night he would walk into the kitchen to find her munching on some crackers or, when feeling particularly decadent, working on a bowl of butter pecan ice cream.

Maybe he would join her, and they would sit at the kitchen table and talk, keeping their voices low so as not to disturb Laura's grandparents. Sometimes they would step outside, especially on a pleasant summer evening like tonight, and smoke a final cigarette together, taking in the last soothing inhalation before heading up to bed.

He hadn't realized how nice it had been, how comfortable it was being with her, until their time together was denied him.

He considered walking around to the back of the house, then knocking lightly on the rear door to get her attention. He had no idea what he could say to her. Or even if she would allow him the opportunity to say anything.

He considered the option, deliberating the pros and cons of the action, when the kitchen light turned off, plunging the house once more into darkness.

It was just a waste of time, he told himself. Laura had left him behind. The family had moved on, re-shaping their lives to one without his presence. He was no longer a part of them. There was no returning to the way things were before. There was no way he could think of to prove his innocence to Laura, and convince her to let him back into their lives.

So, like them, it was time to for him move on as well.

Paige had told him that repeatedly during his time with her, and had stressed it again when he got his apartment. He was finally seeing the wisdom of his sister's words.

Ted started the car, pulled away from the curb, and drove away into the night.

As he left the neighborhood Ted never noticed the dull red glow emanating from the building, a glow that came from the kitchen in the back of the house.

Chapter Thirty-Six:

T HE SMOKE alarm went off at 1:37 in the morning.

Laura Reed was awake instantly, the blaring clatter from the device interrupting her slumber. She sat upright in her bed, eyes snapping open, confused for a moment about what was happening. Awareness came as to the cause of the sound but, still half-asleep, full realization eluded her.

"Damn batteries!"

She took a quick glance at the alarm clock on her dresser, the digital readout appearing more dim than usual. "One-thirty in the morning?"

She plopped back onto her bed, grabbing her pillow to cover her ears, managing to deaden only a fraction of the sound.

But the alarm served its purpose. Its siren call was not to be ignored.

Laura sat upright once again, tossing the pillow to the floor.

Something was amiss. She could feel it, but couldn't immediately put into words the cause of her apprehension. Senses on the alert, she gazed toward the hallway, toward the darkened corridor that led in one direction to the bathroom and in the other to the stairway leading downstairs. Only the passageway wasn't dark. It glowed intermittently, with a soft red light that seemed to flicker on and off, as though someone was manipulating a dimmer switch.

Then she smelled it.

For a moment her mind drifted back in time. She didn't remember much about her early childhood, in the days before her world had fallen apart; a few scattered memories, vague enough now that she often wondered if they were truth or merely something she had fantasized. She recalled vacations with her parents; the camping trips in the woods and the bonfires blazing in the night; grilling s'mores over the open flame; watching, in rapt fascination, as the sparks ascended toward the heavens before winking out into nothingness. The odor of the flames came back to her now, the sweet pungent smell of burning wood on a cool summer night.

Only now a different smell insinuated itself, obliterating the formerly pleasant aroma. It was the smell of melting plastic, and smoldering glues and solvents; the smell of draperies and cabinets and furniture going up in flames; the dying smells of a house being devoured by fire.

Laura sprang from her bed.

"Oh my God!"

She made it to the door in seconds. It never occurred to her that she was wearing only a flimsy little nightgown, a light cover-up she wore on hot summer nights. She didn't bother to step into her slippers. There was no time for such considerations. Her naked feet slapped against the bare wooden floor of the hallway. The planks felt warm to the touch. One thought only was on her mind as she exited the bedroom.

Her children.

"Aaron! Evan!"

She ran to the boys' room, her heart beating a rough staccato of fear in her chest as she moved down the corridor. Her breaths came in excited gulps, as though she was struggling for air, but whether that was due to her growing fear – or something else – she never stopped to consider.

She came to a halt at the door.

For a fleeting instant thoughts flashed through her head, warnings she had read, somewhere, in the past. *In the event of a house fire don't open a closed door. Feel the panel for heat first. Be careful grabbing the doorknob in case the metal is hot. Stay low to the floor where the air is safer.*

She disregarded all the knowledge she had and flung the door open.

"Mom!"

Evan sat upright in the top bunk, his head inches from the ceiling. He looked trapped, as though unable to move. Panic gripped him, the terror increasing at sight of his frantic mother.

His voice, when he spoke again, betrayed the youngster's anxiety. "What's going on?"

"We're getting you out of here!" Laura flashed him a smile, willing herself to be strong for his sake, then reached into the bottom bunk. She rummaged through the blankets, flinging the pillows and sheets aside in her haste. "Where's Aaron? Where's your brother?"

Evan sat in silence, shaking his head, too frightened now to say anything. His eyes glowed, reflecting a red tint in the moisture welling up from his tears. Laura grabbed him, hefting him off the bed as though he was a plaything whose weight was insubstantial. Holding him close, reassured by the warmth of his body, she left the room. Evan wrapped his arms and legs around his mother, burying his face against her chest. The sobbing started as they reached the top of the stairs.

"It's okay, baby. It's okay." She kept repeating the words, more as an attempt to convince herself than as reassurance for the child. Even without looking she realized his eyes were closed, as he attempted desperately to shut out the images around them.

A light blue haze hung over the top of the staircase, a smoky accumulation that stung her eyes before she even reached it. Where at first the odor had been pleasant, almost inviting, the smell had progressed to an overpowering stench that clung to her skin and hair and clothes. It was hotter already. As she moved nearer to the glow emanating from downstairs the heat intensified. It was like opening the door to an oven and crawling inside. Sweat dripped in her eyes as she coughed violently, struggling for fresh air, her chest heaving from the effort.

She knew it was a foolish thing to do so but she had no choice; she had to move forward. Staying where they were was never an option. Shutting her eyes, pressing Evan's head close to her, she plunged down the stairs. She nearly slipped, her bare feet sliding on the worn carpeting, but with her free hand she managed to brace herself against the wall. It too felt warm, like it was heated from within.

Opening her eyes once more, trying desperately to catch her bearings, the acrid stinging of the smoke attacked her. She coughed again, jumped the last two steps to land on the living room floor, and made a rapid burst for the front door, the adrenaline coursing through her body influencing her movements.

It was humid outside, a hot and sticky summer night, but to Laura Reed the air felt cool and refreshing and invigorating. Like a swimmer gasping for oxygen she filled her lungs, enjoying the sweet sensation of the life that poured into her.

Her senses still on alert, wary of relaxing her vigil for fear of missing something important, she took a quick look around. The neighborhood was nearly light as day, illuminated from the activity at the rear of the house. Flames shot from a window on the side, from what she knew to be the kitchen. The red and orange tendrils licked greedily at the clapboard siding of the structure, as though discontented with what had been already consumed and craving new sustenance. Wisps of smoke accompanied the blaze, like the exhalation of a dying beast. She could almost hear the creature groaning as the building began to fall to pieces, burning sections of her grandparents' homestead collapsing to the ground and smoldering in the grass where they lay.

She set Evan down at last, still staring incredulously at the spectacle in front of her. A crowd was beginning to gather already, neighbors having miraculously materialized – from seemingly nowhere – even though it was the middle of the night, faceless spectators eager for the opportunity to bask in someone else's misery.

The frantic mother raised her voice in an effort to be heard above the racket. "Has anyone seen my son? Has anyone seen Aaron?"

No one answered, though it hardly mattered. She was in no mood to listen to them. No sooner were the words spoken then she was headed back into the house.

"Lady! You can't go in there!"

She never heard the stranger's warning. There was no stopping her at this point.

As she entered the house she paused, listening, hoping for an indication of where she should go or what she should do. A sizzling noise came from the kitchen, where the majority of the flames were localized. She was at least aware enough to realize that was an area to be avoided. The smoke alarm still blared, it's shrill tone overpowering everything else, though there was competition now from another sound. At last she recognized the tone insinuating itself onto the scene, the sirens growing louder as the emergency vehicles approached.

It reassured her to realize help was on the way. But there seemed no time to spare. She couldn't afford to stand idly by and wait.

Laura looked to her left, toward an open doorway; toward her grandparents' room. Three quick steps gained her access to the apartment. An accumulation of smoke swirled just above her head, blackening the ceiling. Grandpa Mike lay on his back in bed. His eyes were opened wide, staring yet seeing nothing. He made no motion; she couldn't even determine whether he was breathing.

Grandma Ruth stood beside him, her hands gripping one of his arms as she coughed repeatedly. She tugged with all her strength, urging the still figure to move, but it made no difference. There was no reaction from him.

She refused to give up on the task. Desperate to pull her husband from harm's way, she struggled ever harder.

"Get up, Michael! Get up!" Her voice was a shrill scream of a sound, a tone such as Laura had never heard before from her prim and proper grandmother.

The old woman continued to pull on her husband's arm. Occasionally she would cough yet again, from the smoke accumulating around her, or wipe at her eyes to see more clearly. Then she would resume, with renewed energy, determined not to give up.

"Grandma!" Laura was beside her now, forced to yell so her voice could be heard above the ever increasing din surrounding the two women. "You got to get out of here. Right now!"

The old woman didn't bother to face her granddaughter. "I'm not leaving," she insisted, her attention focused on Grandpa Mike. "Not without Michael."

Laura approached the bed, grabbing hold of her grandfather as well, adding her strength to the effort. The two women pulled, managing to move the form several inches toward the edge of the mattress.

Laura released her hold.

"It's no good, Grandma. He's too heavy."

"I'm not leaving him."

"You have to. It's your only chance."

Grandma Ruth reached for Laura's face, brushing her fingers lightly against the younger woman's cheek. The wrinkled skin of her fingers felt rough – nearly abrasive – against Laura's skin, a reminder of the ravages of age. But the years hadn't diminished her spirit, or dampened her enthusiasm when faced with a task she was determined to follow through with. And this was one duty she wouldn't shirk on.

A single tear slipped gently from the old woman's eye.

She then returned to her struggles with her husband.

Laura didn't know what to do. Panic gripped her. She

realized she had to do something but had no idea what. She couldn't desert her grandparents. But she couldn't help them either. And she still had no idea what had become of Aaron. What could she do? What *should* she do?

Turning her back on the two people in the room she entered the living area of the house once again. The familiar surroundings – the rooms she had grown up in as a child, the place she and her sons had called home for the last three years – confused her. The house had an otherworldly quality to it, the fire from the back of the house lending a hellish glow to the setting. Bizarre shadows danced on the walls, flickering images brought to life by the growing conflagration threatening to consume everything around her. It was disorienting, a dizzying sensation that made her feel sick to the stomach.

And the heat! It was steadily increasing at an alarming rate. She felt as though she was being smothered under the unrelenting glow of a heat lamp. Her skin felt red, the sensation akin to a sunburn.

She tried to ignore the discomfort, focusing instead on what mattered most.

"Aaron! Where are you?!"

She felt a tightening in her stomach that brought queasiness to her entire body. She was sweating profusely, but the droplets seemed to dry instantly the moment they rolled across her skin, absorbed by the steadily rising temperature of the harsh environment within the structure.

She ran to the closet at the front of the house, flinging the door open in desperation, hoping to find her child huddled within the tiny space.

Disappointment greeted her. The barren little compartment mocked her with its emptiness.

She knew time was running out. She felt weakened, exhausted, ready to collapse from the strain, but found the energy to continue her search.

Laura moved once again to the ground floor bedroom.

Grandma Ruth lay slumped on the bed, her still form laying on top of her husband as though her frail body could offer him some sort of protection. She grabbed her grandmother's inert form, shook the woman in an attempt to restore her, but failed in the trying.

Muffled voices reached in to them, the words inexplicably garbled and difficult to comprehend. Laura turned to see two uniformed firefighters approaching. One seemed to be speaking to her, but the words were unclear – whether it was because of the oxygen mask covering his face, or the ever-increasing noise from the fire raging at the back of the house, or just the general listlessness she was experiencing and the weakness that gripped her, she couldn't say.

The second firefighter reached up with a gloved hand to push a button at his collar. For a moment static replied before he spoke into his radio.

"Dispatch. This is Search Team 1. Three victims found. One appears unconscious, a second barely standing. Send in another crew immediately."

As the second figure moved toward Grandma Ruth the first approached Laura. A moment later she felt his hand grip her arm. His protective gear glistened from the wildly erratic lighting given off by the flames that were, inexorably, drawing nearer, imparting a glow that shined with the promise of deliverance. The man's form towered over her as the figure of salvation led her gently, yet firmly, toward the front door.

She moved along with him as though in a daze, hardly aware of what was going on. She passed two other figures on the way out, the second team of emergency personnel heading into her grandparents' room with a steady, yet urgent, motion.

The next thing she knew she was sitting on the sidewalk, holding Evan, and bawling her eyes out.

Captain Timothy Clawson was the first emergency responder to arrive on the scene. While Laura Reed struggled with the recalcitrant figure that was her grandmother, urging her to flee the premises, the Fire Department Captain jumped from his car and headed toward the side of the house. It was important that he make a complete circuit of the burning building to assess the situation, anticipate any difficulties that could be encountered, and take a look for stranglers – or injured persons – around the structure.

Clawson had seen many things in his fifteen years serving with The Toledo Fire Department – from acts of heroism that he would never forget to tragic encounters that haunted him years after the original occurrence. But as he made his way to the back of the burning house he witnessed a sight such as he had never seen before.

The young child sat cross-legged on the grass in the center of the back yard. The fire's glow painted his features in harsh reds and yellows, casting a giant shadow behind him that served to make the child look even more tiny and insignificant than he would have otherwise. The young boy's eyes were drawn to the flames. A look of wonder, of enraptured fascination, danced in his eyes, which never blinked as he continued his silent vigil. He was mesmerized, captured by the spectacle of it, unaware of anything around him.

In his right hand he held a knife; a steak knife, from the looks of it. Never taking his eyes off the fire, seemingly oblivious to his actions, the child drew the serrated blade across his forearm. A trickle of blood seeped from the freshly carved wound, which roughly paralleled the half-dozen or so bleeding marks already on his arm.

He exhibited no reaction following the event. He neither flinched nor cried out. Not so much as a whimper escaped from his lips. Aaron Reed's attention was too firmly attached to the spectacle before him.

Chapter Thirty-Seven:

THE EMERGENCY Room of Toledo Hospital was a flurry of activity, a situation that started at the beginning of the night and continued throughout the shift. The evening commenced with a three-car pile up, the consequence of too much alcohol and not enough common sense, that resulted in four new overnight guests at the hospital.

Things had barely settled down when an attempted suicide arrived on the scene. The patient was a young girl in her teens who had gotten hold of her mother's sleeping pills. Had they been much later getting her to the hospital it would have been too late. It was touch and go for a while, but by the middle of the night she had pulled through the worst of it and was sleeping off the aftereffects of having her stomach pumped.

Dr. Lois Tyrone was hoping things had settled down for the evening when she found a few minutes to sneak away with a cup of coffee and a cold bagel. It was her first break of the evening. It felt good to put her feet up and relax for a moment.

She had barely sat down when one of the staff sought her out.

"Two squads are on the way," the nurse reported. "A house fire on Locust Street. I understand we have at least one victim overcome from smoke inhalation. Vital signs are low. Unresponsive."

"Prepare Trauma Room 2."

211

With that simple exclamation the doctor knew everything would be prepared for the arrivals when they reached the hospital. The necessary staff would be in place; the Trauma Cart would be ready to go. Oxygen would be available, as well as the endotracheal tubes necessary for intubation should it be necessary to clear any blocked air passages. Considering the nature of home fires there would no doubt be burns to administer to as well, so plenty of gauze and silver sulfadiazine would be on hand to treat any open wounds.

Hospital personnel would be equipped to check oxygen levels, in order to assess the possibility of carbon monoxide inhalation, and to administer chest radiographs, X-rays, or other tests to determine the patient's condition. It was a familiar routine, one they had gone through countless times in the past, with lives hanging in the balance, but Dr. Tyrone had no doubt the staff at the hospital would rise to the occasion as they always did.

The doctor watched the nurse walk away, sighed, and took a sip of her coffee. The drink was cold already.

The man on the gurney looked to be in his early seventies; the woman hovering beside him, clinging to his arm, only slightly younger. They both reeked of smoke – from the bedclothes they still wore, from their hair, even from the pores of their skin. Black smudges colored them both, particularly beneath their noses and around their mouths, indicative of the smoke that had been inhaled during their ordeal.

But beneath the remnants of what the fire had deposited on them the man's color was pale. The doctor wondered if this was his natural complexion or an indication of what he'd recently been through. He didn't look the type that exercised much. He was overweight, in particular his legs, which were disproportionately larger than they should have been, as though he spent much of his time off his feet. A mask held over his lower face connected to a tank of oxygen, offering him its rejuvenating breath of life.

"His name's Michael Franklin," one of the attendants announced as Dr. Tyrone drew closer. "There doesn't appear to be any burns on him, but he was overcome from smoke inhalation. He was unconscious when the firemen arrived on the scene."

The paramedic motioned with his head toward the woman beside the gurney. "His wife, Ruth Franklin. She was barely conscious when we got there."

The physician cast a disapproving look at Grandma Ruthie. "You shouldn't be walking around, Mrs. Franklin. We need to be certain you're okay."

"I'm fine." She spoke the words as though there was no denying the fact. "It's Michael I'm worried about."

"We'll do everything we can for your husband. I assure you. What can you tell us about his health? Any concerns we need to be aware of?"

"He had an accident fifteen years ago. Compression fracture of the lower spine. Been operated on three times since then. Gives him some relief, after the surgeries, but never totally cures things."

"Is he on pain medication?"

She actually smiled, as though she was considering something humorous. "He should be, but he's not. Nothing stronger than Tylenol. He's too stubborn to take anything else."

"High blood pressure?"

She shook her head. "No. But he's Type 2 diabetic. I give him his insulin shot every night."

"We'll need to check glucose levels immediately." The doctor motioned toward one of the nurses standing by. "Melanie. Get Mrs. Franklin to an exam room."

"I'm okay. Really."

"We need to check you over, Mrs. Franklin. It's for your own good."

"But Michael needs me."

"There's nothing you can do for your husband right now. And I'm certain he'll feel better knowing you're being taken care of."

She wanted to say more but there wasn't time for argument. They led Grandma Ruth away against her protests, her head turned toward her husband in obvious reluctance to lose sight of him.

The doctor addressed one of the paramedics. "I thought there were two squads on the way. Was there someone else in the fire?"

"Three others."

He pointed to a trio standing by the door. They were just stepping from an ambulance, escorted now by hospital staff into the emergency room. They looked dazed and confused, as though uncertain what was expected of them. It appeared to be a mother with her two sons. The family stood together, appearing none the worse for wear except for a wrapping of gauze around the arm of one of the boys.

Dr. Tyrone paused a moment. The family looked familiar, as if she had seen them before, but she couldn't place where. She saw so many people during the course of a typical day that often the faces tended to blend together.

"What's the prognosis?"

"The mother and one son seem fine. Shook up over what happened, of course, but otherwise okay. The other boy…."

He paused, as though uncertain what to say next.

The physician stopped, halting the forward progress of the paramedic. She watched the gurney carrying Mike Franklin as it continued down the hallway accompanied by several nurses. She realized she only had a moment and then she would have to follow them into the exam area.

"What's the problem? What happened to the boy?"

The paramedic lowered his voice. "They found him in the backyard. Watching the fire."

"Probably in shock," Dr. Tyrone surmised.

She was answered by a shaking head. "The boy was mutilating himself. Dragging a knife across his left arm. Totally unaware of what he was doing."

Something clicked in the doctor's head. A recollection of an event from a couple months ago. And a recent conversation. "What's the boy's name?"

"Aaron Reed."

Dr. Tyrone leaned over the desk, motioning to one of the staff to step forward.

"Contact Dr. Richard Markham. You should be able to reach him through his answering service."

"What should I tell him?"

"Tell him he needs to get down here right away." She took a final look at Laura and her twins. "Tell him one of his patients needs him."

Chapter Thirty-Eight:

THE FLAMES were gone now but the heat remained, as though the fire, once extinguished, was reluctant to release its grip on the house. It oozed from the shattered windows and destroyed doors of the wreckage, assaulting anyone who drew near.

The two men from the Fire Department gazed in from the back porch at the charred and mangled remains of what used to be a kitchen. Strips of wallpaper, miraculously still intact, had peeled away from one wall. The sink rested in the center of the room, thrown there with the collapse of the counter that had originally supported it. A thick slurry of water and ash covered the floor and ran out the door, a miniature river of the gunk spilling outside and onto the back lawn.

One of the men held a metal can in his gloved hands. The can had burst open during the fire, leaving a jagged tear in the side, and much of the writing on the container had been obliterated due to the flames. But enough remained that there was no doubt as to what it was.

"Lighter fluid."

"I'd say so."

"Looks like the wall was soaked with it, along with whatever was in the corner there."

"Magazines, probably. Old newspapers maybe?"

The two were silent for several minutes, taking in the spectacle before them, examining the havoc wrought by the recent conflagration. They had fought fires for years now, these two, and had seen enough of it to realize its devastating potential. Not only the destruction it wrought, but the way it changed people's lives, shattering their complacency, awakening them to the awful potential of how something tragic can alter everything you believed in.

The man holding the discarded can faced his partner.

"This was no accident."

Chapter Thirty-Nine:

"HELLO, LARRY. This is Connie Peters. From Children's Services. Listen, there's been a development concerning Aaron Reed I thought you should know about but, well, it's kind of hard to explain over the phone. Give me a call when you get this."

Larry nearly deleted the message on his cellphone, but then decided to listen to it once again. He took note of the time it came through, which indicated the caseworker had called about twenty minutes earlier. The second hearing offered no more information, no clue as to what was going on, other than the fact that Connie sounded concerned about something.

He considered giving her a ring immediately, to satisfy his curiosity more than anything else, then decided to wait.

He still felt sweaty from his early morning workout. The ten miles on his bicycle was especially grueling in the summer time. That's why he tried to get out early, before it got too hot. He'd feel better after a shower, certain that whatever Connie needed to tell him could wait that long.

He had just finished dressing, was toweling his hair dry, when a rap came on the bathroom door.

"Just a minute," he called through the panel.

"Lawrence? Your father has something to tell you."

"Dad?"

He stepped into the hallway, throwing the towel over his

bare shoulders. Droplets of water glistened on his skin from the shower. The moisture felt cool as he stepped out of the warmth of the bathroom, a pleasing sensation after his workout.

His mother was walking away from him. He followed her to the kitchen, leaving a series of damp footprints in his wake.

His father sat at the table in his police uniform, a grim look etched on his face.

"I thought you had to work today, Dad?"

"I do. But I heard something at the station I needed to talk to you about." He paused, as though reluctant to continue with what he had to say. "What's the name of that family you're dealing with? In your CASA case?"

"You know I can't tell you that, Dad. I'm expected to keep things confidential concerning my cases. You understand."

"Of course." Jeremy Kendall nodded, taking in the information, contemplating how best to continue. "Still..."

His wife moved closer, sitting down in the chair across form him. "What going on, Dear?"

"It's just something I heard this morning at the station. I was thinking it may have been involved with this case of Larry's."

"Why would you think that?" his son asked.

"Something about the situation just sounded..." He paused, searching for the appropriate word. "Familiar, I suppose."

Larry and his mother remained silent, awaiting further explanation.

"There was a house fire last night," the police officer continued. "Early this morning, actually. The story was all over the station by the time I got there."

"Is everyone okay?" Linda asked, catching her breath as she waited for an answer.

He seemed not to have heard her, his attention concentrated on his son. "An elderly coupled lived at the house. They were taken to Toledo Hospital for smoke inhalation. From the sounds of it the old man isn't doing too well."

Larry kept his voice calm. There were a lot of old couples in a city the size of Toledo. Surely this wasn't more than a coincidence. "Where was the fire, Dad?"

"On Locust Street. Off Broadway."

Larry slowly sat down, digesting this latest morsel of information, considering the possibilities. "What was the name?" His voice portrayed no inflection, as though he was afraid to reveal too much with his queries. "Of the people involved?"

"The couple's name was Franklin. Michael and Ruth Franklin."

Jeremy Kendall had conducted enough police interrogations in his life, questioned enough suspects, that he had developed a sort of sixth sense when it came to spotting the truth. He knew his son was troubled. The information obviously meant something important to him.

Jeremy stood and advanced toward his son. "There were three other people living at the house. I'm guessing you know who they were. A mother and two sons."

Linda gasped. "Are they alright?"

"They're fine."

"That's a relief."

"But...." Jeremy hesitated.

Linda reached toward her husband, touching his hand where it rested on the table. "What is it?"

"They're still investigating things, you understand. All the details aren't clear yet. But the fire department has reason to believe this wasn't an accident. That the fire may have been ignited on purpose."

"Who would do such a thing?" his wife asked.

Jeremy didn't look at Linda; he was focused instead on his son. Larry said nothing, waiting for his father's next words.

"They think it was one of the boys."

Larry's expression betrayed his surprise at the words. "What do you mean?"

"They found one of the boys. Sitting in the backyard. Just watching the fire."

"That doesn't mean anything, does it? Maybe he was just in shock? Maybe he just didn't understand what was happening?"

"He was holding a knife," his father continued, the words slow and precise. "He was.... ....cutting himself with it. They say it was like he was in another world. He made no response when the emergency personnel showed up. Like he didn't even know what was happening. Or what he was doing to himself."

Larry immediately called Connie Peters to ascertain what was going on. Her voice was frantic, as though she was still attempting to compile information and didn't have all the facts in front of her. She confirmed what Jeremy Kendall had heard at the police station, concluding the story by reporting that the entire family was currently at Toledo Hospital.

"And everyone's okay?" Larry asked.

"As far as I know. Sounds like it was roughest on the grandfather. With all his health problems they're looking him over pretty carefully, as you can well imagine."

"What about the other thing? I heard Aaron was...." He stumbled over the words, uncertain how to continue.

She responded quickly. "I'm not sure. I'm getting ready to head down to the hospital now. But, from the sounds of things, you may have been right."

"About what?"

"About Aaron. There was more going on with him than we realized. The last I heard his injuries had been treated and they're talking about transferring him to the Psych Ward, but nothing definite on that yet. I understand they got hold of Dr. Markham and he's down there already. Listen, I'm heading out the door right now. Can I call you later?"

"Sure. That's fine."

The line went dead.

Larry, still holding his cellphone, plopped onto his bed.

In his entire life he had never felt so bad before about being right.

Chapter Forty:

L AURA REED paced the corridors of the hospital.

Her mind raced, trying to process everything that had happened since the early morning wake up call from the smoke alarm. Her world had changed, drastically, in the space of a few minutes. Watching the flames attack her grandparents' house had been like watching her world fall apart.

She knew things would never be the same again.

Maneuvering through the hallways at Toledo Hospital – first a left, then a right, then catching an elevator to another floor – she felt like some sort of human rat in a bizarre laboratory experiment, as though her senses were being analyzed and her recall being tested. If that was the case, if some higher power was indeed watching her, assessing her behavior, then they should have been pleased with her progress. She was learning already, she concluded. It was becoming second nature to find the rooms she needed.

The last corridor she traversed was cheery, with colorful animals painted on the walls. A tiny chair and table sat beneath a picture of several frogs, with the words "Frog Town" emblazoned at the top of the painting in a bold colorful script. A vase of flowers decorated the nursing station, unobtrusive yet hinting at the beauty of the world outside. A glass-fronted room she passed, obviously a visiting area for family members, was light and airy. A half dozen people occupied the chamber, sitting together in animated conversation. No voices reached out to her, the sound cut off due to the glass between them. But Laura was certain from the expressions on their faces that a lighthearted reunion was taking place in the room.

The entire children's ward of the hospital was designed to elevate the spirit and brighten the mood.

It had no such effect on Laura.

She slowed as she approached room 507, taking a deep breath to prepare herself for what she had to face. Forcing herself to be strong, she entered the room.

Her brother Paul looked up as the door closed behind her. He acknowledged her entrance with a nod before setting the book he had been reading down on his lap. Across the room Evan sat on a chair, concentrating on the checkerboard in front of him. He waved at his mother, smiling briefly as he performed the action, and returned his attention to the game.

On the other side of the checkerboard Aaron sat propped up in a hospital bed. He looked tiny laying there, like the bed was out-of-proportion to his young body. His left arm was bandaged with a fresh layer of gauze. It lay limp at his side. He stared, not at his brother and the game the two were playing, but straight ahead, his eyes fixated on nothing.

Laura leaned over, kissed Aaron lightly on the forehead, but elicited no apparent response from the action.

There was an empty chair beside Paul and she sat down, grateful for the opportunity to get off her feet. Laura found it a struggle to keep her voice sounding anything but dismal – there were too many unpleasant thoughts and disturbing memories floating through her head – but she forged ahead anyway, doing her best to set the children at ease.

"So how are my boys doing?"

"We're okay," Evan replied, in an off-handed way that implied he hadn't really stopped to consider the question.

Laura turned to face Paul.

Her brother shrugged, presenting a helpless look. "He's doing okay," he answered, his eyes glancing at Aaron then back again to his sister. He kept his voice low, barely above a whisper. "He responds to things around him. He seems to understand the game he's playing. But I'm not certain if he's aware of his surroundings."

Laura nodded, worrying her lower lip.

"There was a doctor hear to see you a few minutes ago," Paul informed her.

"Who?"

Evan looked up from the checkerboard. "It was Dr. Markham."

"Did he say anything? Is he coming back? Where can I find him?"

Paul shifted position, placing his hand on his sister's hand. She was trembling with nervous energy. He gripped her fingers, securely but not too tightly, in a reassuring embrace. "We told him you'd be right back. He said he'd stop again in a few minutes."

"Good. Good."

"How's Grandma and Grandpa?" Evan asked.

She had to pause to collect her thoughts, sorting through the images swirling through her head. "I haven't seen Grandpa yet," she informed them. "He's not doing too good. They say his lungs are pretty congested, from all the smoke he breathed in. It's going to take him a while to recover."

She noticed the concerned look on Evan's face and continued, amending her previous words. "But he's going to be okay, baby. They assured me he'll pull through it. So there's nothing to worry about. It's just gonna take a while, that's all."

"And Grandma Ruth?"

"She's doing much better. I talked to her for a few minutes. You know Grandma. She's ornery as ever and anxious to see you guys. She wants to be sure you're alright. She's ready to march out of her room and head over here but they won't let her get out of bed yet."

Paul smiled at the mental image. "Sounds like Grandma."

Evan rose from his seat. "Then let's go see her. Can we do that?"

"Not yet, Evan. Mommy wants to talk to the doctor first. Okay?"

"Yes, Mom."

He sat once again and returned his attention to the checkerboard.

Laura leaned back in her chair, a long sigh escaping from her lips.

"You okay, Sis?"

She faced Paul and nodded. "Just tired. And confused, with everything that's been going on." She closed her eyes. "But mostly tired."

Laura stepped out into the hallway to confer with Dr. Markham, fearful of what he might reveal to her. She knew now, beyond a shadow of a doubt, that there was something wrong with Aaron. The doctor had discussed the possibilities with her at the office the last time they met, presenting vague references to possible mental illness and childhood symptoms and a slew of things to consider, most of which hadn't made much sense to her. They were concepts she never felt she would have to deal with. She had anticipated problems ahead, and assumed she'd be up to the task of handling whatever situation came her way. But now she could only wonder if she was strong enough.

The fire at the house had changed her entire way of looking at life.

She found herself rambling, the words forcing themselves out in her effort to make sense of things. "They tell me they found evidence that the fire at my grandparents' house was purposely started. They said they found a bottle of lighter fluid, along with what looked like a pile of items stacked in the corner, where the fire started. They tell me...."

She stopped, swallowing hard, forging ahead with the next words. "They tell me they think Aaron started the fire."

Voice calm and clear, spoken slowly as though each word was chosen with care, Dr. Markham answered. "Considering Aaron's present state of mind, it is certainly within the realm of possibilities, Laura."

"But why? Why would he do that?"

"We talked the other day about mental illness. That there were things I needed to consider; symptoms I should be aware of. This is never an easy thing to tell a parent, but I fear Aaron is in the early stages of Childhood-Onset Schizophrenia."

"I don't understand. I thought that was a split personality thing? And something that only happens with adults?"

"It's true that Schizophrenia generally doesn't show up until the early twenties. But with some children symptoms develop at a much younger age."

"But split personalities? That doesn't sound like Aaron."

"Not all Schizophrenics develop dual personalities. But what most have in common, and it's something Aaron seems to be exhibiting to a tremendous degree, is problems separating reality from delusions. They live in a sort of fantasy world. They can't always distinguish what is real and what isn't. As such they have a difficult time determining what behavior is appropriate in a given situation."

"Appropriate? What do you mean?"

"Last night at your house Aaron was found with a knife in his hand. Cutting himself."

"No." She shook her head vehemently, as though her behavior could make the accusation go away. "I'm sure that wasn't happening. I'm sure it must have been something else. It couldn't have been that."

"I'm sorry, Laura. But I believe it is true. It's hard to deny the facts when the proof is displayed on his arm."

He paused a moment, giving her time to consider the words, then continued. "I also believe it wasn't the first time such an incident occurred."

Laura nearly replied, once again denying what she was hearing, when realization dawned on her. She felt herself grow weak, dizzy with the thoughts swirling through her head. There was a chair in the hallway, close to where she was standing, and with trembling fingers she reached for it, steadied herself a moment, then sat down.

She stared at the floor for several seconds before looking once again at Dr. Markham. All signs of resistance had left her. She looked like a conquered fighter, having lost the will to continue and given up the fight.

"That's correct, Laura. The suspicious marks on Aaron that came to light weeks ago were more than likely self-inflicted."

"He did that to himself?"

Dr. Markham nodded.

"But why?"

"It's all part of the illness, Laura. The delusions experienced by a person suffering from Schizophrenia are very real to them. These delusions can take control of their senses, prompting them into actions that seem completely unorthodox to us but, to the sufferer, make perfect sense."

There was another chair near by. The therapist maneuvered it closer to the distraught mother and sat down beside her. For a moment they were both at a loss for words.

"What happens now?" Laura inquired. "Will he get better?"

"I can't lie to you, Laura. Many Schizophrenics suffer their entire life with the disease."

She buried her face in her hands, shaking her head back and forth in denial.

"That doesn't mean we can't do anything for him," the doctor continued. "Now that we are aware of the issue we know how to approach Aaron's treatment. There is medication we can use that will alter his mood, to restore a more normal thinking process, one where the delusions and hallucinations won't be as extreme for him."

"Will it change him? Affect his personality?" Tears were beginning to form in her eyes. "Will I lose my son?"

He answered slowly, choosing his words with care. "It may affect his personality. Some. But the hope is it will only be in positive ways.

"But medication isn't the only answer," he was quick to add. "There are other approaches we can take. We will continue his therapy, with a more aggressive routine tailored to his individual needs. With time he will grow to understand more clearly what is reality and what isn't, allowing him to isolate the delusions so his mind can deal with them in a more healthy manner."

Laura made no response as she attempted to process the barrage of information. There were so many questions. So many things she didn't fully understand.

A sudden thought struck her.

"What about Evan? Is this going to happen to him too?"

"Time will tell. With twins there is a strong genetic disposition when it comes to mental illness."

"I should have known." She stood and started pacing up and down the hallway. "Evan is such a daydreamer. He seems to live in a fantasy world already. Is that part of this? Is that a sign he's going to turn out like his brother?"

"No. I don't believe so. From talking with Evan I feel he's experiencing the normal thoughts of a boy his age. Much of the recent research points to barely a 35% chance, even with twins, of both siblings developing the illness. That means there's nearly a two-to-one chance that he *won't* become Schizophrenic. Those are good odds, Laura.

"Especially since we can be on the lookout and monitor Evan carefully. But we can't be hiding things from him. We need to be honest about it, and explain to him what to be aware of. Not only will this help him with his personal fears and apprehensions, but it will also help him to cope with understanding what his brother is going through."

"So when can Aaron come home? When can we start getting our life back together again?"

He hesitated before answering. "Not for a while. I

would like to see him in a long-term care facility first. So we can watch his behavior and assess him better."

"Is that necessary?"

"I'm afraid so. You saw what he's capable of when dealing with his delusions. You were all lucky to get out of the house alive. Especially your grandfather, considering his poor physical health. We can't take a chance on Aaron hurting himself again. Or others. It's the best thing for him right now.

"Also, we may not have a choice in the matter. There are bound to be repercussions because of him starting the fire at the house."

"Repercussions?" Images flashed through her head, pictures of Aaron in prison gray behind a barred door. "Will they send him to jail?"

"I don't believe so. Nothing as extreme as that. At his age he won't even be sent to juvenile detention. But I'm certain conditions will be put into place, to monitor him and make certain nothing like this happens again. A long-term care facility, where he can be under constant supervision, should be adequate to satisfy any demands put upon him as a consequence of his actions."

She knew what he was saying made sense. It was the logical thing to do. But that didn't deaden the pain. Or remove the guilt she felt, as though she had failed her son and was now abandoning him.

"So what do I do in the meantime?"

"Just be patient. And show both your boys all the love you can. They need their mother, now more than ever. For their sake you have to be strong."

Laura could only hope she would be up to the task.

Chapter Forty-One:

T HE JOINT was a bit of a dive.

Ted Myers couldn't help thinking that as he walked into *Papa Joe's*. The guys at work claimed it was a great place to relax on their time off, but he failed to see the charm of the setting. The lights were down low, giving it a dingy atmosphere, though it probably helped to alleviate the run-down appearance of the place. The bar stretched across one end of the room, a row of stools standing as sentinels before the counter. The surface was scratched and pitted with blackened marks, souvenirs from careless cigarette smokers. The tables and chairs arranged haphazardly in the room were a mismatched conglomeration, as though they'd been obtained over the years from various garage sales.

Ted heard the sound of laughter from the back and followed the noise. Two pool tables filled the small room he entered. Terry and Alan were laughing at something when he entered. Each held a bottle of beer. They seemed in good spirits, relaxed and at ease.

Terry noticed him first. "Hey, Ted. Glad you could join us. Grab yourself a beer and a cue stick."

He wandered over. "Maybe I'll just watch for a while."

"Suit yourself."

Alan took a shot as Ted found a chair and sat down. He wondered again what he was doing there, and realized once more that he'd rather be somewhere else. He missed Laura and the boys. He had felt like part of something with them. Now he just felt so unsure of his life. He went to work and went home afterward, maybe watching television or attempting to read a book; things he had never had time to do before. But it wasn't satisfying. Time dragged. It hadn't been as bad when he was living at his sister's place. At least other people were around. But that had been too awkward, especially with the way Chris treated him – the accusatory looks, the occasional snide comment, the feeling of mistrust that never went away.

He thought things would be better once he was out of there. But now that he had his own apartment it felt even worse than being at Paige's place. The television helped to fill up the emptiness; at least there were other voices to listen to. Still, it wasn't the same as having people around.

Ted had been on his own for years, before meeting Laura, but it had never been like this. He had never had a full time relationship before, so he had been oblivious to what he was missing. His time with Laura had changed all that. He had developed a closeness with the family, a sense of belonging that had grown in the short time they had been together. He even missed the grandparents. Ruth was a bit much to handle at times, the way she spouted Bible verses on every occasion. But Mike was alright, though he often remained in bed for days at a time due to his health problems.

It was a family. And he had been part of it. For a short while, anyway. And now that it was denied him he realized how much it had meant to him.

Ted had been angry with Laura in the beginning. Not only had she not believed him, but she had overreacted in her handling of the situation. He was certain there could have been a better way to work things out.

But now, looking back at things, he understood her position. She felt her children were being misused so she took the difficult steps necessary to rectify the issue. He had to at least give her credit for having their best interest at heart.

He wondered again what was really going on with Aaron. He had never touched the boy, either of them, in any way that would be harmful or threatening to them. The fact that something had happened to Aaron was undeniable, but it was none of his doing.

He supposed he would never know the truth of the matter.

As he mused Terry wandered over to where Ted sat, stopping in front of him with a stupid grin on his face.

"What's up with you?" Ted asked.

"Just thinking about something funny I heard from a friend of mine. From the sounds of it you really dodged the bullet with that old girlfriend of yours."

"What do you mean?"

"My buddy Seth.... Have you met him?"

"Don't think so."

"Well, anyway, he works for the fire department. Went on a call early this morning and he called me at lunch to tell me about it. It was the damnedest thing. Fire started in the kitchen in the middle of the night."

"Is everyone okay?"

"Oh, yeah, they all got out okay. An old couple. And a mother with two kids."

"So what's all this got to do with me?"

"Keep your pants on. I'm getting to that. The mother's name was Laura. And the two kids were twins. Twin boys."

Ted had hardly been paying attention to the story. But with the last sentence he was on his feet, his anxiety obvious. "You don't think...?"

"I sure do. Everything fits. I remember taking you home from work a couple times, and sure enough it sounds like the same place. Pretty wild, huh? And you ain't heard the craziest thing about it."

Ted faced his friend, momentarily at a lost for words. By this point Alan had wandered over, a look of concern on his face, as the story continued.

"They say one of the twins started the fire." Terry was

laughing by now, as if this was the funniest story he had ever heard, unaware of the obviously distraught look Ted presented him. "They say the damn kid was sitting in the backyard, watching the fire, carving his arm with a kitchen knife. Can you imagine that? Kid must be a real fruitcake, don't you think?"

He was laughing again, barely containing his mirth, which continued for perhaps another fifteen seconds before he became aware that he was the only one in the room who found the story comical.

"What's wrong with you guys?" Terry asked at last. "Can't you guys just imagine how ridiculous that must have looked?"

Ted nearly hit him then. He took a step backwards, planting his foot firmly behind him, prepared to weigh in with whatever kind of punch he could deliver. Then he stopped, realizing it wasn't worth the effort. Terry was an asshole and that was all there was to it.

Saying nothing Ted headed for the door, knocking Terry aside on the way out.

Voices carried to him as he headed for the front door.

"What was that all about?" Terry asked, his tone incredulous.

Alan's answer was stern, brooking no argument. "Knock it off, Terry."

Then Ted was out the door.

Chapter Forty-Two:

SHE LOOKED like an old lady.

Standing in the doorway, watching Grandma Ruth as she sat in the hospital bed, it occurred to Laura for the first time how old her grandmother actually was. Her frailty came as a shock. Ruth Franklin had always seemed a formidable presence. Seemingly invincible, the woman was the tower of strength that held the family together.

Even when Laura was little, and she and Paul would spend the day with their grandparents before everything fell apart with her mother and father, her grandmother seemed a force to be reckoned with.

Her strength and fortitude had only increased in the years since Grandpa Mike's accident. Grandma Ruth was steadfast in her beliefs, never wavering and never yielding, sure of herself at all times and not afraid to voice her opinion on any topic. She had no doubts concerning her place in the world; she was aware of her limitations and just as certain of her strengths.

Laura had long been convinced that the woman was invincible. She never seemed to be ill; never took time off from the thousand-and-one chores she found to do around the house. She hovered over the family – Grandpa Mike, Laura, the twins – nurturing each of them and administering to their needs.

But now, recovering in the hospital, she seemed nothing more than an old lady. An old, worn-out, lady. Time had caught up to her, accelerated no doubt by recent events.

The fire at the house had obviously taken its toll on her.

Grandma Ruth glanced up. A smile lit her face at sight of Laura and Evan in the doorway, looking at her.

"Don't just stand there gawking," she prompted. "Come on in."

Evan hesitated.

His fantasies had never prepared him for this type of reality. On unsteady legs, motivated by a slight push from his mother, he entered the room.

"How are you doing, Grandma?" Laura asked.

"Just fine, dear."

The young boy moved closer, standing at the old woman's side at the head of the bed. She reached for his hand and he offered it to her, saying nothing.

"Don't look so sad, young man. Everything will be alright. *Cast your burden on The Lord, and he will sustain you.*"

Evan remained quiet, while Laura found no words to reply. She lacked her Grandmother's strength and was uncertain how to cope with recent events.

"When are you coming home, Grandma?" Evan asked at last.

Ruth hesitated. For a brief instant it was as though doubt had grabbed hold of her, steering her toward indecision. But the moment passed. "I don't think I will be coming home, Evan. I think it's time for me to find a different home."

Laura moved closer. "What are you talking about?"

"You know that old house was getting to be too much for your grandpa and me anymore. And now...."

She paused, for a moment lost in reflection.

"I don't think Michael and I are up to rebuilding the place. The hassle of hiring contractors. And living with the mess of renovations. We're too old for all that nonsense."

"That's not true," Laura suggested. "It could be exciting. Picking out new carpeting. Buying new curtains. And I could help you with it."

"Me too," Evan suggested, anxious to be a part of things.

"No." Grandma Ruth shook her head slowly back and forth, as though resigned to a concept she had a hard time admitting to. "Your grandfather and I have been talking this over for a while now. Before all this happened. We're thinking of finding a nice retirement home someplace, where we don't have to worry about taking care of a yard or maintaining a roof over our heads. It's time for us to just sit back and relax and enjoy the years we have left to us."

Laura wasn't certain how to respond. Her world was falling apart and there wasn't anything she could do about it. She felt helpless, condemned to watch as events unfolded around her, changing her family; changing so many things in her life.

The only thing she could think to do was to crawl away in a corner and have a good cry. But, for Evan's sake, she forced herself to carry on.

"You make it sound so final," Laura commented at last. "Like you have nothing left to live for."

"Don't be silly. We may be old but we're not *that* old. There's a lot for us to look forward to."

She smiled at Evan, who still held her hand, as though he was reluctant to let go. "I have these two wonderful grandkids who still have a lot of growing up to do. I wouldn't miss out on that for the world."

"But Grandma." Laura sat down on the end of the bed. "You two love that house of yours. With everything you've done to it over the years. And think of all the time you spent together in that place. All the memories you have of it."

"We'll always have those memories, Laura. Nothing can ever take that away from us. And we still have each other. That's the important thing. The house was just a house."

Tears began to form in Evan's eyes. "You can't leave me, Grandma. You can't leave me, too."

"Nobody's leaving you, Evan," she replied.

"You and Grandpa are leaving." He looked toward his

mother, glaring at her. "Ted left." His next words were barely a whisper. "And now Aaron's gone."

"Aaron isn't gone, baby." Laura moved closer to him, draping an arm over his shoulder and drawing him near. "You'll always have your brother."

"But he's not the same, is he? He's so different now."

"But he's going to get better." Laura forced back the tears. "You'll see. He'll be good as new in no time."

Grandma Ruth reached over, cupping Evan's chin in her hand, and forced the youngster to look at her. "A big part of living is growing, Evan. And changing. The Bible tells us *a friend loves at all times, and a brother is born for adversity*. You and your brother will always have each other. There will be good times. And bad times. But you'll always have your brother. You must accept the bad times as part of what life gives you. Remember, enduring the bad times makes you appreciate the good times."

He nodded, trying to understand. But it was obvious he was struggling with the concept. So much bad had happened of late that good times seemed only another of his fantasies, something to pretend at but an experience that would never come true for him.

An awkward silence invaded the room. Laura broke it when she stood up to retrieve a package she had left at the foot of the bed. She handed Grandma Ruth the nondescript plastic bag.

"This is for you."

The old woman opened it slowly, her hands appearing feeble as she performed the task. She drew out a book and a glow lit her face when she saw what it was.

Laura continued. "I didn't have time to go to a book store or anything. It's not that fancy, but it's the only one they had at the gift shop."

"A Bible doesn't have to be fancy," Grandma Ruth conceded. "It's the words inside that are important. Thank you, Laura."

"I just wasn't sure what happened to your old one. At the house. With the fire and all. And also...."

She paused, reluctant to continue, but finally forced the words out.

"I wanted to say I'm sorry."

"For what?"

"For the way I criticized you the other day when you were talking to Aaron. I shouldn't have said the things I said."

"Nonsense. He's your son." She reached for Evan's hand again, giving it a squeeze. "You have two beautiful boys, Laura. You have every right to raise them the way you want."

"But I was wrong. I see that now. I think Aaron was reaching out for help. I think he needed someone to listen to him. And I failed him."

"Don't ever say that." The old woman's tone was harsh now, a reminder of her former formidable self. "There was no way you could have known what was going on. Or anticipated what was going to happen."

"But he's my son. I should be aware of what's happening in his life."

"You can't read his thoughts, Laura. You can't know what another person is keeping to themselves. No matter how good of a mother you are. And you are a good mother. None of this was your fault, so don't blame yourself."

"What about Ted?"

Evan's words startled Laura. For a moment, while talking to her grandmother, she had nearly forgotten her son was still in the room. "What's that, Evan?"

"What about Ted? You said before this was all his fault. You said he did the bad things to Aaron. But it wasn't him. He didn't do anything to Aaron. I told you that and you didn't believe me. You wouldn't listen to me. And now he's gone."

He released hold of his grandmother's hand and turned away, refusing to look at his mother

Laura didn't know how to respond. Because, when she considered her son's words, the truth of the matter came through to her. She had been unfair to Ted. She had been so upset with what had happened to Aaron, so angry to think such a thing was even possible, that she had lashed out at the first target that presented itself, accusing her boyfriend of something she knew he wasn't capable of.

"I'm sorry, Evan. You were right. But I made a mistake. I guess I've been making a lot of those lately."

He turned around, a glimmer of hope in his eyes. "Then Ted should come back."

"I don't know whether that's an option or not."

"Why not? You could just call him up and ask him to come back."

"It's not that easy."

She drew closer to him.

"Ted's been gone for a while now. I'm not sure he'd want to come back. Especially after the way I treated him."

"You could apologize to him. Tell him you made a mistake."

An image flashed through her head, of Ted walking out of the house, the door slamming shut behind him, closing a chapter of her life with it.

When she spoke the words came quietly, more to herself than to the others in the room. "I don't think that would be enough."

"Why not? When we do something wrong you tell us to apologize. That it will make everything okay. So why can't you just tell Ted you're sorry?"

"It's different with adults. It's not that easy."

"You are sorry. Aren't you, Mom?"

"Of course I am."

"Then tell Ted. Tell him you want him to come back."

"Let's not talk about this right now, Evan. There's too many other things going on. We'll talk about it later. I promise."

Chapter Forty-Three:

THE HOUSE appeared relatively unscathed from the front. People driving by would hardly notice anything amiss. But were one to walk along the side of the structure, toward the yard in back, the reality of the situation revealed itself.

The rear wall was three-quarters missing. All that remained was a blackened triangle of burnt clapboard at the peak which had managed to escape the fire's full fury. Shattered glass coated the grass behind the house, intermingled with blackened chars of wood siding, partially consumed window frames, and cabinets that had been wrested from the burning conflagration that had once been a kitchen and thrown outside to be extinguished.

Two men, dressed in firefighter's overalls, were methodically dragging articles onto the front lawn, throwing the debris onto an ever-growing heap. They worked carefully, fearful of uncovering a smoldering pile that would ignite the blaze again. They would poke about with their axes first until they were certain it was safe to continue. Then, with asbestos-gloved hands, they would drag more rubble out front.

Ted Myers sat for several minutes in his car, watching their efforts, before leaving his vehicle to step onto the front sidewalk. He was acknowledged with a nod from one of the workers.

The other fire fighter drew closer. "Can I help you, sir?"

"I'm a friend of the family. I just heard about...."

He looked toward the house, then quickly turned away.

"Is everyone okay?" Ted asked.

"An elderly couple was taken to Toledo Hospital. Along with a little boy, I think. As far as I know there wasn't anything significant." He looked back at the house, then again at Ted. "Injury wise, anyway. The house is pretty much a mess."

"I can see that."

Ted stared in silence at the pile of debris, and eventually the two men returned to their tasks. Something caught Ted's eye – a book of some kind – and he reached forward to claim the article. He managed to open the volume, but only partially. The plastic pages were fused together from exposure to the heat. He could barely make out the miniature designs displayed within, the stamps blackened now from smoke, their intricate markings erased to the world.

Grandpa Mike's collection had, like the rest of the house, gone up in flames.

"Hello, Ted."

He turned at the sound of his name. Tony Perkins, from three houses down the street, strode closer.

"Hi, Tony. How are you doing?"

"Better than Laura and her family, I'm sure."

"Have you heard anything? About how they're doing?"

"Not much. The wife says she heard there was some kind of funny business going on with one of the kids. Not sure what, though. Do you know what it might be?"

Ted recalled the story he had heard at the bar. "No. No idea what it could be."

"It's a shame, alright, what some people go through. So how are you doing?"

Ted barely heard him. He made no reply, his thoughts elsewhere.

"Haven't seen much of you lately," Tony continued. "Is everything okay?"

"Yeah."

Ted realized then that he was still holding the ruined collection of stamps in his hands. He let the binder fall at his feet, where it disturbed a tiny cloud of black dust.

"Yeah, Tony. Everything's just great."

He got back in his car and drove away. He never looked back.

Chapter Forty-Four:

LARRY DROVE to Toledo Hospital after dinner that night. He had only been to the facility once before in his life. His last trip comprised an Emergency Room visit following an overly rambunctious basketball game with some of his friends, back in his early teens.

He was startled to see how much things had changed in the duration.

The main structure had been added onto several times at least, and was now part of a complex that seemed to include more than a dozen ancillary buildings. More growth appeared to be on the way, judging from the chain-link fence surrounding what looked to be a recently cleared lot. Construction vehicles were parked haphazardly on the other side of the barrier, idle now but prepared to resume their duties with the start of the next work shift.

Larry maneuvered his way through the parking garage, taking the seemingly endless turns necessary to ascend the structure, until at last finding a space on the top floor. An elevator brought him back down to the street level. Connie Peters had told him Aaron's room number, so armed with the information he was able to locate the proper wing of the facility.

His progress was halted when he arrived at the nursing station.

"Are you a relative of the child?" The nurse had a

brusque demeanor to her, no doubt honed from years of dealing with family members and the drama they brought to her work routine.

"No, I'm not," he answered. "But I've been assigned as a guardian for Aaron, as well as his brother Evan."

Judging from the sound of her voice the concept seemed preposterous to her. "Assigned by who?"

"Lucas County Juvenile Court. I'm a CASA volunteer."

As he spoke he withdrew from his folder the court document, signed by Lucas County Judge Dorothy Harrelson, that presented him as the guardian of the twins. He presented the paperwork to the nurse for her approval. He also removed the plastic card he wore around his neck which identified him as a representative of the court. He always wore it when working on a case.

She examined the information carefully, as though he was attempting to pull a fast one on her and she needed to be diligent. Finally she stood up from her chair to walk around the partition dividing the two of them.

"Please wait here, Mr. Kendall."

She was gone for less than five minutes, though it seemed much longer to Larry, standing idly in the corridor and watching as occasionally someone walked by.

A young girl, probably close to Aaron Reed's age, passed by in a wheelchair. The woman pushing the conveyance was no doubt her mother; there was a marked similarity between the features of the two of them. He couldn't help wondering what was wrong with the girl. He detected no indications of anything, but even had there been something he would have more than likely missed it.

He found himself contemplating, not for the first time today, what he was doing at the hospital. Assuming he could get in to see Aaron, he really had no idea what to say to the boy. There were issues involved here that he had never considered dealing with before.

His mind went back to his youth. He had always admired

his father's role as a police officer. The fact that he was out there helping others, perhaps even putting his own life on the line – every day when he left the house to go to work – said volumes about the type of person he was. Larry wished he could be more like that himself.

He had the desire to help, which explained why he had gravitated to social work. But he had always considered it a safe vocation, one where he could observe others, and assist them, without personally getting involved in their issues and problems.

He had recently abandoned that concept.

He still wanted to help, but he questioned whether he could ever make a difference in the cases he handled. He applied himself, and put forth the effort, but often it seemed like it just wasn't enough.

He couldn't help wondering too if he should have handled Aaron's situation differently. Perhaps he should have said something sooner – to Monica or Connie or anyone – the day of the hearing. Maybe, had he revealed his forebodings, the tragedy at the family's house could have been prevented. They could have at least been on the lookout for any peculiar behavior on Aaron's part.

He had held back, afraid he would appear ignorant in front of others. He had been fearful as well of alienating the family by revealing accusations that he couldn't support. And they had paid the price for his reluctance.

He knew he would need to be more assertive in the future – for the children's sake. At least he had learned that much from his experience.

"Mr. Kendall?"

The voice, coming from right beside him, startled Larry, who had been unaware of the man standing beside him until his name was spoken.

"Yes. I'm Larry Kendall."

"Dr. Richard Markham. We spoke on the phone several

days ago."

The two shook hands.

"Let's find a place where we can talk," the doctor suggested.

Larry retrieved his information from the nurse at the station and followed the physician to an empty room off the hallway. Dr. Markham threw a switch by the door, adding a modicum of light to the room, and motioned for Larry to enter. It looked to be some sort of consultation area, with a desk and several chairs and in one corner, on a table that had obviously seen better days, a computer with a bulky monitor.

"How's Aaron?" Larry inquired, no longer able to contain his curiosity.

"It's pretty early to tell. To be honest, this episode took me completely by surprise. I know we had talked about possibilities, so I had an inkling of what might have been going on. But I never imagined what Aaron was capable of."

"What is he capable of?"

"That's difficult to ascertain. He obviously has issues differentiating between what is real and what isn't. He seems to be susceptible to inappropriate behavior, such as inflicting pain on himself. I think we can assume at this point that the abuse discovered two months ago was indeed of his own doing."

"It's just so hard to believe he could do something like that to himself." Larry paused, his mind drifting back to the photos Dr. Rahid had revealed before the Adjudication/Disposition hearing.

"Isn't there anything you can do for him?" the CASA worker asked at last.

"That's the good news in all this. Now that we have a better idea of what we're dealing with we know how to approach his issues and address his needs. I will continue with his therapy, tailored to his specific condition, while starting him on a regimen of medication."

"So there's a good chance you can cure him?"

"I didn't say that. Schizophrenia isn't like a headache.

You can't just take a few pills and have it go away. It may never go away.

"But there are ways of dealing with it," Dr. Markham continued. "Of making Aaron understand what he's going through, and teaching him how to recognize his delusions and react in an acceptable manner."

"I'd like to see him. Would that be alright?"

"Certainly, though he may seem a bit unresponsive. Remember he's just gone through a trying experience."

The doctor left the room, Larry following him down the corridor. The CASA volunteer tried not to appear inquisitive as they made their way through the hallway, but it was difficult not to glance into the rooms he passed.

One room held a teenage boy, alone and moaning as he lay on his bed. He tossed and turned, his sheets wrapped around him like a cocoon.

A young child, perhaps five or six, occupied another room, sitting next to one of the nurses, who was reading from a picture book. Larry couldn't tell if it was a boy or a girl; the youngster's hair was shaven, lending an almost alien aspect to the child's appearance. At one point something in the book must have struck the child as funny. A giggle followed, in a definite feminine voice. Looking up, seeing Larry standing in the doorway, the child smiled – the picture of innocence – and waved.

She must have been going through chemo therapy, Larry surmised. That would explain the lack of hair. He reflected a moment on what a shame it was, that someone so young had to deal with something so tragic. But to see her smile, and hear the laughter coming from the room, one would think she hadn't a care in the world. It was amazing the resiliency of children, to be able to make the best of such a situation.

At last they reached Aaron Reed's room. Dr. Markham paused several steps from the doorway. "I believe Laura is inside," he stated. "I'm sure she'll be glad to have some company." He turned, walking away, and Larry steeled himself for what he was about to confront.

The television was on, the sound muted. Laura was watching a game show, but paying little attention to the program. Aaron lay on his side, sleeping, looking peaceful and content.

"Hello, Laura. How are you doing?"

She looked up at him but didn't smile, even though her eyes sparkled as though she was pleased to have some company. Or maybe it was something else. Maybe it was merely moisture, the tears she had cried, that gave her eyes their shine.

She looked tired and listless. Her hair hung limp at her side, unwashed and uncared for. She wore no make-up. She looked for all the world like someone that had been through an exhausting day.

"Hello, Larry," she said at last. "I didn't expect to see you down here."

"I wanted to see how Aaron was doing."

"He's doing good." She nodded, as though trying to convince herself of the fact. "Considering."

"And how are you doing?"

"I'm tired," she blurted out. "But I'll be okay."

"And you're grandparents? I heard Mike was in pretty rough shape."

"He was, but they think the worst is over now. They're both still here. Under observation. I think the hospital just wants to be sure they're okay before they get released."

"Will you be taking them home?"

She shook her head no. For a moment she seemed lost in her own thoughts. "I don't think there's much of a home for them to go back to. They're talking about looking into a nursing home. I think Connie said she'd be able to get some information for them."

"How about you? Where are you staying?"

"Here, mostly. They said I can spend the night, so that's what I plan on doing. In case Aaron needs anything."

"And Evan?"

"He's at my brother's. Paul offered to let us stay at his apartment for a while. Until things settle down some and we get back on our feet."

She lapsed once more into silence, and Larry found himself wondering again how much he was even accomplishing by being there.

Chapter Forty-Five:

HE WAS aware initially of sound. A rhythmic beeping intonation registered first, the steady tone reminiscent of a clock due to it's regularity. Something fell in the distance, a loud crash accompanied with the clattering of metal. Voices slowly became recognizable, people speaking in quiet whispers, though the words were indistinct to him.

Things began to appear lighter. Though his eyes were still closed he suspected it was daytime. Or, if not, then he was in a well-lit environment. He considered further. The light struck him as artificial. Not the warm, glowing light of the sun, but rather a harsh light, a cold light that washed over him with its rays but delivered no comfort.

It struck him for the first time that he was laying down on something soft. A pillow rested beneath his head. It was comfortable there, but he resisted the urge to fall back to sleep. He knew he needed to wake up. He felt as though something was calling to him, urging him to open his eyes and take a look around.

Things seemed out of focus at first; hazy. With time the sights became more clear, losing their blurry quality to become more distinct. Initially he could only make out shapes, vague colors reminiscent of something he knew he should recognize. As his eyes became more adjusted to the light clarity developed.

A face, seeming to hover above the bed, smiled at him.

It was enough to restore him to his full senses.

"Hello, Ruthie."

"Hello, Michael."

He felt a sensation and realized it was his wife squeezing his hand. It almost felt painful, her grip was that firm and steady, but it was reassuring to him. He didn't say anything about it. At that moment, in that time, he could think of nothing that would comfort him more.

"How are you feeling, Michael?"

Her words came slowly, as though she had trouble enunciating them.

"What happened?" he asked.

"It doesn't matter." She stroked his cheek. "I'll tell you all about it later. When you're stronger."

Without turning his head, reluctant to pull his attention away from his wife, he began to notice his surroundings, or at least what little revealed itself within his line of sight.

"I'm in the hospital," he declared at last, the truth of the situation dawning on him.

She nodded.

"What happened?" he repeated. "I remember feeling hot. And coughing."

"There was a fire." She spoke the words as though it was the most natural thing in the world to talk about, in a calming voice clearly intended to set his mind at ease.

Thoughts raced through his head, the implications from her simple declaration alarming him with possibilities. "Laura! And the boys! Are they alright?"

"They're fine, Michael."

He became aware at last of what she was wearing, a white hospital gown that tied around her neck and hung on her like an old sack. It made her look pale, like her skin was washed-out. It was hardly a flattering look.

"You're here, too. What happened to you? Are you...?" He failed to continue the words, concern clouding his thoughts.

Ruthie patted his arm and smiled. "I'm fine, Michael.

Everyone's fine. You know doctors. They insist on running all their tests before they can make any kind of decision." She stroked his arm with slow and steady passes. "But everyone's okay. There's nothing to worry about."

He closed his eyes again, for a few seconds only, then they snapped back open. He didn't want to lose sight of the woman he'd been married to for so many years. He wanted to study her face; the way her smile had a lopsided look to it; the fine wrinkles in the corners of her eyes; everything he had grown to cherish over the years. But he lacked the strength.

"I'm tired," he announced.

"You should get some sleep."

He nodded.

"But I'll be back real soon. And then we'll talk some more. Okay?"

He smiled, too weak to reply.

She leaned forward to kiss him on the forehead.

"I love you, Michael Franklin."

He opened his eyes to gaze at her once again. Ruthie's eyes were misty now, glistening with tears.

"I love you, Ruthie Franklin."

She smiled, squeezed his hand once again, and he drifted off to sleep.

Chapter Forty-Six:

T HEY MET at Children's Services two days later, an emergency session to discuss the ramifications concerning Laura Reed and her twin boys.

Connie Peters opened the discussion. "In light of what we now know – and considering the recent turn of events – Children's Services has decided to reassess the case concerning Aaron Reed's alleged abuse."

A startled exclamation answered her. "How can you say alleged?" Dr. Rahid, though maintaining his composure, was obviously distraught. "I saw the boy in the hospital. The marks were clearly a sign of abuse."

"But not necessarily by a family member," Connie replied. "I think it's pretty clear to all of us that there is more going on with Aaron than we had at first realized. There are issues involved here that we had no suspicion of at the start."

Larry, having seen the boy in the hospital and spoken to his mother about what had happened, felt the need to speak up. "Dr Markham informs me that given the boy's subsequent behavior he feels confident in saying that Aaron has been suffering with his Schizophrenia for at least the last year or two. Possibly longer. There's no denying the fact that he has been behaving irrationally. He was actually witnessed hurting himself the day of the house fire. Indications are this wasn't the first episode."

Dr. Rahid refused to see their point of view. "You are talking theories, here. What proof have you that the boy's injuries were self-inflicted?"

"Of course we have no proof," Mark Anochevsky, the attorney from Children's Services, remarked. "Just as you have no proof that someone else was responsible."

"And from what we've been able to determine during family visits," Connie added "the two boys are in a loving environment with people that care for them. We haven't seen anything suspicious or alarming. There is nothing to indicate that a family member is responsible for Aaron's injuries."

Monica Perry, the attorney representing the CASA office, turned to face Larry, who sat beside her. "Do you agree with that assessment? Is that your impression as well?"

Larry hesitated. He had held his tongue earlier, reluctant to reveal his thoughts on the matter for fear no one would believe him. The results had been tragic for the family. He didn't want to make a mistake. There was too much at stake.

But he realized he had to tell them what he was thinking. Whether they believed him or not, whether it altered the course of the investigation, didn't matter. He needed to present the facts as he saw them. It would then be up to the group to determine the next course of action.

"I agree with Connie," he replied. "I think Aaron is a troubled individual. I think he's responsible for what happened, for the injuries that first brought this case to our attention. And, I might add, I had the opportunity to speak with Dr. Tyrone, the physician who treated Aaron at Toledo Hospital following his accident. She admitted that the marks she observed on the boy could very well have been self-inflicted."

Laura Reed, not present for the meeting due to her commitments watching over her family, was represented by her attorney, Emily Landrum, who took the opportunity to speak up. "I feel, in light of the situation and the recent turn of events, that the allegations against my client should be dropped and she should be exonerated from all wrong-doing. I suggest a motion for reconsideration be presented to the courts, and the case be dismissed. The poor woman has enough on her hands now without the added burden of these allegations hanging over her head."

Mark turned to face Jim Richards, the father's attorney. "On behalf of your client, do you have anything to add?"

The lawyer held his hands out, indicating the empty air around him. "As you can see, my client didn't bother to show up today. After several discussions with him concerning his role as a parent – and the possibility of back child support becoming an issue – he seems to have lost interest in his children's welfare. I have no problem with the case being dismissed."

"Then I will contact the courts and set things in motion," Mark concluded.

As they left Children's Services Larry caught up to Monica. "So what happens now?"

"What do you mean?"

"With Aaron Reed. Is he going to be okay?"

She shrugged. "We can only hope so. He's receiving medical attention, the kind he needs, and that's a good thing."

"Should I continue to check in on him once in a while? To see how he's doing?"

She hesitated before voicing an answer. "I can tell you're concerned, Larry. And that's great. You've been involved with this more than I have, so I'm certain this is difficult for you. But once the charges are dismissed that means the case is over. Your job as a CASA volunteer is over. There's no reason for you to be involved anymore."

He paused, considering her words. "Not even to stop by and see how they're doing?"

"It's probably best that you don't. It may confuse the children, wondering why you're visiting them. In the long run I think you should allow them the space they need for the healing ahead. Does that make sense?"

He nodded, his reluctance to agree with her obvious.

"Don't feel like you're letting them down, Larry. Because you're not. As a CASA you fill a special need. You were there for the children, looking out for their interest, advocating for them when they needed someone. That's something you can be proud of."

"I don't feel proud. I feel like I failed them."

"But you didn't. And there are other cases, other children out there, who need someone like you looking out for them. Don't give up, Larry. You have too much to offer."

Chapter Forty-Seven:

A SIMPLE sign adorned the outer wall of the structure.

The Alice Strouthers Home

No further information was presented on the plain wooden plaque. Beside the placard, lower and closer to the glass door, was a smaller sign.

All visitors must check in at front desk

Though difficult to determine the building's purpose at first glance – it could have been a school, or a suburban apartment complex – it was in reality a long-term care facility, located in a secluded area away from the congestion of the city. The fact that it comprised one floor only, and sprawled with assorted wings through a wooded lot, made it appear much larger than it actually was. The parking lot in front was nearly empty, though behind the structure, practically hidden when entering the long drive from the main road, was a paved area that appeared to be set aside for staff vehicles. Benches were placed strategically around the building, inviting one to sit and enjoy the serenity of the surroundings.

Paul Reed pulled his car into a parking space labeled with

a green Visitor sign, shut off the engine, and turned toward his sister. "Do you want me to come in with you?"

Laura shook her head. "No. I don't want him to feel overwhelmed. Or like we're ganging up on him."

She sat, staring out the windshield, reluctant to move.

She felt her brother's hand on her arm and turned to look his way.

"Are you okay?" he asked.

"Yeah. Just wondering. Thinking. What it's like inside. And how lonely it must be for him here."

"Don't think like that, Sis. This is the best place for him. You know that. These people are trained for this kind of thing. They know what they're doing."

"I'm sure you're right." She sniffed, dabbed at her eyes, and exited the vehicle. She turned to look again at Paul. "I'll try not to leave you waiting too long."

"Don't worry about it." He already had his Kindle in his hand, having retrieved the device from the back seat. "I've got plenty to keep me busy."

Laura paused before entering, searching for a buzzer, or knocker, or something to announce her arrival, but saw nothing. In desperation she tried the door and discovered it was unlocked.

The front doorway admitted into a tiny cubicle of a room. A sliding glass window, frosted for privacy, stood above a small counter holding a sign-in book and a bell. Laura rang the bell, which emitted a pathetic sounding tone, and waited.

The window slid open to reveal the reception area beyond. An attractive young woman – her name tag read Maiya – smiled in greeting. "May I help you?"

"I'm here to see Aaron Reed. I'm his mother. Dr. Markham said you'd be expecting me."

"Of course, Miss Reed. One moment, please."

Maiya closed the glass panel and Laura found herself alone once more. This wasn't what she was expecting. It seemed more like a business office than a medical building; so sterile, and uninviting, in marked contrast to the landscape on the outside.

Eventually she heard a door opening behind her. A portion of the glass wall parted, and Dr. Richard Markham appeared from the other side.

"Hello, Laura. How are you doing?"

"Okay. Nervous. How's Aaron?"

"Aaron's doing well. He's just finishing his lunch now. I'll take you to his room and he'll be in to see you in a few minutes."

They walked down a hallway that seemed unreasonably wide, passing a series of closed doors along the way. Each door had a white sign beside it with a stenciled name, no doubt announcing the occupant of the room. The sound of their footsteps through the passageway echoed off the walls, reverberating with a hollow racket. It made Laura feel uncomfortable, as though they were disturbing the silence of the facility.

"Aaron seems to be adjusting quite well," the physician was saying. "There are two other children here, close to his age, which I think is helping him to feel less isolated."

The only word that registered with Laura was isolated.

"Is he feeling lonely? Does he miss us?"

"Of course he misses you, Laura. But he's never lonely. He has some new friends now, and there's a constant flow of staff members checking in on him. He doesn't have much opportunity to feel lonely."

"Has he had any more…?" She paused, her forward progress stopping as abruptly as her words. "Any more incidents?"

Dr. Markham came to a halt, then turned to face her. "As far as we can determine, no. The facility isn't staffed to monitor him twenty-four hours a day, so we can't be one hundred per cent certain. But I'm very pleased with his progress. He seems to be adjusting well to the medication, which is good."

They continued on, at last reaching a door featuring a

sign with Aaron's name upon it. Laura followed the therapist into a compact living area containing several chairs; off to the side sat a table, and two more chairs. A doorway at one end of the room led into what appeared to be a separate bedroom. She could just make out a tiny dresser along one wall and the end of a bed sporting a colorful comforter.

"We try to maintain the semblance of being in a household setting," Dr. Markham informed her. "We find it's less intimidating that way, more conducive to the patient's recovery. Please, won't you sit down."

She chose a heavily upholstered seat, while he selected a wooden chair from next to the table. They had just sat down when a knock came on the door.

"Come in," the doctor invited.

An orderly in hospital scrubs entered, followed by Aaron Reed. Laura was surprised to see him wearing normal clothes, like he was at home instead of in a hospital. She smiled at her son.

"Hi, baby."

Aaron paused. For a moment a look of confusion showed on his face. The expression vanished in a flash, replaced by a smile of his own. "Hi, Mom."

He ran to her for a long overdue embrace.

The visit went much too quickly. Aaron hated to see his mother leave, but it had been a long day and he was feeling worn out. She paused in the doorway, smiling at him once again, and he waved goodbye.

"I'll be back to see you again real soon, baby. Okay?"

"Okay, Mom."

"I love you, Aaron."

"Love you too, Mom."

And then she was gone, and silence filled the room as he realized he was once more alone.

You must not listen to their lies. They are attempting to

corrupt your mind with their false truths and accusations.

I don't believe you.

But you must. We can lead you to the truth.

No. You're the ones that lie. All you've ever shown me are lies. All you've ever done is to hurt me.

We want to make you strong. We want to make you powerful.

No. You don't belong here. The things you tell me aren't true.

You can not deny us.

Yes I can. I don't want you in my life anymore. I don't need you in my life anymore.

You can not abandon us. We are part of you.

I can fight you. I know I can.

You can try. But will you succeed?

Yes. I think I can.

Chapter Forty-Eight:

IT HAD been a long day, and Laura was tired of being on her feet. She still had another hour to go before her shift ended. Normally that wouldn't be too bad, but it had been one of those nights when there weren't many customers and the time just seemed to drag. So she stood at the register and waited.

It would be nice to get home, and spend some time with her family. Or, at least, what was left of her family. It was just the three of them now, with her and Evan still staying at Paul's apartment. It was crowded, but they were making things work.

Laura stopped to consider what had been going on lately. So much attention was given to Aaron anymore, it didn't seem fair to his brother. With visits to the long-term care facility, and family therapy sessions, it seemed her entire world revolved around Aaron. Laura wouldn't change any of that. It was all worth it. To see the improvement in her son, the way he was progressing with the treatment, was gratifying to her.

But she needed to make a conscious effort not to forget Evan's needs. So Laura always made it a point, no matter how tired she felt at the end of her shift, to spend some time with Evan; reading a book, watching some cartoons together, anything to make him feel life was getting back to normal. He was going through a lot, with all the recent changes in his life. He deserved some quality time with his mother.

From the corner of her eye Laura caught a glimpse of an

approaching customer. She looked up, catching her breath with the motion.

Ted Myers stood at the counter, a 12 pack of Pepsi and a bag of barbecue potato chips on the counter in front of him.

"Hi Laura. How are you doing?"

She hesitated, wondering just how much she should say. She couldn't read him anymore. At one time they had been intimate, sharing each others thoughts, dreaming of the possibilities of a future together. But that was all behind her now. They had moved in different directions.

Still, she couldn't help wondering. Was Ted just being polite, or was there more to it than that?

She managed a reply. "Alright, I guess. We're getting by, anyway."

"I heard about what happened." He seemed reluctant to broach the subject. "I wanted to stop by, but I wasn't sure if you'd want to see me or not."

Turning away, ringing up the items, she mumbled under her breath. "You could have stopped by." There was nothing in her voice to indicate how she truly felt about the idea. It was just empty words; something to say to pass the time.

The total came up on the register, Ted slid his debit card through the reader, and the transaction was complete. For a moment he stood there, uncertain what to do next.

"Well, I'm glad everything's okay now. If you need anything...."

She nodded in reply, he cleared his throat, and the awkward silence continued. Without another word he grabbed his purchases and walked away.

He had taken three steps before Laura decided to speak up.

"Ted?"

He turned her way.

"I get off work in an hour. If you're not too busy to.... You know, just talk for a while. I'm not doing anything after work."

"Okay." He nodded. "Maybe I'll stop back then."

"Good. Good."

She never noticed the smile on Ted's face as he walked out the door. She was too preoccupied with her own smile to notice.

THE END

Afterword:

THE COURT Appointed Special Advocates Program – CASA – began in 1977 in Seattle Washington. In the forty years of its existence it has grown tremendously into a truly national organization, with all 50 states now enlisting the aid of volunteers to help children in need. Nationwide, approximately 70,000 volunteers in over 1,000 CASA programs speak up on behalf of the nearly 280,000 abused and neglected children they worked with last year alone.

CASA volunteers deal with issues of domestic violence and child neglect. They work with families whose parents suffer from a dependence on alcohol, or struggling with addictions to prescription pills or narcotics. The children they serve come from all walks of life, covering the spectrum of society, though many of the children they deal with live below the poverty level. These are children who go to bed each day hungry. Or cold. Or alone.

CASA volunteers also deal with issues of mental illness.

The trauma brought to a family through mental disease can be manifested in a variety of forms. Often it is the parents who suffer, struggling to make sense of life while dealing with an often debilitating condition. Raising children is difficult enough under the best of conditions, but when a parent's thinking is impaired through mental illness it increases the burden. Often they are unable to cope, their poor judgment skills resulting in decision making that is flawed at best and, in the worst of cases, dangerous to their children.

CASA volunteers are involved as well with children dealing with mental illness, whether it be Attention-Deficit Syndrome, Bipolar Disorders, Autism, or something as unnerving as Childhood-Onset Schizophrenia. The story told in these pages is extreme, a worst case scenario of a person suffering with delusions and unable to separate fantasy from reality, but it is not beyond the realm of possibilities of what some people go through when dealing with Schizophrenia.

Some liberties were taken with the hearing of voices. From all accounts it is unlikely that conversations such as detailed in these pages occur to most people, but the tone of the voices, the emotions they elicit, are not unusual. A common factor is for the voices to belittle the sufferer, telling them they are worthless and tearing down their self-esteem.

Often the words they hear are nonsensical. One authority I spoke with described it by saying "If the voices tell people something about the world around them, it is often something involving paranoia – my dog is telling me that there are people out to get me. So I become so frightened that I have to get in my car, go on the turnpike, and roar down the road at 100 miles an hour."

Obviously this cannot be an easy thing to live with on a daily basis.

It takes a special person, and a lot of love, to deal with a family member suffering from mental illness, but sometimes even the best-intentioned of adults find themselves confronting situations that get out of control. It has been estimated that children with a disability or chronic illness are twice as likely to succumb to child abuse as the average child, a clear indication of the strain family members endure while caring for children who require the extra attention and understanding necessary to care for someone in this position.

Fortunately society views mental illness differently than it has in the past. Where not so very long ago the mentally ill represented a stigma to the family, something to be kept under lock-and-key and not discussed, the growing awareness of mental health issues has become more widely accepted, alleviating some of the concerns families had to deal with formerly.

There are many fine organizations devoted to the matter. NAMI – The National Alliance On Mental Illness – has chapters across the country to not only assist with the mentally ill, but to support family members as well. These centers can offer advice and guidance, referrals to practitioners, and a wealth of information to guide families along the proper path to understanding, acceptance, and the ability to live with mental illness.

Author bio:

DRAWING FROM nearly a decade of personal involvement working with troubled youth, author Keith Julius creates intense stories that pull readers into an emotional landscape of hopes, fears, and brutal realities.

Growing up in a large family, and raising two sons of his own, Julius has always had a compassion for children. Realizing not everyone has the stability he's been able to create for his own family, it has become his mission to provide a voice for the children in our society who need it the most. This led Julius to discover the CASA program. Founded in 1977, the program enlists volunteers to represent children in cases of child abuse and child neglect. CASA volunteers work closely with families to assure the children in these traumatic situations are placed properly and are well cared for.

In 2015 Julius released his first novel, the suspense thriller REMORSE BY DEGREE. This was followed by his series "The CASA Chronicles," which currently stands at four volumes, including the 2023 release A DECADE ABORNING. Each book focuses on a different family struggling with some of society's most challenging issues, including addiction, mental illness, human trafficking, teenage suicide, and childhood trauma.

Though his books are fiction, the writing brings a compassion and understanding to the stories that can only come from personal experience. These realistic portrayals allow the reader to join with mothers and fathers, and of course the children involved, as they face life's adversities. The author invites you to share in their triumphs, and sorrow in their failures, as they confront their struggles with dignity, determination, and the promise of a better future for their children.

Daniel Jameson was living the American Dream. With a secure job, a house in the suburbs, and a wife and two children, he seemed to have everything he ever desired out of life.

His storybook existence is thrown into turmoil when he witnesses a tragic accident at his workplace. Following the event Daniel begins to question aspects of his life he had long taken for granted. He manages to become separated from his wife Becky and on his own, aimlessly adrift and uncertain of his future.

A chance meeting at a restaurant introduces Daniel to Jackie Somerset, a younger woman to whom he is immediately attracted. His infatuation runs counter to the wishes of Jackie's boyfriend, Brad Wilkens, who unleashes a torrent of violence - beginning with a brutal attack against Daniel - that soon escalates to much more.

Daniel finds himself involved in situations and events he could have never imagined, fighting not only for his peace of mind but for the life of his family as well.

Keith Julius

Aleisha Turner is young and attractive, a wife and the mother of three beautiful children.

Aleisha is also an addict.

Following a heroin overdose that nearly takes her life away her children are taken from her. Aleisha finds herself in a rehab center, the first step in what will prove to be a difficult recovery. She faces a long road ahead to restore normalcy to her life and bring her family back together.

Beverly Stone works as a CASA volunteer, a Court Appointed Special Advocate. Her responsibility is to see that Aleisha's children are living in a healthy environment conducive to their welfare while encouraging their mother to break the deadly habit that has come to monopolize her life. Along the way Beverly must immerse herself in a world far different from the one she is accustomed to, experiencing life from the perspective of the people who reside in inner city America.

When nine year old Aaron Reed has an accident at a local playground it seems like a routine emergency room visit. The case becomes more than routine when signs of child abuse are discovered. The young boy and his family find themselves embroiled in events that threaten to tear the household apart, as suspicion deepens and trust disappears.

Court Appointed Special Advocate Larry Kendall arrives on the scene to discover things are not always what they seem, as the secrets behind the family slowly begin to unravel. The truth, unsuspected by all, at last emerges. It is an ordeal that will test the bonds of family and the strength of faith.

A young girl's life is thrown into turmoil following the death of her older brother.

Fifteen year old Rosaletta Guiterrez finds things turning from bad to worse after witnessing the tragic accident that takes her brother's life. Estranged from the only family she's ever known – removed from a verbally abusive mother who has no concern for her daughter's well-being – Rosaletta is sent to a foster home, to live with a couple she can't relate to as she struggles to get on with her life.

Court Appointed Special Advocate Melanie Cox is assigned by the juvenile court to safeguard the child's interests, a task made more difficult due to the trauma that has infected the youth's thinking.

Desperate for change, seeking liberation from the loneliness that refuses to release her, Rosaletta runs away. But the escape she seeks becomes a nightmare, as the teenager becomes entangled with people and circumstances she could have never anticipated.

A suicide attempt by teenager Pamela Watkins leaves the young girl's family concerned regrading her state of mind and what could have driven her to contemplate such a drastic solution.   No answers can be found from Pamela herself, who has withdrawn into doubts she refuses to express to others. As answers begin to reveal themselves Pamela's life spirals further   downward,   complicating   the   situation   further   and driving her closer to tragedy.

Beverly Johnson, a Court Appointed Special Advocate, is assigned to the case.   Meeting with the teenager brings up unresolved issues form both of their pasts, with the clues to Pamela's mental health and Beverly's recurring doubts buried beneath ten years of family complications and unresolved issues.